THE LAUGHTER IN DJAKARTA

THE LAUGHTER
IN DJAKARTA

By

DERWENT MAY

1973
CHATTO & WINDUS
LONDON

Published by
Chatto & Windus Ltd
42 William IV Street
London WC2N 4DF

*

Clarke, Irwin & Co. Ltd
Toronto

ISBN 7011 1985 3

© Derwent May 1973

Printed in Great Britain by
T. and A. Constable Limited
Hopetoun Street, Edinburgh

To
MY FATHER

I am indebted to Mr Sandy Llewellyn
for the last two lines of the verse on
page 69.

CHAPTER ONE

Leszek Mylski

'SOMETHING I can't identify,' thought Leszek Mylski, 'has just reminded me of' – he hesitated – 'of something I can't quite remember!' He peered into the warm Javanese night from the betjak – the bicycle rickshaw – in which he was riding. It was very dark under the palm trees on either side of the road, but the boy sitting high on the saddle behind him was pedalling fast and confidently. Leszek gripped the arms of the betjak tighter. There was no sound to be heard in the darkness except the humming and whining of a rubber band stretched between the betjak's wheels. Leszek tried again to think what sensation it was that had half-formed in his mind and then vanished. He couldn't pin it down. 'Something I can't identify has just reminded me of something I can't remember' – an extremely precise formulation of an experience almost entirely without content!

At that moment the betjak swerved violently to the left and toppled over. Leszek found himself with his knees on the ground and his face squashed up against the red plastic covering of the betjak seat. His left ear and cheek were smarting. They must have hit the metal framework of the betjak's hood as he fell. He looked up, pushing himself up on his hands. In the starlight between the trees he could see that the betjak driver was already on his feet again, staring down at him. Perhaps he had leaped off and never actually been on the ground. He still had his broad-brimmed straw hat on, all he was wearing apart from a pair of thick white shorts.

7

'Tiger!' the boy said, with a shrill laugh. Though he had laughed, his voice was trembling.

'Tiger?' Leszek couldn't believe him – a tiger in the suburbs of Djakarta? Did he mean a Dutchman? They were sometimes called tigers. But that would be nothing to be afraid of, not now.

'A ghost! A ghost!'

Leszek got up, pressing one hand to the side of his face and dusting his trousers with the other. 'No,' he said, 'no, it couldn't have been.'

The boy seized his straw hat and shook it violently in front of him. 'It's true! It's true!'

'It bit me in the ear then.'

The boy laughed again, but he insisted, though he seemed already to be getting over his fright. 'I saw it! Now it's gone.'

'It won't come back?'

'God knows.'

'Shall we go on?'

'It's been seen here before!' The boy waved his hat again.

'Someone told you?'

'Yes – they say it's the biggest tiger in Djakarta.'

'But shall we go on?'

The boy shrugged and looked around him into the night. Then he put his hat back on. 'All right, tuan,' he said without expression.

They righted the betjak between them. After they had worked together doing that, Leszek felt guilty as he clambered back into the seat again. To let a boy of fourteen pedal you through the streets! – but the driver wouldn't understand such feelings in a white man. He started talking again as soon as they were moving. Leszek was glad to find he understood nearly everything the boy said – he was getting familiar with Djakarta slang by now.

8

'There are a lot of ghosts on this road, tuan. Mostly in the tree-tops, you hear them howling. Sometimes they come in the shape of wild boars. But those are people, they turn into wild boars at night and go into people's homes and find out what they've got in them.'

'Have you seen one?'

'No, but someone saw one in this kampong, tuan.'

There were lights among the trees now, from small bamboo houses, and not far ahead on the roadside were a few trestle tables with paraffin lamps on them, where food was being sold. It was not much further to Sumitro's house. But the night was just as silent. Leszek found he was not much shaken by the fall. The calmness of the night was too pervasive. A bat flew with a sharp clatter into the dead, hanging fronds of a palm tree above their heads, and there was a faint roll of thunder far away; then there was nothing but the twanging murmur of the rubber band again.

No howling ghosts. Yet the boy saw his vision in the darkness; while I failed to see mine, whatever it was, thought Leszek. But the pain in his cheek suddenly did throw a memory into Leszek's mind, one that drained all the strength from him for an instant. On a night almost as warm as this, in Warsaw just three years ago, his wife had smacked his face very hard. A terrible moment, in which they had each despised the other, and each with complete conviction that they were right to do so.

That was early in the autumn of 1954. Leszek was twenty-seven that year, Zosia twenty-four. They had a room in an old bullet-scarred block near the Warsaw main station – a dingy, and still largely shattered part of Warsaw, with the relics of a famous street-market giving it most of the life it still had. There were apple-barrows all the autumn at the end of the street, and the barrow men would often come and sit in the high gateway of the block in the evening to drink vodka. If he was late coming home from the university, Leszek would sometimes be offered apples. He took them, generally – not so much in the spirit in which they were given, namely as bribes to him not to make trouble, but rather because accepting them would be a bribe to the men not to be a nuisance themselves.

That night, though, about half past nine, he and Zosia had been sitting listening to the radio in the dusk when there had been a hideous noise in the porch: loud, grating shouts followed by high-pitched screams. Leszek had rushed down the stone stairs to find a boy shrinking against the wall, one leg of his trousers torn and bloody at the thigh, and a dirty-looking man lying on the ground with three men sitting on top of him. There was a broken bottle on the stone floor. The boy's mouth hung open, and his eyes were wide but dull. Obviously it was he who had been screaming: now he was just whimpering, one hand with spread fingers hanging in front of his wound but not touching it, as though it had emotions of its own, fascinated but fearful. The man on the ground was breathing heavily. He lost consciousness as Leszek looked. One of the men sitting on him said, 'He went for the boy with a broken bottle – the boy was teasing him, saying women didn't like him because he always has his shit sticking to his prick.'

'I'd better do something for the boy.'

'No!' The man looked angrily at him. 'We're getting a taxi. We're getting away before the militia come.'

'He needs . . .'

'No!'

Just then one of the little pale-blue cars with a chequered line along the side that served at the time as taxis in Warsaw stopped outside the gateway, its headlights already on. Another boy ran into the porch, glanced at

Leszek, then put his arm round the wounded boy and led him gently to the front seat of the taxi. He helped him in and got in after him. The men were already dragging the drunkard across the pavement to the back seat. Not more than a couple of minutes after Leszek had come hurrying down the stairs, they had all gone. No one else in the block had ventured out to see what was happening. 'Indifferent beasts,' thought Leszek, as he went back up again.

He hadn't expected to find what was waiting for him. Zosia was standing with her back to the open window: even in her bright red dress she was only a purplish silhouette against the last light, and the rest of the room was very dark, with the tall sombre furniture all round it that his mother had given him from his father's surgery. He switched the light on, and saw that Zosia was staring coldly at him, her chin pointed and trembling.

'Did you call the police?' Her brown eyes looked quite wild.

'No, there was a boy . . .'

'Why didn't you call the police?' She was shouting.

'Zosia, what's the matter?'

'I can't take any more! I want it easier, Leszek! I want it easier!'

It was something she had said once before in the past week – something she had never given any sign of thinking in the first two years of their marriage, before they had managed even to find a room big enough to take his father's furniture. And it seemed one of the worst things a woman could say to a man in the conditions of life in Warsaw then, where few honest men of his age had much to offer a woman except themselves.

'Am I to blame, Zosia?'

'Yes!'

'Oh yes?'

'Do you want to know why? Because you're preaching all the time and never doing anything. Always straining and striving to see the good in things, to be the good man, not jump to conclusions, not condemn anyone. Fuck them! Fuck them and put them in jail if that's how they behave! We only have a country like this because people like you acquiesce in every vile thing anyone does, at the top or the bottom. The people, the revolution, it's all got a moral end so we have shits like that screaming on a summer night outside our door. I'm the only one who's always wrong!'

'You seem slightly confused.'

'Oh shut up! I had a dream the other night about a church with a great black cannon sticking out of it. I thought about it and it must have been you.'

'Thank you, Miss Symbolist. There was a wounded boy down there.'

'Fuck the boy.'

'Oh, you bitch.' He wished he hadn't said it, and started to say almost in the same breath, 'I'm sorry, I didn't mean to say that.' Though at the moment of saying it he had meant it and said it in despair. But before he had a chance she had stepped across the room and slapped him as hard as she could on the cheek. Then she burst into tears and threw herself on the divan bed on the other side of the room.

They spent most of the night repeatedly taking back what they had said, and for the next few days were especially gentle to each other. But it had come out several weeks later that there was more to Zosia's anger than just irritation with Leszek and the conditions of their life. She had begun to fall in love with someone else. In the event it had come to nothing, and Leszek had told himself, as better prospects began to open up for Poland in the middle of 1955, that his marriage would profit by them too. It hadn't done so. Just before Christmas that year Zosia left him for a different man. She had not found herself an easier life: for the past year and a half she and the man who was now her husband – a young, very badly-paid architect – had also been living in a single room, in a Stalin-period block about which the architect hated everything.

It was Leszek who had unexpectedly had a kind of luxury thrust on him. The Foreign Ministry had wanted someone to go out to Indonesia and make contact with the writers there, especially the communist and other left-wing writers. Leszek's knowledge of Sanskrit, the subject he taught at the university, had led to his being offered the job. Sanskrit had at least vague connections with some of the languages spoken in the archipelago – though, in fact, no connection at all with the national language. He had been very lonely without Zosia. She was the only woman he had been out with since she had left him – he'd insisted that they should remain friends. But now he had jumped at the job. He had worked furiously in the empty flat, learning Indonesian from a Russian and an English text-book, and getting on for three months ago – at the beginning of July, with university exams over, and his colleagues beginning to head off to the Baltic, the Black Sea or the sanatoria – he had taken a Russian airliner to Djakarta.

Tonight was the first time he had thought of Zosia for several days, he realised. And already, in a matter of minutes, the pain was subsiding, the scene he had just relived turning into little figures mouthing words that did not reach him, like a television screen with no sound. The betjak turned off the road into a narrow lane between banana plants, with their enormous leaves like ragged green capes. The lights from the houses threw long shadows among the trees and the bushes. Some distance away, electric light-bulbs had been rigged up on poles, and two men were playing badminton. Other men stood around in their sarongs, broad sombrely-patterned cylinders of blanket that they rolled tightly round their waist and legs, or held up, arms apart, like wings, for a moment or two. A little girl in a pink frock strode past the betjak throwing her arms out proudly as she walked, but staring at him with large eyes. It reminded him of three small girls he had noticed as he came out of his house this evening in the sunset. There was a canal running along the other side of the road, and the girls, four or five years old, and all of identical height to within a few millimetres, were squatting in a line on the concrete bank, shitting into the water, and with much laughter comparing their performances. That seemed to express an ease of heart that to him was exquisite luxury; and a luxury just to see.

He got out of the betjak and paid the driver what he had agreed. 'Mind the tiger,' he said. The boy beamed at him. 'I'm afraid of it,' he said blandly, but he showed no sign of fear in his smile now. As he drove off, another betjak came along the lane, with a man in the seat and about twenty live chickens hanging head down either side of it. Some of the chickens moved their heads, trying to look up. Leszek heard the two drivers telling each other in loud voices where they had come from and the fares they had managed to get.

He walked through more banana trees, across to Sumitro's house. Just then Sumitro himself appeared at the open door. It was the same as on the previous occasion they had met: Leszek thought at once how striking the contrast was between the ironical, modern mind one met in his novels, and the face of the man. He had a narrow, very dark brown face, with moist dark eyes that seemed to shine in perpetual emotion. Leszek had been talking at some diplomatic reception to a man from Sumatra who, speaking in English, had said of the Javanese, 'When they look at a cup of coffee, they don't just see a cup of coffee – they see it fa-a-a-ding away into eternity.' And on the word 'fa-a-a-ding' he had pushed the back of his hand slowly and firmly out from his chest until it was stretched as far as it would go. The eyes of Sumitro, who came from one of the old court towns of central Java, gave just that impression of seeing inexplicable and disturbing depths behind everything. Yet of all the Indonesians Leszek had met so far, none had revealed a greater sense of reality as Leszek understood it.

'Hallo,' Sumitro called out. He spoke in Indonesian. 'I could hear the betjak men comparing their fares and I guessed it was you. I came to see.'

Leszek smiled at him and gripped his hand firmly. 'They always seem to be doing that,' he said.

'Yes – well, you see what happens when a crude, uncontrolled money economy hits a simple people. They never stop talking about it.'

'But we saw a ghost tiger too.'

'Did you? Even worse! There are still plenty of those around. It didn't hurt you?'

'The betjak swerved and I fell out. But I'm quite all right.'

'You're sure? Well, come and meet my other visitors. I didn't know they were coming but I don't think you'll mind meeting them. I'm sorry my wife had to go out, she's teaching tonight.'

Sumitro's eyes were gleaming with pleasure all the time he was speaking. He showed Leszek ahead of him into the house. Like the men watching the badminton, he had on his sarong, but he was wearing a white shirt above it. Leszek knew from what he had read that Sumitro was almost forty, but in these clothes, with his smooth, soft skin, he looked ten years younger.

Three other men were sitting in rattan chairs in the

small main room of the house, a white man and two young Indonesians. They got up for Leszek, and all shook hands with him as Sumitro introduced them. The white man was English, a journalist called Coventry Pearce. When Sumitro said Leszek had met a ghost tiger in the betjak, Pearce said, 'I must try and find that betjak man – would you recognise him again?' and rubbed his hands with delight. He was a good-looking young man, with a lean face and luxuriant brown hair. He had on a purple shirt – Leszek, in his blue Dacron suit suddenly felt overdressed, both beside him and beside the Indonesian boys in their white shirts and cotton trousers.

Pearce had spoken in Indonesian, rather inaccurate to Leszek's ear but fluent. He replied in the same language – it was easier than English for him, by now, and politer with the Indonesians there. 'I might recognise him but I wouldn't know where to find him.'

'No, of course. I don't suppose I'd have seen anything anyway. Still it'd be quite interesting to watch someone else seeing a ghost – it might even be more frightening, you couldn't damp down their impressions with your reasonings, like you might your own.'

Sumitro poured Leszek a glass of the pale yellow Heineken's beer as they all sat down again. 'Mr Pearce is enthusiastic about our primitive ways – it's touching for us.' His eyes moved rapidly back and forth between the Englishman and the Pole, flashing with delight and anger at the same time, it seemed to Leszek. 'But Mr Mylski is a communist, so he understands how we are trapped now – trapped between our old superstitions, and the new exotic myth-makers who would free us into capitalism!'

'You're a communist?' Pearce was as enthusiastic about this as he had been about the tiger. 'I thought all you Poles were really red-hot anti-communists and all ready to admit it at the drop of a hat since Gomulka.'

'Did you think so?'

'Not really. But are you in fact a communist, somehow?'

'I could bore you describing my views, I'm sure. But though I know what terrible things have been done in the name of communism, I'm still one, really. I have a sort of bedrock to my thinking, a bedrock of egalitarian ideas, that I like to think is reasonable. But of course it may just be a bedrock of acquired clichés. However, there it is, that's how my mind works today. I try to improve it.'

'Well, I've a pretty big bedrock of my own I've no doubt – an enormous one probably! Dreadful! – oh dear, dreadful now you say it like that. I'll shut up and examine mine for a few seconds.'

They all laughed. Leszek had been thinking that he and Pearce were already starting to exclude the Indonesians from the conversation, and he wondered if Pearce had thought the same. It seemed likely, as Pearce turned his face expectantly towards Sumitro now, at just the same moment as Leszek did. Leszek felt a sudden pleasure at meeting Pearce.

Sumitro looked at one of the young Indonesians. 'Achmad, tell them about the tiger in your well.'

Achmad's eyes widened, but he drew back his lips, pressing his lower teeth against his top lip. Pleasure and shyness were warring visibly in him. At last he swallowed, and started to speak, beginning rather gulpily. 'My brother was poisoned up in Sumatra by a man who wanted his land. But the *dukun*, that's the magic doctor in the village, you know, he said it was some evil influence, and he went down the well and came up with a handful of tiger's hairs. He must have been paid by the man who killed my brother, but everyone in the village believed him, except me.'

'And yet they're not political, these boys, not in the least!' Sumitro laughed, but he was speaking passionately.

'They know all these things, and they're good boys, but they're not political! They read my books and come and say flattering things to me about them but they haven't got a political thought in their heads!'

The boys were also laughing. Achmad gulped his laughs out through gritted teeth, while the other, Subekto, evidently a Javanese like Sumitro, laughed softly with his whole, round, smooth face.

'We love your art, tuan,' he said, in a voice as soft as his laugh.

Sumitro's eyes glistened again. 'I'd better give up writing, then!'

'No!' said Pearce. He shook his curly hair. 'No, you see, the trouble with all you moralists, communists or whatever, is that you want everybody always to be living for everybody else. But it can't be done. And it'd be so boring if it could. Of course you can put wrongs right sometimes but that's not what concerns most people. What's important is for people to live through everybody else, as I see it, not for everybody else. Through everybody else! All be individuals and all enjoy the extraordinary fact of other people's individuality! Sumitro, that's what you help us do as a writer, you know. You may think you're asking us to change things by telling us your stories but really you're just helping us to get more pleasure out of things as they are! That's what these boys like. They see things they've never seen in their country through your eyes and they worship you for it – it's terrific!'

'I see. I think I'm a revolutionary, but objectively I'm just a reactionary bourgeois, then. That's what your diagnosis amounts to, Mr Pearce. I don't think you're right but I'd better reconsider, hadn't I? Perhaps I really had better stop writing that sort of thing and just become an activist.'

Sumitro had sat very still, staring at the foot of Pearce's

chair, while he had said this. His whole slight body was
tense and steely – the other men in the room were like
feathers, in comparison. It silenced them all for a minute.
In the quietness they could hear shouts from the badminton
players through the open door and windows, and near the
top of the wall facing Leszek a small lizard lifted its head
and made angry ticking sounds. Leszek's emotions were
quite turbulent. It seemed as though he might be witness-
ing a man about to take a step back into mental habits
that Poland, with a great convulsion, great danger and
great rejoicing, had just thrown off. Could this gifted
man become the kind of simple propagandist that most
Poles were at present vowing never to tolerate again? There
was a joke he'd heard in the embassy only the other day.
'Who are the socialist realist composers?' – 'Those who're
dead and those who say they are.' That was the nation-
wide mood of scepticism about such matters at the present
time.

But there was a more personal clash of feelings going on
in Leszek as well. Sumitro convinced him, in a few words,
what in any case his eyes told him plainly enough: that
there was poverty and humiliation everywhere about
them, as they sat talking in the warm tropical night. Yet
he had to make an effort to resent it. The world was
charming him as he had never been charmed before. He
had not heard so much laughter in his life, it seemed, as
he had heard in the last two months. And he had never
felt less desire to change things, more desire just to see
them. He looked again at Pearce. The Englishman was
just starting to speak again, leaning forward in his chair,
spreading the fingers of his left hand in front of him.
Leszek couldn't remember ever having heard such a
calmly unmoral view of life put forward by such an
attractive person. No one with any pretensions would have
dared make such an unsophisticated defence of pleasure

in Poland. Poland seethed with morality, at any rate publicly. And now Pearce was repudiating even the mild agreement he'd expressed with something Leszek had said earlier:

'You know best for yourself, Sumitro, but I go to the other extreme! I don't think I even agree with what Mr Mylski just said, after all. I don't believe in digging around too much in bedrocks – let bedrocks lie! I like the frost that glitters on the bedrock sometimes!' He had said the word 'frost' in English. 'Do you boys know what frost is?'

Achmad grinned excitedly, keeping his lips tightly pressed together, as though he knew perfectly well but could never get the acknowledgement of it past his modesty. Subekto simply said with a slow smile: 'In the cold season . . .'

'They're lucky they only know the word,' said Sumitro, all the tension gone again. 'Our people might be tempted to forgive the Dutch if they'd all had their faces frozen off them in Amsterdam.'

Leszek suddenly remembered a morning in a small town in the Tatra mountains: icy air coming in round his head through the window of a wooden boarding-house as he and Zosia looked out at a fountain below that had frozen in the night – twelve feet of water arrested in mid-air. 'It's like a great silver bush,' Zosia had said, staring in amazement. She could glide under his defences at any moment, still.

But his thoughts were called back by Sumitro's servant coming into the room, carrying a large plate. She was another very typical Javanese, with a small round head on a slender neck, a muslin blouse and a *kain*, a cloth of dark blue and brown batik wrapped tightly round her from her waist to her ankles. Her pouting mouth was like the place where a stalk had been broken off a fruit. She must have been about twenty.

She came up to Leszek smiling, and offered him one of the skewers of meat on the plate. 'Tuan is the Polish Dutchman?' she said, her voice soft but ringing.

'Yes – yes I'm Polish,' Leszek answered. He looked at Sumitro and saw that all the others were doing the same. They were obviously thinking the same thing. In one of Sumitro's best-known stories there was a servant girl who spoke of an 'English Dutchman'. But no one said anything, and Sumitro only smiled faintly back at them with his eyes.

Just then there was the noise of a car stopping outside the door. 'Oh my God,' Pearce said, in English. He looked at the two boys. 'It's Bill.' He started to explain to Sumitro, 'I'm sorry, I think it's a friend of mine, a journalist.' At that moment a tall figure appeared in the doorway. It was a young white man with his hair already balding unevenly, thick glasses and a missing top tooth. He was grinning broadly. 'Tuan Sumitro's house?' he asked in a raucous voice with, it seemed to Leszek, an American accent. 'O.K., Cov, O.K., I know I've seen you so it must be but, Jesus, I must be polite. Introduce me.'

Pearce, who had got up, sighed loudly and said, 'Sumitro, this is Bill Macpherson, he's a Canadian journalist working for an agency. I told him I was coming here and he said he had to come and meet you. He's heard about your books – he hasn't read them.'

Macpherson shook hands vigorously with Sumitro, said the Indonesian word for books – '*buku-buku*', it was not difficult – and winked at Sumitro with a nod of the head and a further grinning grimace. 'Cov,' he went on in English, 'tell him I hear he's a genius even if he is a communist. That's the story, eh? – the communist genius from a little unknown land.' He slapped his fist into his palm. 'I hope he'll give.'

'Please invite your friend to sit down,' said Sumitro.

'Do I have to?'

'I welcome him.'

'All right, sit down,' Pearce said to Macpherson. 'But you'll have to come with me some other time if you want to talk to him, it's no good tonight.'

Sumitro indicated to the girl to offer Macpherson something from the plate, and this started Macpherson off again immediately. He did not seem to have any idea that a conversation might have been going on, and apparently assumed that no one wanted to start one, since he spoke loudly in English in a way that made it clear he thought he was not understood.

'Ay! ay!' he said, looking the girl hard in the face, 'Always a cunt around to keep your eye up, eh, Cov, you and your two boy friends.' He winked at the girl, who smiled equably back at him. 'And who's the other fellow, sinister by Christ! – must be another commy, eh, a Russky?'

'Mr Mylski is a Pole and I think he understands what you're saying.'

'Oh sorry, Mr Mylski! My apologies. One's got to be spry with you commies, eh?' And he gave Leszek a big, friendly-looking grin in his turn. 'But I'm surrounded by commies!' Suddenly he looked round him nervously. 'I'm not afraid of *them*, but by Christ! what about the other side, Cov? Put a match to this little matchbox and they could roast us all alive in a couple of minutes! I don't like it when I go in for a quick suck with little bints, let alone in a commy's wooden house!'

'You can go if you like.'

'Oh, I'll take a chance.' He seemed to speak quite seriously. 'It's not happened yet.'

But Pearce persisted – he had evidently seen his opportunity. 'Look here, we're having a conversation all in Indonesian. Why don't you eat your stick of *saté* and go home, and I'll bring you again another day? We could even sit outside.'

'All right!' Macpherson put the whole small skewerful of meat in his mouth, then dropped the stick on the floor and got up waving both hands in the air. 'Goodbye, everybody. Goodbye, Tuan Sumitro, I'll see you again. Bad omens tonight, I feel them in the air! Keep your powder dry for me and next time shoot! Heh, heh! Thanks!' He managed the last remark again in Indonesian – '*Terima kasih*' – and went, half-running, through the door. The car engine roared and they heard the car race away.

The Indonesians had sat patiently through Macpherson's visit, except that Sumitro had got up when he arrived and again when he left. Now both the boys began to laugh uncontrollably – they obviously knew Macpherson and his ways. 'Difficult but amenable,' said Pearce, but Sumitro smiled silently, his eyes gleaming, as he poured out more beer. Leszek could only guess what asperities were running through his mind, firmly barred expression, even in this free-thinking man, by Javanese ideas of hospitality and discretion.

They talked a little longer, but when Pearce said he had to go, and offered Leszek a lift back into the middle of Djakarta, Leszek accepted. He told Sumitro he had arranged to get back fairly early. The truth was that he didn't want to miss the chance of talking to Pearce a little more. He hadn't managed to discuss with Sumitro the translations he was thinking of doing, but Sumitro seemed to accept that that was unavoidable tonight. They promised to meet again in a few days' time. The boys lived in a students' hostel near Sumitro's house, and said they would walk back.

Pearce had a small, rather dented Morris which he had parked round the side of the house. He shot off with Leszek as fast as Macpherson must have done. From the car they could see very little in the kampong. The badminton was over, and many of the houses were in darkness by now, though it was not much after nine.

'Have you been here long, Mr Pearce?' Leszek thought he'd better speak English now. But he found himself more uncertain when talking to Pearce than he would have supposed.

'Almost a year. A good year, though.'

'You like Djakarta?'

'Oh, it's a horrible place but I'm enjoying it. And you?'

'I'm enjoying it, though I agree with you.'

'Where did you see the tiger? I mean not see it.'

'Just about here, I suppose.'

They stared out of the car windows, but there was nothing visible in the headlights except the trunks of the palm trees.

'There's nowhere I know that's more like nowhere than this,' said Pearce. 'Obviously no use trying to find that tiger by earthly landmarks.'

'As hard to find the boy.'

'Exactly!'

They were silent for a moment or two, then Pearce went on, 'Look here. Would you like to come up to the hills one weekend? I'm going up in a week or two to stay in a bank bungalow. Not an embassy bungalow, you needn't worry about your secret policeman who cleans out the lavatories reporting you to your Central Committee.'

Leszek was so pleased, he was amused at himself. It was like being a schoolboy again. 'Well, yes, that'd be very nice. And I'm sure it will be all right. Yes, thank you.'

'Good! We'll have a better chance to talk, eh?'

They were already out of the trees and on to a broader, better-lit road. Old Dutch houses with urns on their gables and verandahs stood at the far end of gardens without fences – you could scarcely say where the road ended and the gardens began, or which encroached on the other. A few minutes at Pearce's speed brought them into the Dutch district that had been built just before the war, where as many rich Indonesians and Chinese as white people lived nowadays. Here, quite suddenly, they were among well-painted buff or white houses, shining in gardens full of roses and magnolias, with high banyan trees often rising some distance from the house to put half the garden in moon-shadow tonight. Leszek shared a bungalow here with two other men at the embassy. He pointed it out as they turned into his street.

'I never thought I'd live in a house like that.'

'It's pretty awful in Warsaw, eh?'

'I see now that it is, from certain points of view.'

Leszek got out of the car, and Pearce smiled at him with his long face through the window. 'Well there you are,' he said. 'And now I've got to work while you can do whatever Poles do at night. There's no justice! Luckily!' He nodded, still smiling, and as Leszek said 'Thank you' the car shot away again.

Leszek remained in the garden. He didn't like the men he shared with much, and tonight he had done things he had no desire to talk about. The sense of pleasure he had set out with had grown and grown – he seemed to have touched new life at every moment, this evening. He walked about on the grass, which was slightly dewy by now. One or two betjaks passed along the road, their wheels hissing, their rubber bands humming. The moon glowed on the ornate pink wall of the garden and the leaves of the hibiscus bushes alongside it. The red bells of the hibiscus were closed, narrow and wrinkled and limp to the feel, but he stroked one of them between his thumb and finger for a long time, looking out over the wall, before going in.

CHAPTER TWO

Coventry Pearce

WHEN Coventry Pearce left Leszek, he was balancing on the brink of a decision. Would he go and look for a girl tonight? To balance on this brink was, he knew, almost always to fall. But he went through the process every time, every week or ten days. He decided. He would. But it meant moving fast now. The glamour began to fade after half past nine, as the search started to grow more difficult. This heat encouraged lust, but quickly subdued it again if it entailed tramping up and down the streets, hoping for any sight of a moving figure in the dark. First, though, he must hurry to the Cosy Corner. The few English and American correspondents in Djakarta had a good working arrangement at present: if one of them got a story, he cabled it immediately, then told all the others. Coventry hadn't a thing himself tonight, but Gerald and the Dutchman Willem who always cooperated would be at the Cosy now and they would know if there was anything going on. Achmad and Subekto had said there was nothing in the evening papers, so even allowing for their exiguous interest in things political he knew that at least President Sukarno had not been assassinated.

He drove along the edge of Medan Merdeka – Independence Square – an old field of coarse grass where he had even heard skylarks singing, with a few fine colonial houses round it. There was a squadron of red betjaks standing under the tall trees that lined the square here. In some, the drivers were already asleep, draped across the seats with an arm hanging over the side here, a leg over the back there, contorted figures that seemed to be the contents of nightmares rather than – as they surely must be – the dreamers of them. He was glad to notice one or two girls in pink and red dresses standing about among the trees still.

The Cosy Corner was in the only street in Djakarta with anything like a European line of shops, though even that had a slow-moving canal running down the middle, twice as broad as the road for traffic either side of it. The Cosy was a narrow bar between two large stores, outside each of which a line of ragged guards sat on the pavement all night. He parked the car by the canal opposite, then walked with his usual feeling of slight amazement into the long room. A few Chinese and Eurasian boys, all of them male prostitutes, were sucking Coca-Cola through straws at the bar in the darker end of the room near the door; but deeper in, the room broadened, and figures like British bank managers and senior American diplomats sat at white-clothed tables eating expensively with their wives, while their subordinates clustered round the second bar. The scene was looked down on by a five-foot-high photograph of the head of the Italian owner, his balloon-sized eyes crazed with drink, and a giant cigar standing out stereoscopically, it seemed, from his mouth. Gerald and Willem were at the second bar, under the picture.

'Nothing?' said Coventry.

'On the contrary, we'll each have a double whisky,' said Gerald.

'No news is the most expensive news,' said Willem.

Coventry ordered three double whiskies. 'Did you see Bill?'

'He was in here a few minutes ago,' Gerald said. 'He'd had a fabulous interview with some Indonesian communist writer.'

'My God!' said Coventry. '*Buku-buku*' and '*terima kasih*', he thought. 'Yeah, I was there. It was my interview in fact. But I was doing it for love, he can have it.'

'Generous.'

'It'll be in my book. Cheers!' He drank his whisky quickly.

'In a hurry, too?' said Willem.

'Too?'

'Bill wouldn't let the waves die down.'

'Oh! Yes, well, I'll see you tomorrow.'

As he went back through the dark bar, he heard Willem's voice behind him, squeezing all the English vowels flat. 'You try your luck on the night life of Djakarta?'

That's it, he thought. He felt a fresh excitement and, at the same time, something eased deep down in him. He got into the car and drove through some small streets behind the Cosy Corner. He parked on the edge of another broad street, with the low silhouettes of Chinese shops and workshops each side of it, and the rails of a tramline gleaming along one edge. It was dark and quiet here, but some way along the road there were lighted stalls. The still air was full of smells – petrol and cloth, he thought, and faint frying smells and fruit. At Oxford he had once said to a rowing man in his college, 'I imagine you enjoy the river smell.' The man had exploded. 'The smell! We don't notice the smell!' The only possible point of contact between them lost!

He walked into the light and heat of the stalls. Here there were more people than he had seen all the evening: Chinese families of six or seven grown-ups and children, sitting on chairs or on the ground round some of the stalls, selling Hong Kong-made toys, mountains of combs, soap, little silver metal boxes of French letters. All action was desultory here, Indonesian men in white shirts and trousers and small brown fezes studying the wares of a stall for minutes on end, voices soft and twanging but repeatedly raised in laughter on one side, then another. Beyond the stalls were the girls. For fifty or sixty yards they sat in their betjaks along the tramlines, where less light – but enough light – reached them.

He walked slowly along beside them. Betjak drivers in vests and shorts leaned with their elbows on their saddles, or squatted on their heels: some of them said to him, 'Want a little girl?' or, more plainly, 'Want *mek-mek*?' The girls sometimes smiled and cocked their heads daintily to one side but said nothing. Most of them were heavily-built girls from West Java, the villages round Djakarta – Sundanese, as they were called. Their hair was thick on their shoulders, and they wore cheap white or pink cotton dresses under which the swell of their big breasts was visible. But there were one or two girls like Sumitro's servant, dressed as she had been, with tiny faces and round, brown eyes. Beyond the betjaks, where it was very dark, there was a cluster of taller women, standing up – even there you could make out their harder chins and heavy eyebrows. They were the *bantji*, the hermaphrodites, whatever that might mean – Coventry had never had the desire to find out for himself, though he reflected that he wouldn't mind knowing. They made no attempt to pass themselves off as normal women, at any rate, so there must be customers who knew what they were and wanted it.

He turned back, and as he stopped in front of one of the small-built Javanese girls he finally felt his stomach turn over with awe and excitement. For a moment he could hardly find the breath to ask her what she wanted.

'A hundred rupiah.'

'Fifty.'

'Oh, a hundred.'

He was about to acquiesce – the bargaining was a ritual, really – when suddenly the betjak man jumped to his feet and the girl, snatching his arm, said, 'All right, fifty.' The man started to push the betjak forward while Coventry, puzzled but complying, was still standing on the step in front of the betjak seat, and as he turned to sit down he fell beside the girl. He saw that all the betjaks were moving. Some of the drivers were pushing them wildly, half-lifting them across the tramlines; most, like his own, were running to gain momentum before jumping on to the saddle. His betjak was one of perhaps forty that were now pounding down the street into the darkness, spreading out across the road and scraping each other's wheels. The night was filled with the noise of them.

'Police,' the girl beside him said, laughing, and clutching his arm. 'Razzia!' So that was what it was! Looking round him at the shadowy stampede, Coventry couldn't see a man in any of the other betjaks. A lucky break for this girl, then – and a pity, really, that it hadn't been a lucky break for a man short of money.

'All right, a hundred,' he said. He put his arm round her and felt the cold skin of her upper arm. Waves of relief suddenly ran through him: this moment was always one of the most intense. His body sank into the hard betjak seat, pressing against hers.

'Thank you, *om*.' She used the Dutch word for 'uncle'.

'What's your name?'

'Sri.'

'Where do you come from?'

'Madiun.'

That was a town in Central Java where there had been a massacre of communists in 1948, after they had attempted to take over the newly independent Indonesia. Only a few days before, Coventry had mentioned the name of Madiun in some connection to a cheerful English librarian who had been in Djakarta for several months putting the University's books in order for UNESCO. 'Where's that,

Cov?' 'Oh, it's where the communist revolt took place.' 'Ah, that must have been when I was in Singapore for a few days.' The girl could have been no more than eight or nine at the time, and probably knew as little. He asked her if she'd heard of Musso, one of the communist leaders killed at Madiun.

'Don't know him, *om*.'

The betjaks were thinning out now, and his turned alone off the main road into an alley, a *gang*, between very small bamboo houses. They went for a long way through this shack district, lit only by the moon shining in narrow canals, hardly more than ditches, alongside the paths of packed earth. The betjak driver said to Coventry, 'Tuan understands our language, then?'

'Yes.' It was as well to establish the fact. Betjak drivers with white passengers on such business were liable to shout to passers-by, 'He's going for *mek-mek*,' which was embarrassing, even positively risky, for one's reputation at least. They were not so likely to do so if they knew that the passenger understood. Coventry asked the girl if she could do Javanese dancing – she came from one of the districts famous for it. She said, 'No', laughing shyly – a funny, twanging little word in Djakarta dialect, '*Ng-ga.*'

'Can you sing then?'

'*Ng-ga!*' This time she spoke more shrilly, and laughed more heartily.

'Of course you can,' the betjak driver said above their heads. 'There's a moon tonight.'

The remark set the girl off screaming with laughter, while Coventry pressed her arm harder. And she was still laughing several minutes later when they stopped outside one of the houses. He got out of the betjak with her, holding her hand, which was as cold as her arm. She called through the wall to someone inside, then led him through a bamboo door that opened directly on to a small room. The only furniture was a chair, and a wooden bed with a mattress and sheet, but the wall was covered with coloured pictures cut out of magazines, Indonesian film stars and political leaders. There was also a framed portrait of President Sukarno. The girl turned to face him, looking straight up into his eyes. 'Do it slowly,' she said.

The appeal was so touching he couldn't move for a moment. But she immediately took off her thin blouse and her white brassière, and unwrapped the cloth from the lower part of her body, on which she was wearing nothing else. She took a pin out of her shiny black hair and suddenly it fell down her back to her waist. Then she lay down on the bed. He stepped over to the bed, and with the palm of his hand rubbed the top of her arm again where he had been holding it. She looked up at him, unsmiling but with soft eyes, and pouted slightly – invitingly, he supposed, though he was not sure. Her little, almost violin-shaped body was milky-brown in colour, except for her small breasts which were pale round the nipples, and her dark knees. He ran his hand over her breasts: they were as cold as everywhere else he had touched. These moments were moments of tense but pure happiness, and he leaned forward and pressed his face into the side of her thick hair, with its pungently sweet smell of coconut oil. What followed as he undressed and lay on her was really just like some final tidying-up of an operation now, necessary to give any sense of satisfaction, yet far from the high point of pleasure, which he had already lived through as he looked at her lying on the bed. He did not excite her, just kept his hands on her slight, soft breasts. His moment of coming gave him just a sensation of completion. It didn't matter that she got up quickly afterwards. He sat on the edge of the bed while she washed herself from a bucket of water she pulled out from under it. She smiled at him now, at last.

'Nice?' she said.

He nodded. Then he got up and washed himself in the same water. He had to take a small chance there. Sometimes he tried to hop up first.

'Are you married?' he said.

'Divorced. My husband took a second wife.' She was suddenly quite friendly.

'Were you married very young?'

'As soon as I started bleeding, *om*.'

'Will you marry again?'

She giggled. 'In the New Year. A chauffeur.'

'You'll have rides in a car.'

'No! It's not allowed!'

He gave her a hundred rupiah note and some other small notes that were in his wallet. As he dressed, with her passing him his clothes, a small girl, six or seven years old, came into the room and took the bucket out. She stared at him with big eyes when she brought it back again, full of clean water, and he gave her some coins out of his pocket. Her whole face broke into a smile. It doesn't cost much to buy gratitude here, he thought. Although there was no doubt who was the worse off, he was not sure who was the most humiliated. He asked Sri if she wanted a lift back to the street he'd brought her from, but she said she was staying. He pressed her to him before leaving, then went out to find the betjak man still on the road. They drove back in silence this time.

Coventry decided he must go and have a glass of beer before going home. Everything felt flat now. It was restful, but to feel really calm he needed to have just a little more subdued energy in him, just as much as might be provided by a bottle of Heineken's.

He took the car to another district, the Pasar Senen,

similar to the one where he had found Sri tonight. There was a Chinese eating-place there that he was fond of: not much more than a brightly lit shed, but if you sat outside it earlier in the evening, around six o'clock, you started by feeling you had a table in the street, then as dusk came up the light from the shed seemed to grow around you and the street fell back.

There was only one other person sitting outside tonight, an enormous smooth-faced Chinaman in white shirt and trousers whom Coventry had seen there before. He was called 'Tuan Gemuk' – 'Mr Fat' – by the owner, who was almost as large, and both men obviously regarded this as normal and proper homage. Coventry, sitting in a low rattan arm-chair, watched Mr Fat's puffed-up hand gripping his beer-bottle like a weapon that he thought he was in danger of losing. Everywhere greed, coarseness, violence. No doubt he had been guilty of all three himself tonight – he could pick them out and inveigh against them as well as anyone. Yet he felt at peace with the world as he drank the cold yellow beer, and men passed by at the edge of the light, kicking up the dust of the street. Even the sexual stresses of the last few years, all that dreamy, bullying passion over Charlotte in Oxford, all that anguish over Susan in Brighton – Brighton of all places! – had slipped away during these last months. Probably they would return in some form or other. But for the moment he didn't seem to want anyone except girls like Sri. There was a tall, good-looking Dutchman here the other night with a girl he had obviously been down to the shacks with – absurd, some people might have thought, for him to be picking up whores when he could clearly cut a swathe through women wherever he liked. But when this greasy-haired girl with the cold limbs had given the man two firm pats on the balls as he had stood half-facing her, just before they took a table, Coventry knew the fullness of satisfaction that the girl had recognised and wanted to symbolise.

He ordered another bottle of beer. What would that man Mylski make of Djakarta? he wondered. It seemed unlikely that he would ever know these pleasures, 'try his luck on the night life of Djakarta' as Willem had put it. But he had fascinated Coventry: you didn't often meet people who kept their thinking in order as steadily as Mylski seemed to. You could see it in those steady blue eyes of his. He was strong. That was why Macpherson, who combined a very sharp eye with an unfailingly wrong judgment, had thought him sinister. But Macpherson was also strong in his volatile way, it had to be said. And he, Coventry, was strong too, for that matter. They all were, these sociable solitaries who gathered in Eastern capitals far from home.

When he got to the car, after drinking a third bottle of beer, Coventry realised he was rather drunk. He was wondering whether he ought to make a further check on the news by going to the Indonesian press agency, but there seemed a lot to be said now for driving straight, and slowly, home. He hadn't wanted to meet anyone, anyway – he never did after being with a girl. He didn't want any vulgar guesses and quips from the Willems of this world. He'd rather have Macpherson's frank, insatiable envy. It was a great advantage working for a Sunday paper, in normal conditions, not having absolutely to file anything till Wednesday or Thursday, and filling things out with those long reports for their special subscribers more or less when he felt like it. Still, on what they paid him for the copy he despatched it was lucky his father had left him a few pounds.

He turned homewards, into another street with a canal along the side of it. The city was really deserted now. There were probably some eyes on him from the gardens of the small houses on the other side of the road, night guards sitting with their backs against the trees. Though as they were really only camouflage for the protection racket, they probably hadn't bothered to stay awake. In the distance, across the canal, a red light shone at the top of the lacework cathedral spire, just visible as a dark black silhouette in the sky. That was another district where the girls strolled at night, and an Englishman he knew at the university had had his class rolling about with laughter, so he said, when he made some dry allusion to the place in discussing Yeats:

> Night walker's song
> Under great cathedral gong.

Looking out at the spire through the car window, Coventry suddenly felt his front wheel scrape up against the stone wall of the canal, and there was a loud, dwindling clatter. Curse! It was his hub-cap that had been spun off by the blow, he knew. He stopped the car and got out into the silent street. None of the guards, if there, had stirred. But he could see it lying several yards behind the car. When he got there and tried to pick it up, though, it wouldn't move. He could only just squeeze his finger nails under the edges of it, and then he couldn't lift it. Slowly it came into his mind that he was kneeling alone in the night, trying to pull up one of the studs that marked the middle of the road.

CHAPTER THREE

Jane Summerson

IN the month she had been in Djakarta, the most
remarkable event Jane Summerson had taken part in
had been an evening of strip poker, at the end of which
two men had been sitting in vests, trousers and bare feet,
the most careless player – a married woman of forty – had
been lying on a sofa, hiding her underclothes under a pile
of yellow and orange cushions, and Jane herself had
managed to get away with forfeiting a number of remov-
able two-headed buttons. But this morning she would
have been willing to admit there had been some point in
coming all the way from England. She and Bertrand
Hobley, to whose children she was acting as nanny while
she thought about what to do with a degree in French,
were walking along a mountain path which looked over
miles of deep valley to the slopes and peak of a mountain
opposite. All the lower part of the distant mountain was
glittering and shining this morning. It was cut into
hundreds of terraces with rice growing on them, and a
sheen of water trickling down the side of every terrace
caught the white rays of the early morning sun. Where she
and Bertrand walked it was cool, and damp underfoot,
the sun's rays not touching these slopes yet, and the tea
bushes on either side of the path were dark and dewy.
They stopped now and then to take deep lungfuls of air,
then laugh breathlessly.

After these interludes Bertrand continued with the
subject he had been talking about ever since they had left
the bungalow. He was a man with a large head made

still larger by solid brown-rimmed spectacles. His upper teeth sloped slightly forward, and as he spoke his top lip continually climbed up them and slid down them again. Jane was very conscious of this, as also of a jagged hollow in his neck where his razor did not easily reach and small hairs curled. For this morning's walk he was wearing a white shirt and long white shorts.

'Mind you, I'm not saying I've been anything but extremely lucky to marry my good lady, but there, one must face facts, when one marries one not only chooses a wife but without knowing it at the time one chooses a whole style of life that excludes other styles of life, just as one's wife excludes other women. Ha ha! – "The fecundity of the unexpected far exceeds the statesman's prudence," that's a phrase I remember learning from my first ambassador, it's a remark of Proudhon's, I think. But it also exceeds the husband's prudence, yes! You don't know what you're letting yourself in for when you let the mysterious magnetic force of a woman play on you day and night!'

Bertrand struck a tea bush with his new red Javanese-cherry walking-stick, and laughed again. It was not a violent blow, it was more like writing an exclamation mark at the end of a sentence, Jane thought, having a propensity to write a lot of them herself in letters home to her sister and mother. The mountains had released something in Bertrand. Perhaps he did have other confidants, but down in Djakarta she had never heard him breathe a complaining word. In his stiff way he had seemed the most good-humoured and attentive of husbands.

But when Jane thought of the breakfast they had just had in the bungalow, she understood him. She remembered another breakfast, when she was staying overnight in Dublin with an elderly couple, friends of her grandparents, on her way to the west coast of Ireland. This old school-

38

teacher and his wife threw jokes at each other across the table all through the meal. But it did not tax their resources very heavily, because after each remark there was several minutes' laughter – each laughing in turn, picking up a laugh as it subsided in the other, like a couple of boats at their moorings rocking each other. It had seemed to her, ever since, a perfect expression of what a marriage should become.

At the embassy bungalow, fifty miles out of Djakarta, that they were staying in this weekend, it had been very different. The embassy staff took it in turns to come up here, but Angela, Mrs Hobley, gave up some of the weekends when she had a right to part of the bungalow, in return for the exclusive use of it two or three weekends a year. And her Sunday morning breakfast in the bungalow had obviously been especially important for her. Under Jane's supervision, the children – Rupert, aged six, and Charlotte, aged four – had had to make toast over the embers of the log fire Bertrand had got going on their arrival yesterday afternoon. Two toasting forks had been sent out from England for these weekends. Their prongs had come through the wrapping paper, and had caused a certain amount of damage to the mail in the embassy bag, which Jane had been surprised to learn really was a sack carried across a man's shoulder at the airport.

The bacon and eggs had given no trouble this morning, since the Indonesian cook they had brought up with them had been minutely trained by Angela in that dish. But Bertrand had been sent to make the coffee all over again after having made it too weak in a new and unfamiliar jug. Angela had come nearest to showing annoyance when it was discovered that only a jar of inferior marmalade had been brought up to the bungalow. However *coki*, as they called the cook, had immediately discovered a pot of Oxford Marmalade which, she claimed, had been left by previous visitors, and it was decided to borrow that and replace it later. Jane was fairly sure it had been brought up to the hills as intended by *coki*, who had hoped to suppress it first and sell it subsequently at a Chinese shop.

Apart from her anxious 'What's this?' when the offending marmalade jar was brought out, Angela had just organised the whole meal with simple seriousness – no excitement, no drawing attention to what she was doing, absolutely no hysteria. Her small face, more tightly-drawn than in photographs Jane had been shown of earlier years, was constantly moving, her eyes fastened on the many procedures she wanted under way; but she did not say much, and that was said quietly and firmly. It was as though everything was being done for someone not present, who in due course would come and give his approval. But even when there were guests in the Hobley household, it was never their approval that was sought. They too, it seemed, just provided desirable procedures for Angela to guide calmly to their conclusion. All Jane could think was that Angela wrote about it in the long letters – where, perhaps, she, too, finally gave way to exclamation marks – that she sent to her mother, even more frequently than Jane wrote to hers.

Yet in the end breakfast, it had to be admitted, was very good and pleasant. The dining-room looked out through broad windows to the mountain Bertrand and she were now passing in the distance, and as the family sat there they watched a tiny feather of pink cloud that lay across the very tip of the peak slowly spread, its centre darkening. The children enjoyed the toast they had made, carefully scraping off the few burnt patches and polishing it to what they considered perfection. Bertrand, already in his white clothes, sat facing Angela in her black woollen dress with an air of delight, as if he had just stepped into the dining-room for the first time that morning, and found everything waiting for him exactly as he liked it. He particularly praised the marmalade. After breakfast, which, in spite of all the preparations, they had sat down to punctually at half past eight, Angela had suggested that Jane and Bertrand should go across to the bank bungalow a mile away, and invite to lunch a journalist called Coventry Pearce who was staying there, along with anyone else who wanted to come. If they went straight-away, she said, they would catch the bank visitors before there was any danger of them going out. This was what Jane and Bertrand were now on their way to do.

Jane tried to find an answer to what Bertrand had just been saying. 'But you have style, you know, Bertrand, you really do.'

'Ah! An outer style, a public style, yes, I get glimpses of that.' Bertrand again struck excitedly at a bush. 'But it's not the same as inner style, you know, intimate style, the style of your soul calmly orbiting, if I may put it that way. I've thought a lot about this. My style's really just a parody – I get glimpses of it, as I say! – yes, a parody of the upper middle-class diplomatist, licensed to show a strictly controlled sort of extravagance, licensed to be a parody in fact. You've read your Proust, I'm like a Monsieur de Norpois with secret doubts – and what would he be with those, just ask yourself!'

'No – no, you've got something else, you know, you've got a sort of gentleness. That comes from inside.'

'Oh! Well, Jane my dear, it touches me, it touches me very much to hear you say that. Yes. It does. But what I've been saying is true, all the same, and peculiarly true for us diplomatists – we who are thought to have such fine freedoms as we go unburdened with much work about the capitals of the world. It's all right for an unmarried man. But in no career is a wife really so thrust into the warp and woof of one's days! You've seen it for yourself – you've seen it for yourself. I remember a colleague of mine in Istanbul – the ambassador at the time there was a single man and he had his mother out for a while doing the entertaining for him. This chap I speak of, he was first secretary then, chancellor I believe now, he liked to squire the ambassador's mother round a bit too, and one day he left a note for his secretary which I happened to see: "Shan't be back till late this evening since I'm taking my wife" – small "w" – "and H.E.'s Mother" – capital "M" – "to the Bosphorus". "My wife", small "w", "ambassador's Mother", capital "M"! Oh! Oh!' Bertrand's laugh boomed across the valley. 'I wonder what was in his head! There was more than mere tuft-hunting there!'

'But he still put his wife first,' said Jane.

'My God! Yes! I never thought of that. Oh my God, yes! How terribly sharp of you! Wife with a small "w" but coming up first – he couldn't help himself! My God, that makes it a gem! Oh, you're sharp, my dear!'

It was becoming difficult for Jane. She wished she'd never made the remark, especially as it occurred to her that it was just as likely that Bertrand had put the two women in that order and not the original note-writer at all. She looked out across the valley to find something to say about it and change the subject. The sun was touching the slopes below them on their side of the valley by now, and a river far away was sparkling brilliantly. They could make out water buffaloes in it, with some small boys swimming around them or sitting on their backs and washing them, the sun gleaming on their wet skin. For a moment Jane had been saddened by Bertrand's story and his pleasure in it, but her elation at being in this country-side could not be marred for long this morning.

'Just look at those boys!' she said.

Bertrand stared into the valley. Then he said 'Yes, when the autumn thunderstorms begin soon you'll see them running out into the streets naked at four o'clock, that's when it comes down, you know – little fellows, they dance about naked in the pouring rain and push and pull the cars out of the lakes that form in the streets.'

It sounded a delightful sight, better than anything she'd seen in Djakarta yet. She had one of those travellers' pangs of hoping she wouldn't miss it through some quirk in the seasons. Risking further pangs of the same sort, she managed to keep Bertrand on the subject of the Javanese climate till they turned a bend and saw another large wooden bungalow in the trees above them, and in front of it five or six people on a terraced lawn that was bright green in the sunshine. In fact the whole garden, and the front of the bungalow, was lit up with sharp yellow light.

'There it is!' said Bertrand. He laughed his booming laugh again. 'And that's Coventry!' He did not need to be more specific about the person he had named. One man was standing up, waving a large, ragged banana frond in the air above him. Everyone else was sitting in chairs round a table, looking at him. The scene leaped at Jane's eye, like a needle she'd been searching for with a magnet. Bertrand's laugh obviously reached them since they all turned and looked. Coventry lowered the frond and seemed to shake it admonishingly at a stout young man in a white T-shirt who was sprawling back in a chair. Then he dropped it and came running and jumping down the garden towards them.

'Hello, Bertrand,' he shouted. 'Come and support me against these dinosaurs!'

He opened a wooden gate for them in the thick hedge at the foot of the garden, then looked rather shyly at Jane and smiled. The smile seemed to crease up the whole bottom part of his narrow face. She found herself liking so much the contrast between his extravagant gestures

43

in the distance and this sudden self-consciousness. His abundant curly hair and bronze shirt both shone in the sunlight. His shyness seemed hardly to last a moment and he stood there very alertly, gripping the top of the open gate, his eyes holding hers until Bertrand said, 'Jane, this, as I announced from afar off, is Coventry Pearce – Coventry, Jane Summerson, who's staying with us.'

They shook hands, Coventry smiling still more broadly. 'Unexpected relief from our envoy in Djakarta! I hope you'll both come and help me make a few dents in the hide of a monster from the bank. He's not my host, by the way, so I'm allowed to be rude to him.'

They went up the path on to the lawn, and Jane was introduced all round before she sat down. The object of Coventry's scorn – the stout young man, as she had supposed – was called Thomas. A blonde girl called Christine was sitting on the grass by the side of his chair, with an arm curled round his calf. Thomas was leaning back looking pleased with himself, but at the same time rather defiantly determined not to let that self-satisfaction be shaken. Despite his languorous posture his elbows were resting stiffly on the arms of the chair. There was another young bank employee, slim and heavily freckled, called Toby. He grinned and nodded silently at her – he had a glass in his hand and, to Jane's surprise, a bottle of champagne and a Guinness on the grass by his chair, whereas the others had breakfast things round them. A tall girl called Jenny was sitting next to Toby. Lastly there was a man introduced to her, and to Bertrand, who knew everybody else, as a Pole, Leszek. He was a short man, very blond, and more formally dressed than the others, in blue trousers that evidently belonged to a suit: he got up and kissed the back of her hand, his lips barely touching it, and looked at her with a sharpness that might as much have meant a frown as a smile.

44

'Now, Thomas,' said Coventry, picking up the banana leaf from the grass, 'repeat in front of Her Majesty's representative and this lady what you'd just said to me when we heard them.'

Thomas's arms stiffened still more. 'I said they're all *orangs* to me.'

Coventry waved his leaf in frenzy. 'Listen to that! Have you ever heard such a classic utterance? Miss Summerson, shall I spell out the meaning to you, if, as I understand, you're a new arrival?'

Jane smiled with due awkwardness and Coventry went on. '*Orang* is the Indonesian word for man. This dinosaur is talking about Indonesians and what he's doing is delightedly pouring back into the word the meaning we've given it in *orang utan*, which means really "man of the forests". To him all Indonesians are *orangs*. Oh, you dinosaur!' He shook the leaf over Thomas's head. 'Here have I for weeks been untangling all the subtleties in Djakarta's political scene, here's Leszek translating wonderful Indonesian novels, and what do you see trotting through the streets of Djakarta – nothing but *orangs*!'

'I don't know anything about the novels,' said Thomas. 'That's as may be. But the politics is all fancy dress. It all boils down to "We want, but the only way we know of getting is to grab".'

'All politics are "we want", Thomas,' said Coventry. 'All banking, anyway. Well, I'll concede you one thing, truth obliges me to, or half-truth anyway. Correspondents in Djakarta never throw a cable away just because some sudden change in the political scene has made it out of date – they always reckon they may be able to use it again a week or a month later.'

Everybody laughed. But Leszek spoke for the first time. 'Careful, Coventry. When we talk with someone like Mr Thomas we see eye to eye, and it would be a pity if our united front at such times should open to reveal the gaps beneath.'

Coventry wheeled round and looked Leszek straight in the face, laughing. Then he looked back at the others. 'He's my conscience, you see, and a very good gentle one too – steering me gently. But I said it was a half-truth, Leszek, didn't I now, a joke permitted?'

Bertrand had been looking pained while this conversation was going on, holding his glasses in front of him by the rims and rocking the ear-pieces to and fro. 'You see, Thomas,' he suddenly said, putting his glasses back. 'You can't – well, you can't, you know, put it quite like that – I mean, really, it just isn't like that, is it? I mean, we wouldn't get very good marks, would we, if that was the kind of despatch we sent back to London? – it wouldn't look too good on the South-East Asia desk, would it?'

Thomas himself had to join in the laughter at this, and Jane noticed what a rapid change of feeling she had had in the brief time during which Bertrand had been speaking. She had started by being extremely embarrassed for him. She'd noticed already how helpless he was at engaging in serious discussion on any level except his own scrupulous one, and it seemed she was going to witness a dreadful example of that. But in mid-sentence the issue itself had been dropped, the actor had taken the speech over, and the perfect rebuke had been delivered – perfect because it made the speaker seem a comic figure even as it registered the recipient's foolishness.

As they made their way back a few minutes later – Angela was anxious to learn as soon as possible what had been settled – Bertrand showed that, all the same, he had not felt easy about his performance. 'Coventry can talk to anybody,' he said, stopping to poke at the root of a tea-bush. 'He's clever but I'm never sure if he believes a word he says. I say, the Pole pounced on him, didn't he? – very

46

earnest, wasn't he, but very quick too. I wonder who he is. We'll find out more over lunch.'

'He was quite shy for a moment when he spoke to me first.'

'The Pole?'

'No – no, Coventry.'

'Oh! Oh yes, perhaps he's a bit shy with women, yes, you're sharp there, Jane, he takes a little time to get on with them. It was the same with Angela, I think, but they get on very well together now.'

An extraordinary pang cut through Jane at Bertrand's words. In a horrid flash she saw a truth that she could not for one moment believe in: Coventry as Angela's secret lover, Angela's calm as a sort of sleep-walking, her mind on Coventry. But it was impossible: she knew how Angela had been occupied during almost every minute of the last month, and there had not been the slightest scope for the attentions of a lover. Coventry's name had been mentioned from time to time, but he and Angela had almost certainly never been near each other. It was a fantasy – and it could only be a jealous one. What had Coventry done, then, running down the garden like that, and pausing shyly?

All the rest of the morning she found herself suppressing her impatience for the visit of the bank bungalow people. Coventry, Leszek, Toby and Jenny were coming – Thomas and Christine had other plans. Jane had to play with the children in the garden till lunch, but she left them to themselves. Rupert, who was always asking for his hands to be wiped, was making his sister dig a ditch. Jane sat in a deck-chair looking over the valley. The walk across to the bank bungalow already seemed a distant experience, she had been so affected by the meeting with the people there. And the scene across the valley seemed to record the change. The sun was high in the sky now, the sky

47

almost white with its brightness, and the valley was no longer sparkling but rich and heavy with deep greens and browns. The cloud on the mountain had spread out further across the sky and the peak was hidden in white swirls. But here in the garden it was perfect under the trees, with the air beginning to shimmer over the sunlit lawn. She was trying to read a novel called *Room at the Top* that everyone in the embassy was talking about, but her thoughts, repeatedly deflected from Coventry, kept turning to other men she had known. She recalled them now with tenderness and indifference. John, her first serious boy-friend, so charmingly incapable of seriousness himself, who would turn the crack at the end of his penis into the shape of a mouth, and make it say pert things to her in a throttled voice. And Frederick, last year, who had kept her frightened nearly all the time, and made love to her in a cold, masterful way that gave her an extreme pleasure she sometimes quite resented. She thought of them both now with the friendliness of freedom from them. Both men seemed arrested in their ways, with nothing to offer but diminishing charm, diminishing power.

About half past twelve she heard the visitors. The road by car from the other bungalow went down into the valley, then with many turns wound its way up to the embassy bungalow. Jane could hear the car a mile away, in the silence where only parrots squealed in the trees above her head, and Rupert's voice rang out, 'Don't splash me, Lottie!' The murmur of its engine came and went, then quite suddenly it stopped, and there were voices and the banging of car doors. It was like the moment, Jane thought, when she and Bertrand had first seen the bank people sitting up on their high lawn in the yellow light, only now the scene was about to be floated up to her where she sat. The children ran round the drive, Charlotte happily throwing down her shovel, but Jane stayed where she was. In a moment the Hobley family and the bank visitors all appeared round the side of the bungalow.

The newcomers looked much as they had done a few hours ago. Only Jane herself had changed, from a blouse and skirt to a white dress with light blue edging that stood out prettily below the waist, she thought, showing off her slim calves. Coventry was talking, but when he saw Jane he stopped and strode across to her ahead of the others. 'Hallo,' he said. 'Toby will babble to you about bandits we saw in the bushes on the way up but don't worry, they were only girls picking tea.'

'Are there bandits, then?'

'Oh there are, terribly fierce Muslim ones, but Toby's private visions are more to be feared today. We couldn't get him off the black velvet. But perhaps he'll just pass out.'

'What happens to him?'

Coventry laughed. 'Oh, some grief or other – we shall never quite get to the bottom of it, I'm afraid. It's a great pity, he's a man of the most liberal views when he's in a fit state to express them. No end of a help.'

Jane was just about to concede a touch of disappointment at this apparent heartlessness when Coventry, for an instant, looked solemn. 'We did try this morning,' he said softly.

Toby's head was lolling on his shoulder, and Jenny was holding his arm and steering him, but there was still a grin on his tilted face. 'No bandits?' he murmured. And as Jenny lowered him into a wicker chair Bertrand had fetched for him, he closed his eyes.

'Very disappointing for him,' said Coventry. The others standing around laughed awkwardly. But after a moment they all started to turn their attention from Toby and talk of other things. Angela began to organise the considerable labour now available – it did not take her long to get a table, spread with cold chicken and salad and wine, out into the garden under the trees, and chairs round it for everybody.

A man from a nearby village came over to the bungalow at Sunday lunch-time to serve drinks. He went round the backs of the chairs now, in a khaki suit and his little brown fez, poking them each in turn in their shoulder – rather than risk rudeness by looking in their faces – in order to offer them gins and whiskies. Toby's head rose slowly when his shoulder got a second, particularly firm poke, but they were relieved to see it subside again. Bertrand, who never liked to let a subject drop while there was life in it, came back to the bandits.

'Jane, you know, we didn't like to tell you because we thought it might frighten you, but that was silly, I see – me being silly, I hasten to say, not Angela, she just went along with me. Anyway they do sometimes come here and talk to *coki* at night and get a bit of food from her, but they're pro-Western, they're rather fiercely anti-communist Muslims, the Muslim Brotherhood, you know. You don't need to worry. They're rather theoretical bandits, anyway, not quite sure what action to take – just the remains of a movement for a religious government, a theocracy, you know. I wonder if Mr Mylski has found his side of the fence – I won't say curtain! – troubled by them?'

Leszek smiled. 'We don't have any bungalows,' he said.

Bertrand laughed loudly. 'No, well that really does deny them their last possible *champ de gloire*.'

'They've met their Bungaloo,' said Coventry.

Jane found herself laughing immoderately at this remark, and stopped abruptly. Throughout the rest of lunch she watched both Coventry and Angela more covertly. Angela was unmistakably pleased to have

Coventry there, but her main aim seemed to be to ensure that he should have ample opportunity to talk. She once interrupted Bertrand to say, 'Let Coventry go on with his story.' Bertrand replied, with a show of mountain spirit that pleased Jane, 'You're Boswelling, my dear.' Coventry looked uneasy at this: in any case, he didn't need Angela's help, for he dominated the lunch table without difficulty. He was a competitive talker, not if he could help it allowing anyone to say anything amusing without using it as a springboard for something amusing of his own. However, Angela did not seem to look for any particular attention from him in return. It was as though keeping everyone filled with his conversation was the same kind of charge on her hospitality as keeping their glasses filled with wine. She'll be busy at her writing desk tonight, thought Jane with a growing sense of relief.

But the best, and most unexpected snatch of conversation that she heard between Coventry and Angela came to her from a distance, when she was concentrating on something else. Rupert, speculating further on what he had heard about Muslims, announced while they were eating their strawberries – flown in from East Africa – that he was the Sultan of Java. 'Then Lottie must be the Sultana,' Bertrand had said encouragingly. Lottie had taken this all wrong. 'I'm not a sultana!' she had screamed, and Rupert, grasping the situation at once, had said, 'Yes, you are, and I'll roll you into the pastry with my rolling pin.' Jane had had to walk to the end of the garden with Lottie to calm her down. It was a depressing moment. Charlotte was tired and hard to soothe, and as Jane stood with her looking out over the valley she realised that the sunlight was getting weaker. The cloud over the mountain now stretched across the sky all along the horizon, and its fringes were reaching out above their heads, just beginning to obscure the sun. But as she was returning to the lunch-table, holding Lottie's hand, she heard Coventry say to Angela, 'Perhaps Jane would like to come swimming with us this afternoon – this is only local, this cloud, it'll be sunny further down.'

There had hardly been time for Jane to take the words in before Angela had said, sounding as unemotional as usual, 'That's very nice of you, I'm sure she'd love to.'

An hour later Jane was sitting in the front of Coventry's car, with Cov driving and Leszek in the back seat, on their way down to the foothills in fierce sunshine. After dropping Toby and Jenny at the bank bungalow – since Toby, it turned out, was nominally in charge of the bungalow this weekend – they had left the cloud behind. They were driving right past the rice terraces now. Once Coventry stopped the car so that they could sit and listen to the deep whisper of the water trickling down the whole of the sunny hillside, the only sound in the silent afternoon. Far above them women were working, bent double, thinning out the young rice on several of the terraces. But no sound reached them where they stood by the car.

'That peacefulness – it is overwhelming, and not quite believable,' said Leszek, as they drove on again.

'You can't tell what it means to them, can you? Or even if they notice it,' Jane said. She had not spoken much since they left the bungalow; she'd been daunted by her ignorance compared with what these two men obviously knew. But she had to talk if there was to be any point in her being there at all, and she'd found that men didn't mind too much what women said at first, provided it seemed sincere.

'Oh, they're people,' said Coventry. 'They have as many different reactions to their own scene as we do to ours. Some of them find it peaceful, I've no doubt.'

'I suppose we do generalise about them dreadfully all

the time, in spite of ourselves,' said Jane. 'Perhaps it's no better than Thomas, really.'

'Well, all of us here find it peaceful, don't we?' said Coventry. 'Here we can generalise with a clear conscience, thank God. Such a relief.' He took his eyes off the road for a moment and looked at Jane. 'I've quite changed since I've been in Djakarta, let me tell you, Jane. Here I am, in the middle of poverty and squalor far greater than I'd ever dreamed of – I have to admit it – yet I'm almost at peace with the world. Like today. My super-ego's just flown off. Watch out for the same thing yourself, I'm not sure it's the best thing, really.'

'I don't know,' said Jane. I really don't, she thought, I hardly know what my super-ego is.

'Super-egos come and go,' Leszek's voice came, laughing yet firm at the same time, from the back of the car. 'But moral situations remain unchanged. Remember that too, Cov. When you start noticing the moral situation again after a little holiday you find nothing's changed – except perhaps it may have changed for the worse because of your holiday.'

'Hah!' Coventry gave a shout of delight and looked at Jane again. 'That's why I like him, Jane, he's nothing if not unsparing. Though what it's done for him I've yet to find out.'

'I too.'

Jane turned to smile at Leszek as he made this reply. But she saw that he was not smiling now. His mouth was straight, and falling slightly open, and his eyes were fixed far away. She turned back again quickly.

It did not take them long to get to the swimming-pool. And from the road they saw a scene Jane could not have imagined in the countryside a few moments before. The rice terraces rose into the distance on all sides of them, but here, on a small piece of flat land, Chinese and

Indonesian boys and girls were shouting and splashing in a square concrete basin full of water, with yellowing grass all round. There was a wooden restaurant in the shade of an isolated clump of palm trees, and people were sitting round on the grass eating, and drinking what Jane had soon realised was almost the national drink of the Indonesian middle classes, orange crush. There were a few cars, some coaches and many bicycles parked just inside the gate – there were even a few betjaks, though according to Cov it was several miles to Bogor, the nearest town where betjaks were likely to ply in the streets.

'Don't be put off,' he said to her and Leszek, as they stood looking at the scene. 'The water's clean and it's absolutely lovely to be in it. We can change in those changing rooms and bring our stuff back and lock it in the car.'

He was right about the water. Jane couldn't remember when she had last had a sensation like it. One's back had only to be above the water for a few moments before it was burning, but then to sink into the cool water again was delicious relief. Swimming and splashing about produced the contrast continuously. She noticed she was easily the oldest woman in the pool – none of the local girls was older than fourteen or fifteen. And she was the tallest – she also seemed to be half an inch taller than Coventry. But as she had dived in she had been confident that her large body was trim enough to be noticed favourably, and she was glad her fair hair was clipped short so that she did not need a bathing-cap.

The three of them swam around for a few minutes, then Leszek decided to go and sit on the grass with a shirt on his shoulders – she had noticed how pale his skin was in the pool. Coventry's head came up, spluttering and smiling, close to hers. 'Best not to swim,' he said, 'just dangle one's body under the water and leave one's head above like a

54

water-lily – beg pardon, a lotus. Then have a good conversation.'

Jane laughed. Whatever would she say now? She was behaving like a fool, but she thought she might ask him some more about Indonesian politics, if that's what he spent his time studying. Her mother had once said to her, 'A woman's life consists of adapt and enjoy,' and she'd pounced on the remark and torn it, as she thought, to shreds. But she suddenly wondered if life was not going to be, in the end, much the same for her. At least she really would like to know more about Indonesian politics. She snatched a satisfaction from that thought as she steadied herself in the water and said, 'Who are the people here today, Cov? I mean would they care about politics at all, like you were talking about?'

'Oh, it's all very fluid – I don't say that because I'm influenced by my surroundings at the moment.'

'But these people wouldn't feel very strongly, would they? It would be watered down among people like this?' She was pleased with herself.

'*Touché* – or rather, *douché*.'

'Oh!' She went under, laughing, and came up blowing water out of her nose.

'Sorry!' Coventry had swum up very close to her, and was looking in her face. 'Just let me go down and cool my head for a moment, then I'll try and talk seriously.'

The next ten minutes were the most enjoyable lesson in politics she had ever had. She learned about the big Muslim party whose leaders were apparently very modern-minded and liberal, and the other, quite mediaeval, Muslim party of religious teachers; then about the Nationalists, the party that probably had most real power and flirted with the communists, and the communists themselves, who had a great following in the Javanese countryside and were quite willing to admit that they

were only using their association with President Sukarno
and the Nationalists for their own purposes. All this was
imbibed (it was her joke) between frequent underwater
plunges. These political parties seemed to her like the
scoops of light on the water all round her, rising up
towards her on a wave, breaking up, sliding back to form
some elusive pattern again. They seemed to have scarcely
anything to do with people on this languorous afternoon.

Later, when they were getting near Djakarta, she
remembered this feeling and was ashamed of it. They had
stopped again, at a fruit stall, to eat some pineapple in
the shade, and to buy some bananas to take back home
with them. *Pisang*, she learned, was the Indonesian word
for banana: 'Toby says this place is pissing with *pisangs*,'
remarked Coventry. They sat on a wooden bench at an
old table, with a plantation of dark palms hissing behind
them. Around them on either side of the road here was
woodland: small bamboo trees, with bamboo houses in
the clearings. The man who had sold them the fruit went
back to lie down on a table in the shade by his door. Beside
him was a newly-planted garden – he kept a hand on
one end of a long pole threaded through a loop of rope
that hung in turn from a stick in the ground, and with
a light movement of his hand swished the far end of the
pole across the garden every time chickens started to
wander on it. A sharp noise behind Jane startled all of
them: but it was only a monkey, with small earrings,
tethered to a slender tree-trunk and shaking it furiously.

After laughing at the shock it had given them they were
silent for a while. But suddenly Leszek looked intensely
at Coventry and said, 'It may be a rash and dangerous
thing to admit, but I trust you, Coventry!' He drew his
breath in sharply, as though he had really sensed danger.
'I hope Miss Jane will forgive me talking about it, but
this moment seemed just the right one – perhaps she'll

understand her presence even helped me to say it.' He paused and his look went from one face to the other – he was very tense, yet his eyes were shining with strange pleasure. Both Jane and Coventry made murmuring sounds at the same moment – obviously Coventry felt the same as she did, not wanting to make an inadequate comment on what Leszek had just said, not wanting to press him to say more unless he wished to, but wanting to convey that they felt its importance. Leszek went on – it seemed to Jane that he would have done no matter what their reaction had been. 'I was very suspicious – I hate to say it but I was, I was very suspicious of that invitation to Mr Hobley's bungalow. We've had it impressed on us so much. But now I'm – I'm just so glad to talk without any fear, though I'm still a bit afraid, you must have seen. I don't want to say anything different from what I've been saying to you already, that's not the matter, but I want to say this so that you'll know the tone in which I talk. I'm not guarded, I'm sincere.' He laughed sharply. 'It's ridiculous! One doesn't say such things. But perhaps I should thank God for the existence of underdeveloped countries where they can be said!'

This was the point at which Jane acknowledged humbly to herself that politics were not just lights flashing on the water. But she couldn't say anything. It was up to Coventry anyway. And he was wonderful, she thought. He looked as hard at Leszek as Leszek had looked at him. 'No danger,' he said. 'Not for you. You can believe me. Oh – I feel I insult you by saying that – but one gets into the habit too, you know. I'm the one in danger now – by God that's the truth of the matter! If I take you too seriously I'll really have to behave myself!'

Leszek's smile conveyed an ease and relief that Jane could not remember seeing on a man's face before. 'Don't worry, Coventry! Really I don't want anything! – I'm sure you know that. I just wanted to tell you how I feel, so you should know the frame of mind in which I talk to you!'

'I do know now. And I'm glad.'

They got to Djakarta just as the sun was going down, and tall white clouds with silent pink lightning shuddering through them were rising in the direction of the sea. Coventry said he would drop Jane first, at the Hobleys' house, which was very near where Leszek lived. The Hobleys were due back from the hills about this time, but they had evidently not arrived yet – their car was not there. Jane was miserable suddenly. The last part of the drive had been different from the first. After Leszek had spoken so unexpectedly at the fruit stall, both he and Coventry had been rather silent. They had seemed to Jane to be letting their feelings get to work digesting this new intimacy, to which her presence had apparently helped to give birth. It was an uneasy pleasure, to have been there and played this part. In the intervals, longer now, between conversations, she had been even more conscious of Coventry sitting beside her. She kept glancing at the back of his left hand on the driving wheel: his knuckles moved slightly all the time and little shadows ran under his skin. When he spoke it was now about things that caught his attention on the roadside – a stationary line of camouflaged armoured cars, with the soldiers in their green uniforms scuttling about them like lizards; or, as they came into the suburbs, a notice in a wall-less garden saying that a doctor living in the half-deserted house behind was a 'Specialist in Rheumatism and Impotence'. 'Damp, sex-mad city,' Coventry had said. Outside the Hobleys' house, getting out of the car, Jane felt even jealous of Leszek. What a ridiculous lot of new jealousy in one day, she thought. But when she had thanked Coventry he said, 'It was a lovely day. I'm glad we met. I'll ring you tomorrow.'

'Oh good!' The words came out before she could stop them. Her depression lifted as suddenly as it had come. She looked round with delight for the first time at her tropical garden suburb, with the wrecked kites of Chinese children adorning all its telegraph wires.

CHAPTER FOUR

Coventry Pearce

ONE morning in the middle of November, Coventry was sitting with five other journalists in the garden restaurant in the middle of Djakarta Zoo. There was more dust than grass under their feet, and a high hedge backed with coconut palms ran in a circle all round them, preventing them from seeing any of the animals except a llama: this animal stared earnestly at them over some wire where a bomb, aimed at Dutch diners, had removed a slice of the hedge in 1947. All six of them, however, were sipping beautifully-shaken *alexandres*, a liqueur blended of curaçao and cream that the Indonesian chef at the restaurant would drop everything to make, so certain he was of the appreciation that would follow. He had brought them out on a tray himself, not leaving it to the waiters. He was an old man with thick grey eyebrows and a blotchy brown face, who had cooked in the past for a Dutch officers' mess. With these journalists he liked best of all to praise the Indonesian political leaders for their Dutch education and their Dutch virtues.

An armoured car passed, roaring, behind the hedge, and sent a cloud of red dust sailing over the top of it, though on this windless morning it dropped quickly again and hardly any of it reached the journalists' table. Many monkeys shrieked. The animals were no more used to such a noise than Coventry had been until the last few days. But Djakarta had changed since the Indonesian case for taking Western New Guinea from the Dutch had got nowhere in the United Nations. Sukarno had

declared to an enormous crowd in Independence Square
that the West would be isolated if it went on ignoring the
legitimate claims of the Third World, and tanks and
armoured cars had started rumbling, or racing, through
the streets. They were often to be found in pleasant places
like the zoo. But who they were meant to intimidate was
unclear. Sukarno's followers and the communists were
eagerly using the rebuff to strengthen themselves still
further politically, and their enemies were frightened.
Which way the armed forces would lean was the question
of the hour. A sinister-sounding 'Body for Co-operation
between the Youth and the Military' had been set up in
Djakarta: it might have been intended to control the
wilder elements among Sukarno's supporters, but the signs
were that it was going to give them the army's encourage-
ment and protection.

This was one reason for the presence of new faces in the
Zoo restaurant this morning. Besides Coventry, Gerald
and Bill, and an American wire-man called Frank who
lived in Djakarta, there were two visitors looking round
for stories – a young Englishman from one of the English
dailies who was normally based in Singapore, and a
middle-aged American who was always circling about the
Far East. But the political situation was not the subject
of their conversation at the moment. The American visitor
was lecturing the rest of them on another topic, and they
were all listening anxiously.

'It's true, till you've had kids you don't understand
women. All that resistance, all those tantrums, it's all
wind, I'm telling you. Just hold them the right way, rub
them right – they coo again, they go down. It pays
dividends, having those kids on your knee, thinking they're
going through some damned trauma, beating their backs
hopelessly then hearing the wind slurp up. You get stuck
into women feeling you know what you're at, at last.'

He sucked a little of the *alexandre* from his glass, lifting his face and tilting the glass at it. No one answered for a moment. He was presenting these bachelors with an unexpected and difficult choice – risking the dreaded trap of fatherhood, or risking not getting what they wanted out of women at all. Hopeless if it's true, thought Coventry, himself very struck by the observation, even if it didn't much affect his present way of life.

Bill Macpherson was the first to speak. He snarled, and said, 'Christ, I treat all women like children, what the hell else?'

The American looked calmly at him. 'Do you? I don't think you do. I don't think you do at all, son. You treat them like you think people treat children. You don't know anything about it.'

'Aw, fucking shut up!'

'Have it your own way.'

Coventry decided it was time to leave. He murmured to Frank, 'I'm off to get myself a nipper.' It was too wide an opening for anyone to give. Frank's black eyebrows dipped towards each other: 'Have one for me too, man.'

Outside the Zoo, Coventry stood on the roadside and considered the scene. This was as mixed-up a district of Djakarta as any. Small white houses, shining in the morning sunlight, sat in gardens full of red hibiscus flowers and neat signboards decorated with paintings of hibiscus flowers: the boards announced ladies' hairdressing, parcels from Europe, parcels to Europe, book-keeping courses – one house even claimed to have a university in the front parlour. The minor members of the Javanese aristocracy who had moved into these houses were making all the money they could to keep up their style. But a hundred yards down the road a dark cluster of palm trees showed where you could get round the houses to the kampong – a sort of village in the city – on the muddy river behind.

The betjaks went by swiftly on the broad road past the Zoo, with a lot of excited laughter and shouting, and ringing of their harsh bicycle bells. One Chinese passenger stuck his own arm out frantically as his betjak turned across the traffic. The names painted on the mudguards of the passing betjaks told a story of the city's mind: 'New York', 'Sarawak', 'Freedom' and 'Tiger', Coventry saw – also the name of the brothel district where he had been with Sri. A man was sitting on a chair having his hair cut by a barber who had hung his mirror on a roadside tree: the barber snipped coolly round the edges of the man's hair for a while, then made a rapid, uncontrolled assault on the hair of his crown. Other men squatted silently on the earth pavement, chauffeurs in khaki suits waiting for their employers, pedlars resting the large aluminium tins of soya cakes and fish crisps that they carried on the ends of long poles. A moment in Coventry's life seemed to have corresponded with a moment in the history of this country, he thought: the tanks might be starting to appear in the streets now, but even if they meant that changes were coming, it was the end of a real honeymoon in Indonesia's post-war history, a short but peaceful run of years in which the new rulers had all managed to get something of what they wanted, most of the people in the country were still tasting a sweet new blend of freedom and stability, and in the outside world even the Dutch had been discreetly restored to favour. This last week there had been a few slogans about New Guinea painted on Dutch property, but not all of these had shown a particularly clear or impassioned grasp of the situation. One he had seen had read 'Dutchmen Go Back to New Guinea' – just the kind of joke, in fact, that Achmad or Subekto might have made, but he thought not intended as a joke in large white letters. The Indonesian State Bank had also had a slogan appear on its walls, the painters obviously assuming that all banks must be Dutch property, but he had actually seen the word 'Sorry' painted in smaller letters under the slogan when he had passed this morning.

He drove to the house of the woman he was going to interview, a larger house than those outside the Zoo. It stood on the edge of a large triangle of grass, with a canal at the far end of it, and another kampong of bamboo houses across the canal. Here, the city was extraordinarily quiet. A cockerel crowed from the kampong, where Coventry could see one or two women moving about silently in the shade. Then there was nothing at all to be heard. Yet, after all, he wondered how far he didn't read this calm, this lack of ardour, into the city from his own state of mind these days – it seemed impossible to tell. He was a good journalist when it came to facts, even quite good at predictions – though he had noticed that that never did him much good, since predicted events when they happened obliterated all memory of the prediction in people's minds. But he tried on top of this to convey the atmosphere of the country in his pieces – and he was never sure how much it was just personal fantasy, an indirect portrayal of himself. Yet, again, it did seem as if there had been some lucky correspondence of moments of life here, as he had thought standing outside the Zoo.

Mrs Rijono received him in a cool room with a floor of exceptionally beautiful tiles, a gleaming brown-black lightly flecked with white, making him think of a fresh fall of snow. Daylight came only through one set of long, white-curtained windows and some small trefoil openings in the walls. A few dark blue and brown Indonesian decorative cloths hung on the walls, but all the furniture was made of steel and black leather. Before the sofa Mrs Rijono stood slim and straight in her long batik *kain* and low-cut pink jacket.

'Hi!' she said to him.

It was her only Americanism – still, what an unfortunate one, thought Coventry. 'Hello,' he said, shaking hands with her.

'Come and sit down. You weren't frightened in the streets?'

'Oh, they still tolerate the English.'

'For how long?'

'You tell me!'

A grinning boy in a white shirt and shorts and a little brown cap brought them glasses of iced syrup with a sweet, elusive taste. 'I found this one half-starved, selling ice-cream in a cinema in Semarang,' Mrs Rijono said, looking at the boy. What slavery does she exact from him in return? thought Coventry, his suspicious mind working furiously. But the boy skipped cheerfully away. Mrs Rijono was the type that all the liberals in the Western embassies went for, and you could understand why. Her husband was prominent in the small, intellectual Socialist Party, and no one Coventry knew could break down the political situation in terms as congenial to the Western mind as Mrs Rijono: all economics and the struggle for democracy, with a little Indonesian folklore thrown in. But she knew things, and he had to admit he quite liked her too. Not that she had any natural feeling for him. A man at the embassy had told him she had inquired very carefully about the standing of his paper after their first meeting, and before he had received any invitation from her.

He thought he might begin by saying something in praise of Sumitro to her, and see what sort of reaction he got.

'Ah, a good writer. I don't know him but I've read some of his stories. Close to the people because he's near to them in mentality. He's been to China.'

Neat, thought Coventry. He'd noticed a painting on the wall at the other end of the room, and asked her

E   65

THE LAUGHTER IN DJAKARTA

about that. Her enthusiasm was more convincing this time.

'Oh yes, Affandi, the greatest Indonesian painter. We know him well. Come and look.'

It was a very good painting indeed: a European city scene at dusk, the high buildings on the sides of the boulevard rocking with suppressed violence, a tram with gleaming yellow lights coming down the middle of the boulevard like a shell.

'Not just Van Gogh,' she said. 'Indonesian history. After centuries of Islam with no art you expect it to break out with that kind of force. Like other forces have broken out too.'

'The armed forces, now?'

'Oh, your questions, yes! No, they stay under control, they will. It's all right. They'll move with the current but they'll remain – what is it? – an anchor, too.'

It was well said, he thought, plausible and quotable.

'Who's been talking to you?' he said.

'Ha!' She laughed for the first time, pleased at him being the blunt Westerner again. 'Everybody talks in Djakarta. Or at any rate I talk to everybody.'

'What's this youth body?'

'A compromise. You know, the army won't go communist, don't be afraid. It has its communists but the price of their freedom is their good sense, and they know it. Sukarno's going left, the army's going with him so that they're there. There may be a few symbolic victims on our side but the communists will never take over.'

'You have the assurance of at least one general?'

'I have the assurance of at least three.'

'You have the assurance, if I may say so, Mrs Rijono, of at least ten.'

She caught his meaning after a split second, and sent him off with a delighted smile for that. Her conversation, he thought, was made for her for days. Also, before he left, she rang up a cousin in the Nationalist Party, formerly Sukarno's own party and his favourite till the communists had really stepped up their flattery, and this cousin had said he would be prepared to see Coventry for five minutes now. His house was just a few hundred yards away, an even bigger one than the Rijonos', not far from Leszek's place.

However, Sudarmo, the cousin, was of no use at all. He sprawled in a chair just like the Rijonos', in a blue silk shirt and his sarong, all curling smiles; but 'Wait and see', the only English phrase he seemed to know, was what each of his comments on the situation amounted to. The only certainty in his mind seemed to be that he would survive, whatever happened. A boy dressed like Mrs Rijono's brought in glasses of beer for them, and it was then that Sudarmo made his one memorable remark. As the boy went out he said, 'I found him selling peanuts on the station in Tjirebon. Half-starved, he was.' My God – what is one to believe when these people talk? thought Coventry. It made him feel as though Mrs Rijono's confident analyses were of no more value than her cousin's evasions. But he'd have to use what she said, all the same.

When he came out of Sudarmo's house the sun was beating down. There was no movement in the streets or gardens. A few round yellow leaves were drifting down from a tall blue-green tree, as they did, in their ones and twos, all the year. A restlessness began to stir in Coventry. Perhaps it was all that mixed drink, he thought. He'd better go home. He too lived in this district, in a pavilion, a little house in the grounds of a large one, supposedly built by the Dutch family who had lived there for their eldest son, so that he could have a life of his own once he was twenty-one. A shallow front terrace, two rooms one behind the other, a kitchen at the back. It belonged to the British embassy as a result of some chance occupation at the end of the war, but they had condemned it without wanting to lose it, so they let him have it for a nominal rent. One day they hoped to swap it for something else; meanwhile Coventry lived there with the cockroaches that swarmed glistening over the kitchen floor each night.

He was thinking about these cockroaches as he walked up the path to the pavilion – probably because he'd been contemplating his lunch, which Rochmet would be cooking in the kitchen now. In turn they made him think of the giant snails which careered at a visible speed over the lawn at dusk. Then, as he felt a globule of sweat drip from his armpit on to his ribs, he suddenly remembered a winter's morning in London, in St John's Wood – November it must have been. Walking on sodden leaves in the early light as a raw wind blew under the trees, and some sparrows flew up from under his feet. But they were ghost sparrows – whirring wings lifting nothing but a grey glimmer. It must have been a few days before he left for Indonesia. Let me see the ghost sparrows again, he thought.

Rochmet came smiling out of the kitchen in her ragged green dress, as he went into the bedroom and took his tie off. '*Selamat pagi*, tuan.' The food was ready. I didn't find her selling anything anywhere, he thought, as she went to fetch it, she at least was just here – though doubtless she'd sell herself to him for next to nothing if he wanted. Better not, he'd always considered, if he wanted to go on getting his lunch on time. In any case, her complexion was terrible, as though she'd been carved out of solidified brown cooking-grease. But he liked her for her smiles and harsh chuckles, and was slowly teaching her to read in odd moments after lunch.

He ate well, sitting in the front room looking out at the lawn. Vegetables, cooked but still firm, in peppery water,

Rochmet's original but healthy attempt at soup: then a steak, beef from Bali, where because of a smack of Hinduism in the air still, they tended the bulls well and sent them to the Javanese to eat. Bananas, papayas, black Javanese coffee – simply called 'Number One' at the Chinese shops. After that, while Djakarta slept, he drafted his next long piece for the News Service, heavily depending, as he'd known he would have to, on Mrs Rijono.

At half past four he had a bath, throwing pans of cold water over himself in the little bath-house by the kitchen, before driving down to the British Club. He'd promised to have tea with Jane there. They had met several times since that day up in the hills, and it had made quite a difference to him. Apart from Angela, with whom his relationship was an odd, very formal one, Jane was the only Englishwoman in Djakarta he'd really liked the company of so far. And she was the only one at all he'd been able to take around and show places. But his relationship with the girls of Djakarta caused him some uneasiness when he was with Jane: you never knew what people knew in this city, or what they might have learned since you last saw them, as John Grayne, his friend at the university, had warned in a ballad he had written on this subject. Coventry knew its envoi by heart:

> Prince, in a hot May, or a hot December,
> Beg you I would most carefully to remember
> That all illicit assignations are
> Caught in the headlights of a passing car.

He found Jane, this afternoon, sitting on the broad terrace of the club, facing the playing-fields. It was the tennis hour for the British, and for the French, Ceylonese, Brazilians and Persians as well, it seemed to him, studying the white-clad figures dotted closely over the courts at the side of the cricket-pitch. Jane, and a man standing up talking to her where she sat at a table, were also in tennis clothes. The man, a swarthy young chap who worked for a British tobacco firm, had last been seen by Coventry leaning out of a car and speaking to a girl in a betjak, a hundred yards along from the Cosy Corner one night. 'Prince!' Coventry silently admonished him. But, rather impertinently, he hoped Jane would have no truck with the fellow. The smile took charge of her whole face when she turned her head and saw him, and the man, nodding to Coventry, said, 'See you' to Jane and walked off. He wouldn't have known Coventry had noticed him down by the Cosy: his departure must simply have meant that Jane had mentioned she was waiting for him. As he came up to the table she spoke to him without greeting him further.

'I've ordered tea for when you arrived. They're good, aren't they? They said they know you and I'm sure it's on its way by now.'

'Thanks! I do feel honoured, and famous.'

She was very welcoming but she was tense, Coventry thought. He didn't know if it was right to speak a little tenderly to her, and put her at her ease – if, as it seemed, that might do it. Anyway, he smiled at her and she gave him a quick, nervous smile back.

'What have you been doing all day?' she said. She laid her hand on the small round table and pressed it.

'Oh, working, mainly. What about you? Have you been playing tennis?'

'I'm going to.'

'With that chap?'

'Yes – yes, I know him slightly, through the Hobleys.'

'He's a tobacco man, isn't he? Don't let him lure you into bad habits like smoking.'

'I'm not easily lured by anyone!' She spoke more

brightly, relaxed suddenly. 'I'm a bit bored, actually, by most of the people I meet here. The Hobleys are by far the most interesting.'

'Yes, I'm afraid I can well believe it.' Yet, he thought, for most of the people at the club this evening it must seem an extraordinarily good life. He himself could only stand a few minutes of it at a time, but look at those leaping tennis players! Little boys shot across the courts to retrieve the tennis balls for them, on the terrace white-coated waiters lingered till darkness should come and the bar begin to grow busy; over the gate of the club Coventry could see clusters of large balloons, where men waited for the children to be taken home, and behind them, he knew, all along the roadside, boys sat on the grass verge guarding the cars parked along the other side. A whole township seemed to be mustered for service, as the yellow light of the setting sun streamed across the cricket ground. But Jane, though dressed for the part, was not looking for this.

'Still, I mustn't complain,' she said. 'I'll bore you if I do that.'

'No, we can have a good old grouse together. It's bad out there too. A passing tank sprinkled red dust into my liqueur this morning.'

Jane laughed, and Coventry found himself laughing with her, with a calm, confident feeling he couldn't remember having for quite a long time. He looked Jane over, covertly. She was a solidly-built girl but dainty in her movements, like a stanza out of some poet like Chaucer, he suddenly thought, a real smack of lively civilisation about her. Tonight he was going with Leszek and the boys to see a *wayang*, an old Hindu-Javanese story acted and danced by a famous company from central Java, and he wondered if he shouldn't invite her to come too. But he couldn't: it would be a different sort of evening from what he'd intended for the rest of them – and for himself, to be honest, a modification he didn't want in something he'd been looking forward to. But he felt he must take her out again in some way soon.

'You don't really find it so bad out there, do you?' she said. 'Better than here, where we are.'

'Well, I suppose yes. But even as I say it I wonder slightly. Anyway let's go out again – come out with me and Leszek one evening in a day or two and I'll take you to a lovely place for dinner.'

'Well – thank you. Of course I'd like to.' She blushed as she spoke, and he read into the blush some disappointment at his having included Leszek, and also a fear that she had shown that disappointment. But he had proposed what, when he spoke, he felt like proposing – should he have done anything different? This was a real small-colony situation, he thought, one you'd never get into in England.

The waiter brought the tea just then and Jane poured it out. Coventry was already feeling like going. Over tea he told her about the servant boys working in Mrs Rijono's house and at her cousin's. She said, 'It's always pretty safe here to say things were worse before you did anything, isn't it? There's plenty of cheap virtue to be picked up here.' She looked at him steadily as she spoke now, her blue eyes and faint frown seeming to ask for confirmation of her words from someone she believed in. He remembered the little girl who had changed the bucket of water after he had been with Sri, and was glad, at least, that he'd thought something similar then.

But he had to be off: and he felt cheerful, a few minutes later, as he stretched back in the driving seat of his car outside the club gates and felt in his pocket for a coin for the boy who'd been watching it. He drove to the Chinese café where Mr Fat exacted obeisance. He was just in time for that moment he especially liked, as the glare from the electric light began to enclose the tables on the street and draw them into the café's bare bright cube. It was the moment too when the great fruit-bats streamed across the darkening sky: looking up from his table, he could see six or seven beating their way over, with that sinister, deliberate-looking pause at the top of each wing-beat. Subekto and Achmad appeared out of the passing crowd, Achmad ahead, grinning nervously at Coventry with closed teeth and twisting his shoulders from side to side, Subekto, taller than Achmad, gliding softly behind him. Achmad lifted a finger in greeting, Subekto merely smiled at Coventry more richly.

'Have you seen John today?' asked Coventry, as they sat down.

'He was lecturing on John Donne,' said Achmad, 'making all the girls faint.' He laughed, bending forward, as though unable to stop. Subekto said in his deep voice:

'If ever any beauty I did see
Which I desired – and got – 'twas but a dream of thee.'

'You would have liked to hear him pause before "and got"!' said Achmad. 'We've been practising it all the way here.'

'And the voice rising on "got",' said Subekto, laughing for the first time. He had a surprisingly high-pitched laugh for a man with his bass voice.

'Ah, such devotion to lust and art in the same breath,' said Coventry. 'What a place it must be to teach in! Look, even the fruit bats know how to pause for effect.' There were still some passing over as he glanced up at the sky. 'But I'll tell John, he'll be pleased, I don't suppose you're brave enough to tell him.'

It had been a stroke of luck meeting these two boys through John Grayne. It was remarkable how they all got on together, how much they had gained, very quickly, out of knowing each other. Much the same goes for Leszek too, Coventry added to himself, as a betjak stopped and they saw the Pole's narrow face thrust forward at them, small blue eyes shining.

Leszek had lived up to his declaration on the way down from the hills. He seemed always at ease with Coventry now, and was a wonderful source of information and carefully weighed opinion. He said something to the betjak driver that Coventry couldn't quite hear but that the boys evidently did, for both smiled simultaneously and looked away from Leszek to Coventry. He frowned at them inquiringly. Subekto whispered, 'He's sending his best wishes to the betjak man's wife.' 'An old whore,' Achmad hissed, his cheek muscles trembling with suppressed laughter. But the boys liked Leszek too. Subekto pulled out a chair for him, saying, 'We heard you send your wishes to his wife.'

Leszek smiled. 'She's ill, he told me.'

Coventry could see Achmad fighting with another fit of laughter, and guessed what ailment he was attributing to the woman. Subekto went on: 'Perhaps you should kiss the café owner's hand?'

'When I know him better. Let me improve the acquaintance by ordering more beer from him.'

Coventry laughed with delight. 'We'd better drink it up quick,' he said. 'We don't want to be late. It's being organised by some fierce Djakarta ladies who're raising money for the New Guinea campaign – they might think it insulting if we were late.'

'You have tickets already?' said Leszek.

'Yeah.'

'Once again, you see, Coventry's wonderful productive touch,' Leszek observed, nodding to Subekto and Achmad.

Subekto nodded slowly too. 'Oh yes, that's it. Yes, a productive touch. That's what we Indonesians don't have. We don't have it, no. Cov has such great energy, look, he brings us all together. How would we all be together without him? We wouldn't be.'

Achmad was feverishly nodding agreement, Leszek smiling. Coventry felt abashed for a moment. 'My pleasure,' he said, thinking that even that was unbearably sententious a remark. Yet Leszek and Subekto could speak as they had with perfect naturalness. Still, they were speaking of somebody else, not of themselves. He supposed he wasn't in fact all that self-conscious a man – he didn't really know what he did or why he did it.

The *wayang* was to be performed in a marquee that had been erected in a field near the zoo. There were no empty seats visible in the marquee when they went in – at the entrance armed police in steel helmets had been helping to turn people away. Whole rows were taken up by some family parties: some of the servant women, sitting at the ends of the rows with the children, and with their own children, were among the most strikingly dressed people in the marquee, with silver combs in their piled-up hair, and jackets of glowing red or orange-gold velvet. Coventry felt a touch of pathos in this, which was increased when he saw a large safety-pin holding together the torn neck of just such a gold jacket on a girl in front of him. But he had noticed before that the ordinary people of Djakarta had this capacity to let their imagination patch up imperfections – a poor people's skill. Leszek sat on one side of him, the boys on the other; the boys were very excited. Leszek was quietly attentive. He said to Coventry, 'There are some serious East German communists behind us. We were told that the clowns will give us some anti-American

75

humour – nothing else could have brought them.' Coventry glimpsed over his shoulder the tense white faces surrounded on all sides by lustrous Javanese eyes.

The curtain went up – it was painted as a mountain with huge sunrays coming from behind it – and two girls kneeling on the stage rose to perform a dance in which not only their arms and legs but also their fingers and necks moved in delicate rhythms. They had jewelled crowns and brocaded dresses, and from their waists hung bright sashes in the shape of an M. Sometimes they would lift the hanging ends of the sashes with their fingers, and the sashes would seem to fall again with the same slow grace as there was in their body movements. On the ground between the dancers and the audience, the orchestra of gongs and wooden xylophones, violin and flute, produced climax after climax of high, trembling notes that gave way each time to melodious plaints and booming murmurs.

Throughout the marquee there was silence. The children stared as rapt as the other spectators. After the opening dance, the play began – an elaborated echo of an incident in the Indian Mahabharata, the story of how Ardjuna's wife Sumbadra was carried off by a demon. Ardjuna was the most prominent character, and very evidently the most popular, though he was by no means the hero of the story: he was played by a girl, and danced frequent brief, sad dances, his fingers describing sorrow in the air. Once he was lured into a dance of pleasure by another girl, once a girl mocked his tears with a dance-parody of his own performance. It was his brother, Gatotkatja, who danced violently through the sky to the land of the demon, then took on Sumbadra's own form to comb the strength out of the demon's hair.

All the dancers had clothes that were variations on those of the first two girls, except for a pair of clowns who wandered continually through the action with their white-striped faces and rough blue trousers. They threw flowers about and hit the other characters in the eye; left alone, one of them tried to sell a dancing-girl to the other, and when he had driven his bargain took a mask off her face to reveal that one side of it was black, the other side white. She laughed shrilly at her purchaser.

The expected anti-American humour came when the clowns followed Gatotkatja into the demon's palace: both were disguised as American women tourists, with strips of black cloth on their heads for hair, and black spectacles which they found difficulty in seeing through, tripping and stumbling as they peered about and took their ungainly steps. There were some energetically-danced fights before Sumbadra was restored to Ardjuna, who had taken part in none of them: he fainted with emotion and was teased by the same girl as earlier in the play, before finally having his wife seated at his side again.

The four men came out of the marquee silenced by what they had seen. The others acquiesced in Coventry's suggestion that he should drive them to a little drinking place that he and the boys liked to go to late at night sometimes. This was just a dark shack with a few tables and chairs outside that tonight had their legs resting in thin mud. A few oil lamps glimmered here and there in the street and one hung on a string above the drinkers' heads. Coventry scraped the soles of his shoes on a bar under the table and left his feet resting there: he resented the mud tonight, after the beauty of the *wayang*. He was less cheerful than the others now – he spat out the warm beer when it came. Leszek was questioning the boys about the play.

'Who's the father of Sumbadra?' he said to Subekto.
'Krishna.'
'Oh yes, of course. And who's her mother?'
'I don't know!' Subekto answered, laughing.

'They are not long, the laughter and the ignorance,' Coventry suddenly said, slightly surprised himself at the remark. At that moment he noticed an Indonesian at the next table looking at him – a burly young man with a large chin and a bright red shirt hanging outside his trousers, whom Coventry had seen there before. This man suddenly got up and walked down the street. In an instant Coventry realised where he was going. Coventry had sat at this table a couple of months ago with a girl he'd picked up, and she lived, or worked, in a wooden house no more than a hundred yards along from here. The man was certainly going to fetch her. Coventry touched Achmad's arm and said to him, 'I'm going for a pee, keep me company.' They only had to go to a ditch behind the shack and as soon as they were out of sight of the others, Coventry said to Achmad, 'Look, that chap who was sitting next to us has gone to fetch that girl, Siti. Go and stop him, I'll give you twenty rupiahs for them. I don't want Leszek to know.'

Achmad was delighted by the mission. 'Maybe I bargain with her myself! She had a soft skin! I desired her but I didn't get her!'

'No, it's not enough, you just give it to her and come back.'

The others asked where Achmad was when Coventry sat down again, but did not appear to give the matter another thought when he said, 'Oh, he's talking to someone.' Staring over Leszek's shoulder, Coventry saw the figure of a man and a girl appear some way down the street, and Achmad's figure as he stepped from the shadows in front of them. All three of them stopped. Then the man in the red shirt came on towards the tables, and the other two figures disappeared into the darkness.

CHAPTER FIVE

Leszek Mylski

'VIOLENCE is coming closer and we're unprepared,' said Sumitro. On the terrace of his house the reflected afternoon sunlight struck across his head, showing glints of white in his hair. His eyes were tired and he tapped a folded newspaper continuously on the back of his hand. He looks so much older today, thought Leszek, watching him with concern.

The third man sitting on the terrace, a tall, lank-haired Indonesian who was always making freer, wilder movements with his body, flung his arms up now. 'Oh, you're a pessimist, Sum-sum. Working with Sukarno is paying off at last, it's just the moment when non-violence is proving to have been right for us.'

'Nothing will happen. Only a fresh act of the play, to provide fresh interest for foreigners. Pardon me, Leszek. But it will frighten people who are well prepared for violence. We'll play and play and play and suddenly we'll find we've lost. And lost in blood.'

'Ay-eh!' The other man laughed and slapped his knee. 'You're doing your best to provoke, aren't you, anyway? "I can speak Arabic"!'

These last four words were the title of a story which Sumitro had just published in one of the communist newspapers – it was a copy of it that he had in his hand. Leszek had been translating it. It described a Canadian sociologist enthusiastically taking notes at a school run by a *ulama*, a Muslim teacher, in a Javanese village. The pupils, all grown men and women, read from the Koran

79

in Arabic to the sociologist, first singly, then all chanting together. After his departure it became clear that though they knew how to pronounce words written in Arabic, they did not understand any of them. And at the same time as feeling proud, they were also feeling mutinous towards the teacher: not because they did not believe what the Koran said was true, but because they were not convinced that the teacher was telling them the truth about what it said. The portrait of the teacher was a hard-hitting one, and Leszek had heard a number of Indonesians speak about the story. He wondered if Sumitro had made the sociologist Canadian in revenge for Bill Macpherson's visit.

'Just a pin-prick,' Sumitro looked still graver as he spoke.

'But deep, and in the balls! Oh they won't like it, those old daddies!'

'I was circumcised,' said Sumitro to Leszek. 'I was ten, I was taken on a dying donkey with an old man playing the flute going in front. I thought everything was going to be so wonderful, so different, afterwards.'

'Like my first communion,' said Leszek. He remembered standing on the church steps with the other boys in his thin white suit, and blurting out, 'You're silly!' to a boy who was laughing and saying, 'We can have a drop of wine now.' It had been a late spring, with a chill blue sky that day. The night before, he had walked with his father through the streets of the town on the frozen snow, which creaked and squealed under their feet as his father told him, in a soft voice, how from now on he must try to be worthy of Christ's great sacrifice, and how confession and the Mass would help him. Six months later his father was dead, killed in Warsaw by one of the first German bombs. But somehow or other – he suddenly thought about it – he and his mother had managed to go on living in their

house, among all that dark furniture. There must have
been some money put aside somewhere. He wondered why
he had never talked to his mother much about that time.
Perhaps he'd felt guilty at having been so protected by her.
But the Resistance had not been very strong in his town,
and there had been no scope for boys of his age to do
anything – they had just been encouraged to work hard
in the brief mid-afternoon classes of the clandestine
schools, preparing to serve the country when victory
came.

After the other visitor had said goodbye – he was the
Communist Party secretary for the kampong – Leszek ran
through his translation with Sumitro. There were some
words he didn't understand, and Sumitro's anxious look
slowly left him as he explained them. Leszek also had a
question about the degree of irony to be read into certain
phrases: this made Sumitro laugh.

'Always read the maximum irony into what a writer
says!' he said.

'Yes, it's true,' Leszek replied. 'With things in a foreign
language one's always inclined to doubt the presence of
irony – I don't know if it's because one doesn't want to
be over-clever and laugh at something that's not there, or
because one has a stubborn conviction that foreigners are
really simple.'

'I must admit it, with the Dutch I couldn't believe for
years they were really capable of anything like irony!'

As they sat bending over the pages on the wooden table
on the terrace, Leszek found it getting harder and harder
for him to gauge the reasonableness of the fears Sumitro
had been expressing earlier. Art might engage itself with
politics, feed or offend the passions of struggling men, but
its creation, and even this kind of absorption with its
creation, were pacific activities, putting one into harmony
for the moment with the world about one. Fears faded at

F
81

such times. The first touch of afternoon wind made the banana leaves tremble, then they were still again; over towards the badminton court a boy was singing a student song. Leszek glanced at Sumitro as he turned the page of the newspaper. He did it with such a quick, graceful lift forward of the fold in the middle of the paper, then as he pressed the pages either side back to back his hands came together as if in prayer. Leszek was suddenly filled with bitterness, to think that such a man felt obliged to begin preaching violence, in order to protect the people and the qualities that he loved. He wanted to help Sumitro, at the same time he dreaded the thought of violence raging through this land again; but he could do nothing about one emotion or the other.

The sunlight was yellow and soft by the time he got home. He found a party starting in the house. For the moment only one or two men in light suits and women in silks were standing about, rather stiffly, in the big front room of the bungalow; but he knew there were hours of party ahead. A man in the house was leaving, and an early evening cocktail party to which people outside the embassy had been invited was going to continue as a long, more normal Polish night of eating and drinking. Leszek was going out later with Coventry and Jane, so he thought he had better have a shower, and then join the party until Coventry came to collect him. But he found himself in no mood to be there at all.

By the time he got back to the room it was full. Most of the Poles in Djakarta were there, some Russians and Hungarians, even two tall Americans sipping their vodka appreciatively over everybody else's heads. It was dark now, but the windows were open on the night, deep blue outside. Leszek was fastened on by Rybacki, a little stout man with various administrative functions at the embassy, including that of laying on provisions on occasions like this. He was a maniacally tidy man, and even as he noticed Leszek he also noticed a tray of canapés that he felt he had to align with the edge of the table it was standing on. He pushed it back with his hairy knuckles, then ran them along the edge of the tray and the table together. The others always laughed at him, which he didn't seem to notice, but he disconcerted Leszek, especially since he had caught himself one day recently tapping some magazines into a squared-off pile while he was talking to an Indonesian visitor. Leszek had another reason for disliking him, which was renewed immediately. Rybacki was a busy Catholic as well. 'Panie Leszku,' he said now, 'when gay bachelors like you go out they must expect to find the house filled with strangers when they come back – no wife to guard the door.' Ever since he had learned that Leszek had had a Catholic wedding Rybacki had been making allusions like this to his divorce, smuggling them in under the pretext of seeing Leszek as an irresponsible but delightful charmer. Of course he knew all the facts. 'Are you sure there are no strangers calling at your house even though you have a wife there?' – that was the obvious reply. But it was one that Leszek couldn't make.

'Excuse me,' he said, 'I must go and speak to the *chargé*.' Rybacki threw his head back and stared insolently at him, but said no more. The *chargé*, Idlinski, was standing on one side of the room studying the scene through his black-rimmed spectacles. There was no one very high-ranking to whom he needed to be attentive tonight. Like both Leszek and Rybacki, he was a man you would not have seen in a Polish embassy two or three years earlier. Unlike Leszek and Rybacki, he was a Party member, but he was a liberal-minded man, a hard-working lawyer who had moved into the upper ranks of the Foreign Service after the events of 1956. Leszek liked him better than anyone else in the place. He walked across the room and greeted him.

'Panie Leszku!' Idlinski looked at him sharply through his spectacles, a slight smile on his face. 'You're not living too Bohemian a life with those writers? Is your productivity steady, are your resources being used?'

'The best of them, you know, that Sumitro, I've been seeing him today, he's not very Bohemian.'

'A pity for you!'

'But very interesting.'

'That's something!'

Leszek laughed. But there was another anxiety beginning to play on his mind now. Since he had come to Indonesia, he had accepted the obligation to pass on any information that might be useful to the embassy in assessing the political situation. With his contacts, and his knowledge of the language, he'd sometimes been useful to Idlinski these last few months. Now, for the first time, he hesitated. Sumitro wasn't alone in the Indonesian Communist Party in wanting a more militant policy, but this was not the current Soviet line – it wasn't even clear if it was the current Chinese line – and these dissidents had already been in some trouble. No doubt Sumitro's views were well enough known at home, but it occurred to Leszek that if they were more formally minuted by the embassy and communicated to the Russians, the matter might end up being treated with quite a different degree of gravity. He decided to say nothing.

Jan Tarski, a man who worked for the Polish press agency, joined them. He sighed. 'Ah, these damned cocktail parties. How can you drink vodka without proper food? And I don't want to drink anything except vodka.'

'Don't become a diplomat,' said Idlinski.

Tarski turned to Leszek, 'I hear you know an English journalist, Pearce.'

'Yes.' As Leszek spoke he saw Idlinski's eyes half-close, and murmuring an apology the *chargé* moved away. Leszek knew what it meant. Idlinski was uneasy about this connection of Leszek's, but he did not feel there was any need to interfere at the moment and didn't want to take up any position on the matter.

'Idlinski knows?'

'Of course. His eyes didn't open. You saw, they closed.'

'Not too far, I hope. That's also dangerous.'

'Don't worry, Panie Janie. The Englishman's just a personal friend. It's a category officially recognised again since last year.'

Tarski laughed. 'Panie Leszku, don't misunderstand me. I just want to meet Pearce myself, that's all – I wonder if you could arrange a meeting.'

It was the last thing Leszek wanted. But he had to say he'd try. He didn't mention that Coventry would be calling at the house in a few minutes, and hoped it would pass unnoticed. It seemed to be an evening of traps. But there was another still to come. One of the embassy wives waved to him across the room with her fingers and beckoned him with a little lift of her head. Leszek had known her in Warsaw – she'd been at the university with Zosia. But Zosia would scarcely have recognised her, she'd grown so much fatter, a fact not disguised by her heavy green shantung dress cut close to her body. She sang her first words out flirtatiously at him. 'Leszek! Kiss me! For our days in Warsaw!' He kissed her lightly on both cheeks, and she squeezed his upper arm. 'I had a letter from Anna.' This was another friend of hers and Zosia's. 'She saw Zosia in our café in Nowy Swiat. She was with – you know – her new husband. She looked very well, she was still eating meringues.'

'Good. I'm glad she looks well.'

'And so do you, my dear.'

'Oh, good!' said Leszek. 'And you – marvellous! But forgive me, I have to go, I'm going out this evening. Make yourself at home, this is my house, you know.'

Inside, he was in turmoil. Meringues! In that very café, they had had such a quarrel over meringues. Zosia had eaten a couple of them with her coffee one afternoon and when she had said she'd like another he'd replied, 'Are you sure? Meringues go straight to the arse, you know, you can see the affinity in the shape.'

Zosia had turned white, as white as the meringues she had already consumed. 'Christ! Let me look after my own arse!'

He had meant it as a joke, he had meant it entirely for her own good, it was a purely speculative reflection, he didn't grudge her anything – nothing he had said could soften her that afternoon. Only now did he see, or think he saw, what at any rate one of his mistakes had been. He had not realised the weight a person's words carried with someone who loved that person – even, perhaps, with people who simply liked him. And Zosia, he thought, had still loved him then. He said such things without any particular belief in his influence – with a feeling, rather, that people would always do precisely what they wanted to unless his words just happened to strike them as worth consideration. It was a kind of self-distrust, really. But in this way, without realising what he was doing, he must have bullied Zosia again and again. Well, he thought, all that's now just matter for remorse at worst, for reflection at best. It was one o'clock in Warsaw, Zosia would be beginning to think about going to lunch with her husband in the Architects' Club, and perhaps in a couple of hours she'd be fattening her arse with meringues again, doing the same to her figure as the woman who'd evoked all this memory. He still hoped she'd avoid such a fate.

One of the Indonesian servants touched his arm at that

moment. 'Tuan Piss is here,' he seemed to say. Leszek had learned that English word from Tuan Piss himself – people name themselves, he thought. 'I'll go,' he said. It didn't matter about Zosia, nor did it matter about Idlinski's half-closed eyes or Tarski's hints or threats, whichever they were. There was no need to put a coat on: he just walked out and found Coventry in the garden, talking to one of the night-watchmen who was sitting under a magnolia tree, a twisting black shadow against the sky.

'Good evening, Tuan Piss.'

Coventry spun round. 'Oh, that insult has reached the Polish Embassy, has it?'

'It comes fresh to our ears.'

'That's all that can be said for it. It stinks otherwise. Come on, Jane's in the car, I've got something to show you in my pocket.'

The old man with his back against the tree-trunk laughed. He'd been watching them, though he couldn't follow their English. 'That one's a proper cockerel,' he said, nodding towards Coventry.

'Mind your hens, then,' Coventry said to him. Laughter came back not only from the old man but from the shadows under the hedge – looking, they could see another dark human shape sprawled on the grass there.

'They're meant to be reassuring but they're terrifying, those guys,' said Coventry. It made Leszek think of Sumitro's words.

'I saw Sumitro today, you know – he's really afraid of violence coming,' he said, as they moved towards the gate.

'It's something about Sumitro I've got to show you.'

'I was trying to tell you of his fears rather than just remind you of his existence.'

'Hey! Don't you put me in my place like that, you Pole! I'll hear all about it in due course. Come on now, Leszek,

87

Jane's waiting.' He vaulted over the metal gate, and opened it behind him. 'Thanks.' Leszek smiled to himself. Not one of the people at the party in the house tonight would vault over that gate.

Coventry's car was standing under a high tree on the roadside. Clouds in the sky showed themselves as the silent lightning glimmered in their rolling silver depths, then the night was dark again. The only sound was that of the voices coming from Leszek's house. With them suddenly came some music, a melancholy tango about Monte Cassino. Jane greeted him through the open window of the car.

'Hello Leszek. Are we dragging you away from a party.'

'It would be harder to drag me back to it.'

'That's nice!'

'What's this Coventry's got to show us?'

'Won't he tell you either? – he won't tell me.'

They soon got to the restaurant Coventry was taking them to. It was in a side street behind the Hotel des Indes, a district of older Dutch houses than those in which these three had all found themselves living in Djakarta. There were high hedges round the gardens here, and the restaurant had a large outdoor terrace inside such a hedge. It was already crowded but they found a table and Coventry ordered some chicken done in what he promised would be a quite unfamiliar way. Then he took a folded sheet of newspaper from his pocket and laid it on the table.

'Jane! – now you'll know why I was telling you all about Macpherson and Sumitro. Leszek, I've got Bill's article about him, it's been syndicated through God knows how many obscure American papers. He didn't go back to see Sumitro again, he told me he was scared I'd get in first.' Coventry laughed. 'You'll see!' He started reading from the paper where it lay.

LESZEK MYLSKI

' "RED BAMBOO SALON

by

Bill Macpherson

Djakarta, Indonesia, Wednesday.

"In the steamy bamboo woods surrounding this decaying capital, there is a new place of pilgrimage. It is a small
bamboo house, built from trees that once grew around it.
This is the home of Ali Sumitro" – Ali! – I asked Bill why
Ali, he's not Ali, Jane, he's just plain Sumitro without any
other name, like most Javanese – Bill said he had to give
him a first name because Americans feel uncomfortable
without one. So he just made up "Ali", it's short, it's
common, it'd do just nicely – "Ali Sumitro, known to
everyone of his acquaintance as plain 'Sumitro', leading
novelist and short-story writer of Indonesia – and one of
its leading communists, albeit not figuring in the Party
hierarchy. To Ali Sumitro's hut flock the would-be
equivalents of those radicals who crowded the great French
literary salons of the eighteenth century, thus paving the
way for the French Revolution. On a typical afternoon
at the beginning of this week I found there two young
Indonesian writers, already outstanding in their student
generation, a Russian and a Pole, both conversing with
writer Sumitro in fluent native language, and a well-known
pink-tinged English writer-journalist who had spent
many weeks in the capital trying to effect an introduction
to him.

"Who is the man who now commands such audiences
day by day in his remote Asian suburb? He is a wiry
little Javanese whose sardonic sketches of the Dutch and
of the decadent Javanese aristocracy are known throughout his native land. His big liquid eyes as he sits in his

89

bamboo chair have something of the charismatic appeal of his fellow Javanese, Indonesian President Bung Sukarno. Using a mixture of languages, we talked together about his books, and the importance he attaches to his harsh, inflammatory portraits of the effete Javanese aristocracy and the Dutch.

"He offered me Dutch beer and goat-meat on skewers. With a dry laugh, he pressed on me the famous Javanese magical titbit, the male goat's sexual organ – for like all Asian communists he is fully conscious of the superstitions of the people and the ways in which they can be exploited.

"I left his miniature house feeling it had been a sinister honour for a newspaper man to be there. For such genial afternoons in Ali's salon could prove in the sight of history to have been intellectual milestones on the road to the Red Domination of Asia." Leszek, you were there, you saw how long he was there! It's a bloody masterpiece!'

'Evidently I'm the man he mistook me for, as well as myself.' Leszek turned to Jane. 'Probably Coventry's told you, there was no Russian there, only me, but he took me for a Russian first.'

'God! I look forward to showing it to the boys – they can hardly write an essay, I believe, so John Grayne tells me, though it's true they write poetry, both of them, I must have told Bill that.'

Jane smiled. But she didn't laugh, it occurred to Leszek. He watched her as she spoke.

'Wasn't he ashamed when he knew you'd seen the article?'

She was ill at ease – diffident about speaking, eager to join in, yet, Leszek got the impression, feeling that this was very much a private joke between him and Coventry. It must have struck her that Coventry had waited till he was there before bringing the article out. But Coventry did not seem to be at all troubled by her tone. He smiled delightedly – smiling more though, perhaps, at his thought than at her.

'He was a trifle abashed, I think, but he put on a bold front. In fact he poked me in the ribs and said, "Got to gild the lily, boy, eh?" He said he hoped I wouldn't mind getting the pink tinge but no one had any reason to think he was writing about me.'

Jane seemed more surprised than amused by Macpherson's article: Leszek found himself neither particularly amused nor particularly surprised. Since he had got to know Coventry he had accepted the fact that he now had a foot in a world where nothing followed a familiar course any more. In Poland, vice and extravagance seemed to observe rules as firm as those prescribed by virtue for its adherents. With Coventry, and the people he knew, nothing could be confidently predicted, yet nothing they did seemed to startle Leszek. That day when, coming down from the hills, he had made that declaration to Coventry he had felt he was taking an extraordinary step in his life. But in some ways it was like becoming Zosia's lover, a few months before they were married: once the amazing event had occurred, making love soon lost its strangeness – lost its strangeness more and more, the better it became. Just so, with Coventry, he had entered a state that had quickly become strange, only – when he thought about it – because of its ease and familiarity.

Their chicken arrived and Coventry put the paper away. 'More magic titbits,' he said, 'though not quite what Bill claims to have had, Jane.'

Jane looked straight at him. 'I can eat anything, you know,' she said. Leszek saw Coventry stare at her in surprise for an instant – obviously wondering how sexual the allusion was – and he studied her quickly himself. She seemed suddenly mistress of the situation, and he was impressed – as though she would not play any more the role, slightly patronised, that she had been given so far, and would let them see clearly that she was in no way put out by anything they said, merely ignorant sometimes of what they were talking about, and that entirely through their discourtesy. All this he had read in a second into the way she had looked and spoken.

Coventry's voice was softer when he answered, 'I think you'll enjoy this, Jane.'

She smiled back at him with quite a fresh look of happiness. 'I'm sure!'

It proved indeed to be an exceptionally delicious dish, the chicken cooked with the sweet pink leaves of the breadfruit. They were just finishing it, and Jane and Leszek were praising Coventry, when there were shouts from the road the other side of the hedge. It seemed to be something about Sukarno. Then they heard clearly – a long, loud, wailing cry – 'Bung Karno's dead!'

'My God!' said Coventry. He translated the words for Jane, and rushed to the hedge with several of the waiters and other diners. 'What's happened?' many voices were calling loudly. Another voice answered from the street, 'Bung Karno's dead – he's been shot.'

'Where?' shouted Coventry.

'At a school in Tjikini, they say.'

Coventry came running back to their table. He was very excited. Again he translated quickly for Jane, then said, 'Look, I'll have to go. Would you mind coming with me, it'd be a terrific help – the others will have to cable for the evenings before they know anything but I can leave it for an hour or so – if I get a good piece in by midnight that'll be terrific! Do you mind leaving your dinner? – it's almost finished. We'll come again.'

Jane and Leszek had got up together. 'Of course!' said Jane. She was staring hard at Coventry.

'It might be a bit dangerous for whites, I'll have to tell

you that – I mean they may already be blaming the Dutch or something.'

'Never mind!' Jane's voice was eager now.

'For me – of course,' said Leszek.

'Good, I'll get you to make a phone call for me in a minute.' He put some money on the table, called to a waiter, 'More than enough,' and led them out, walking fast. Many of the other diners were also leaving – Leszek heard them speaking to the betjak drivers and gathered that some of them were also going to Tjikini, a district of Djakarta about half a mile away. Betjaks passing along both ends of the small street noticed the group of people outside the restaurant and turned into it. Bringing the vultures' wings, thought Leszek, as they all came gliding up. There was no knowing what the news would mean for the country: yet apart from the first clear cry they had heard, there had been no further sound of alarm or sorrow – the crowd in the street were chatting and joking.

They drove down ill-lit roads, the headlights occasionally picking up the red shine of a drifting betjak, or a group of men squatting on the roadside, their sarongs pulled up to their shoulders. It was not until the car was approaching a main road that anything happened. Then some policemen in steel helmets stepped into the middle of the road and halted them. One put his head to the window: 'Where are you going?'

'On to the main road,' said Coventry.

'You can't pass. Let me see your papers.'

While the policemen examined their identity cards, Coventry asked them what had happened. But none of them would say anything except that they could not go through with the car.

'Can we walk?'

'On the roadside. You can't cross the road.'

'Come on, then,' said Coventry. 'We'll park.'

When they got to the main road, a few yards farther along, it was evident why they had been stopped. There was a stream of police and military cars, and small ambulance cars, passing up and down the road under police direction. But there were many people watching – this was the district of small houses near the Zoo, and the gardens and pavements were crowded.

'For God's sake, we must find out what's happened!' said Coventry. 'This stall!' From the owner of a little meat and tea stall that was doing good business on the pavement they at last learned what everyone else at the stall seemed to agree were the facts. No one had been shot: hand-grenades had been thrown at an exhibition of children's work at the school a hundred yards down the road, which the President had been visiting because his own children attended the school. Many of the pupils and some adults had been killed or wounded; but the President and his family were unharmed, though he had clearly been the target.

'He's a cockerel!' said the stall-keeper, grinning. Second aspect of the character this evening, thought Leszek. 'He's home in bed now giving it to Hartini.' This was the President's latest and youngest wife. 'Got a bit of extra bang in it tonight.'

Coventry laughed. 'I'll fill in the details for you later, Jane,' he said. 'Or Leszek will. Look, I'll try and get closer to the school now. Will you do something for me now – will you go back up the road to that cinema we passed, you'll find a phone there, and ring up the Press Agency?' He gave them the number. 'Say you're speaking for me – I've got a chap there who speaks English – and find out exactly what they say happened. You speak, Jane, you mustn't involve yourself, Leszek, it might be difficult for you. And meet me here again in twenty minutes.'

Jane and Leszek found a betjak to take them to the cinema.

'Who would have done it?' said Jane, sitting pressed tightly against Leszek's side.

'I don't know. Probably on the right wing, people who don't like him getting closer to the communists. But it could be more complicated. Chinese communists, communists who don't want an alliance with Sukarno. Everyone seems to be enjoying it, anyway.'

Jane looked at him for a moment before speaking. 'Yes, they do seem quiet, they do seem to be taking it quietly, at least.'

'Is Cov enjoying it, do you think?'

She answered quickly this time. 'Oh, he's got a job to do, it isn't a question of enjoyment. You want to know what's happening, so do I, so does everybody else. You can't do a job unless you put yourself into it.'

'Of course, you're right. I'm glad we can help him.'

'Yes.'

After this exchange they were silent till they reached the cinema, where they had no difficulty in getting through to the Press Agency. Leszek offered to speak but Jane said she'd prefer to do as Coventry had said – she didn't know all the implications so she'd rather leave it to his judgment as they were doing it for him. But she let Leszek prompt her over what questions to ask. The man at the other end who worked there for Coventry in the evenings confirmed most of what they'd heard at the stall. There were thought to have been three bomb-throwers but none of them had been caught yet: the official view was that they were young Muslim fanatics.

'You were right then,' said Jane, as she put the phone down.

'It's what the government would want to believe at the present time, it must be said, but probably it's true.'

'How uncertain everything is here, isn't it?'

'You're right! Though I mustn't get led into taking the view of things that Cov was taking that day we met in the hills.'

'Whatever was that?'

'You remember, his cables for all seasons.'

She laughed. 'Oh yes!'

When they got back to the stall there was no sign of Coventry, so they sat down and ordered some tea. There were still a few ambulance cars passing along the road: some of the unharmed children, Leszek gathered, were being taken home. The number of people on the roadside and in the gardens had diminished considerably. The stall-keeper, a brisk man whose shiny face gleamed in the oil-lamp as he bent over the table with the tea, smiled at Leszek. 'It's terrible,' he said. 'The price of rice, now this.'

Leszek nodded. He refused to smile at the man, then couldn't help smiling slightly to himself.

'What did he say?' said Jane.

'It'll only dismay you more if I tell you.'

'All the same tell me.'

She sighed and shook her head when he did so. 'It's no use us judging, I suppose.'

'Perhaps it's a luxury.'

Just then they heard Coventry's voice, and they looked up. He had Bill Macpherson with him, his broken teeth as prominent as when Leszek had first seen him at Sumitro's, and a torn battledress jacket round his shoulders.

'Jesus, it's the Russky, I mean the Pole.' Macpherson sat himself on the table. 'What a night to come across him. Your boys behind it? – I don't suppose so, not now they've got their little old finger up. Did you tell him about my piece, Cov?'

'I showed it to him.'

'Heh-heh,' Macpherson cackled at Leszek. 'You've got

a Russky buddy tucked away somewhere, haven't you? I know, I didn't just make him up.'

'What did they say?' said Coventry.

'Yeh, shoot,' said Macpherson.

Leszek gestured towards Jane, of whom Macpherson only then seemed to become aware.

'Who's this? Cov, who's this? We're going to hear the news from this lovely speakerine?'

'Jane Summerson, Bill Macpherson.'

'Oh yes – oh yes! I've heard of you. Down at Bertrand What's-his-name's?'

'Yes.'

'Well be a good girl, tell us very quick. I've got to put my next wire together as I drive back now. Of course we're all hours ahead of Cov, the lazy bastard, we all got our first wires off within minutes. Playing crap in the Agency, luckily, heh-heh. We couldn't find this joker.'

Jane told them as succinctly as she could what she and Leszek had learned from the Press Agency.

'Muslims, eh, Cov?' said Macpherson when she had finished. 'They'd guessed that before—it's official now, is it? Not much new there, it fits though. Come on, Cov, get your pash-wagon.'

Coventry lifted his hands in the air. 'I must go, I'm afraid, I must write my piece down at the Agency. We'll all meet tomorrow, eh, we can talk about it all then. I'm awfully sorry, Jane.'

'Ach, she can take it,' said Macpherson. 'Can't you, speakerine?'

Jane answered Coventry. 'Don't worry about us, Cov. It was – well, not nice, but you know.'

Coventry leaned over and patted her hand. 'Thanks,' he said softly. 'Goodnight Leszek, many thanks. I'll ring tomorrow. You all right?'

'Yes, thank you.'

'Come on! Christ!' Macpherson's shout came from the darkness in the side-street, and Coventry disappeared after him.

'I'll take you home in a betjak,' said Leszek.

'All right – thanks.'

This time, sitting beside Jane in the betjak, Leszek felt there was more sympathy between them. They sat more comfortably. Perhaps it was because they had both now been finally deserted by Coventry. This heavily-built, unflirtatious English girl was so unlike Zosia; but he began to think that he liked her, to feel her rather dependable. He had never really given her a thought till she had spoken out at the restaurant. She suddenly said:

'I'm sorry if I rather bit your head off when you spoke about Coventry.'

'That's all right. It's true, one does want to know – I wish I knew what he found down at the school, though I expect it would appal one.'

'Yes.' She shuddered. 'You suddenly realise, don't you?' She was silent for a moment, then spoke more shrilly. 'But I can't criticise Cov, I don't know him, how can I say he should or shouldn't do anything? What do I know?' Her voice dropped in pitch again. 'You like him, don't you, Leszek?'

'I need hardly tell you.'

'No.'

At her gate, she invited him in for a drink, but he said he had better get back – he ought to make himself available at the embassy as he knew something about what had happened. So they said goodnight, and he went on home himself in the same betjak. He said to the betjak man as they drove through the still streets, 'Did you hear about the bombing?'

There was a shout of laughter from above him. 'Fireworks tonight, tuan!'

CHAPTER SIX

Coventry Pearce

THE events of the night had left Coventry feeling sexually restless, and the following afternoon he decided there was nothing for it but to drive down to the brothels. It was a brilliant afternoon: everywhere red hibiscus gleamed in the gardens round the pavilion. When he got near Independence Square, the sense he sometimes had of the frailty of all that constituted the city in this pastoral land suddenly came to him again strongly and pleasantly. There were water buffaloes, like bulky sheets of grey tarpaulin, struggling through a broken hedge into one garden, and immediately afterwards he saw five coolies trotting in single file across the road, digging-tools over their shoulders, just as though they were treading their way along the strip of earth between two wet paddy-fields. Later, on a wall on the roadside, he saw a white goat standing with its ears, feet and tail all tipped with black – an obituary card in the flesh.

Memories of the previous night forced their way back into his mind with the thought – though he didn't want to think about it. He'd not been able to get past the police cordon round the school, but in this respect he'd been like several distraught Indonesian men and women. They had been shouting that their children had been in the school, but they had no identity papers on them and were not allowed to pass. He'd been glad to get away from them; but in fact he'd seen nothing worse. What had struck him most was the way that the whole event, bloody though it was, had hardly broken the calm of the night. Many people had gathered round the school and along the main road leading away from it, but they had watched quietly and most of them had soon gone. A few yards off the main road the streets were empty and silent under the high trees. There was no trace of the angry mobs he had warned Jane about. Both he and Macpherson had been ignored except when they asked people questions, and then they'd been answered good-humouredly enough. He wondered if this atmosphere wasn't producing some atrophy of his own feelings. Or perhaps he'd never really had any, and he was now discovering the fact in a sympathetic environment. This wasn't the kind of self-doubt, it occurred to him, that Leszek was likely to be troubled by.

He was going to a different part of the town today from the one he had been to with Sri. As he turned into the street he'd been heading for, he at once noticed the smell he associated with this district, hot cooking oil. Along the edge of the broad road here was a line of sturdily-constructed wooden stalls selling fried chicken, mainly to the clients of the girls. Behind them were dusty gardens in which only the largest trees had survived, and, at the end of these, a long way back from the road, stood some peeling white bungalows, each with a square terrace in one corner where a girl or two sat or leaned out over the wall. Coventry stopped the car and as he looked up the road his resolution wavered. The kind of imagination that could overlook safety pins was sorely needed here in the middle of the afternoon. The fierce sunshine allowed you to see all the cabbage stalks littered in the roads and gardens, the pale patches of skin-sore on the faces of three boys who stared at him as they passed, the big front teeth and the syphilitic sadness in the eyes of the one who walked behind the other two. A girl on her own on the terrace of the house nearest to him had a very dark face and a thin pink dress – it made Coventry think of a dry, cheap, iced cake in an English baker's window. Just a single water buffalo would do something pretty big for this landscape, he thought. He had a better idea suddenly: he would go and call on Sumitro, who lived only half a mile from here. He'd got Macpherson's article in his pocket – he'd show it to Sumitro and also find out what he thought about last night's events. A twinge of lust came at him with precisely the same kind of sharpness as a pang of conscience, a reminder of a failed opportunity, and his pleasure at the thought of seeing Sumitro faded momentarily. Then it rallied and triumphed, and he started the car with a firm push of the button.

His road took him into a greener district, and he noticed another change before he'd driven far: clouds were coming up and the sun was getting fainter. At this time of the year, especially, that mounting afternoon heat could lick in wet winds from the sea in no time. A few minutes later the sky grew distinctly dark and heavy drops of rain began to fall. Instantly the air was full of sweet pungent smells, detectable through the open window of his car even as he drove along. The dust and the leaves alike were dispensing a richness of which they had shown no trace in the heat. Before long the rain was pouring down, so thick it was like a white mist all round. He stopped the car. The road was awash, even if he could just about have seen enough to go on. A small boy and girl ran splashing along the road each holding a banana leaf above them and shouting with pleasure: after a moment they dropped the leaves – their clothes were already soaking – and jumped about in a deep puddle before running on. The banana plants were thick on either side of the road here and the rain bounced off their leaves in a high spray. The smell had gone again, drowned by now, and the whole land around roared with the sound of falling rain.

Suddenly a man's head appeared between the banana

THE LAUGHTER IN DJAKARTA

leaves only a few yards from the car. The man stared at
Coventry for a moment, then his head went out of sight
again. It had been a most remarkable head. The man's
hair was sodden and matted, his shining bronzen face
narrow with a neat square jaw; from a spot on one side of
his chin hung a thin twisted strand of black hair, obviously
cultivated on an otherwise hairless face, and now dripping
with water. The man's eyes had flashed at Coventry; then
they had opened wide, apparently whitening into fear,
before the head had disappeared. Perhaps because of the
man's sign of fear, Coventry himself felt fear slowly
creeping over him now. He looked up and down the road
through the dense rain, wiping the condensation off the
car windows, and studied the banana plants on either side
of the road carefully, his hand on the starter button. He
hoped the engine had not got so wet or cold that it
wouldn't start. But there was no sign of a living soul along
the road. He remembered stories he had heard about men
turning into boars – Leszek had told him such a story
quite recently. Had this man just metamorphosed himself
back into human shape? He'd have coped better with the
rain in his boar's skin.

A few minutes more and the sky brightened again as
quickly as it had gone dark. Water still dripped heavily
from the trees but the rain had almost stopped, and the
puddles on the road were draining rapidly into the red
earth either side. The sun was already warm again on
Coventry's head as he drove on, the starter giving him no
trouble; a betjak splashed by him and both the driver and
the old man sitting in it grinned broadly as Coventry
swerved to try to avoid spraying them. No one minded
these warm afternoon storms when the sun came out
again so quickly afterwards. Something more than the
rain had been troubling that man whose head he'd seen.

When he got into Sumitro's kampong he noticed more

people than usual outside their houses and in the road. He supposed it was the freshened air and the warm sun that had brought them out, women with their long black hair hanging to their waists, men pulling sarongs up round their shoulders. But there was shouting coming from the direction of Sumitro's house, and more people were to be seen there than elsewhere. Something more interesting was evidently happening. He stopped the car and made his way towards Sumitro's house through the people standing about in the thin layer of mud on the ground. There were several people on Sumitro's terrace, but there was no shouting now. He was just about to climb the steps when a boy turned his face to him, his large brown eyes open wide, and said, 'Tuan Sumitro's dead, he's been killed with a knife.' A young woman by the boy's side added a long, confirmatory wail. Coventry stared at them, then went on up the steps. No one on the terrace stood in his way. He gently pushed open the wooden door, and there at once saw Sumitro's body lying on the floor. A green and red striped sarong had been laid across the body up to the neck, but they had not covered his face. His head rested on one side, the mouth open with his tongue in one corner of it, the eyes closed. It seemed smaller than it had been and its stillness was dreadful. It was already a greyer brown than it had been in life.

There were several people in the room. A woman – Mrs Sumitro, he supposed at once – was sitting in one of the rattan chairs in the corner of the room, making a thin trembling squeak again and again. Coventry had never seen her before: she was dressed in a pale blouse and *kain*, but her hair hung to her ears, curled, in Western style, and even though her eyes were glazed and unseeing, and her small mouth half-open – the sound coming from inside her without the lips moving – he could see the intelligence in her face, a tension and alertness of the muscles that even this grief could not wholly dissipate. A boy was kneeling on one leg at her side, a hand on her knee – his posture immediately recalled a sight Coventry had seen on the way, just before it rained, a boy kneeling like this on the ground by the side of a large cockerel, gently stroking its wattle between thumb and finger. There were also two men standing in the room – they turned their eyes on him not challengingly but inquiringly. One was familiar to Coventry – young and fierce, though now he had a slow, beseeching look. Coventry remembered that he was the Communist Party secretary of the kampong. The other, older man, barefooted and holding his sarong tight round his whole body, stepped uneasily forward.

'I was coming to see Tuan Sumitro – he knew me,' Coventry said.

'I've seen you,' the old man said. 'You were a friend.'

Suddenly the face of the man in the banana trees came back to Coventry, and he started trembling violently.

'Sit down,' the old man said. 'Sit down, tuan.'

Coventry let the man take his arm and sit him in a chair in the opposite corner to Mrs Sumitro. Even as he did so, he noticed away in the back of his mind that a white man – at any rate, a white friend – was treated even in this house with a special kind of unquestioning respect. He couldn't bring himself to ask any questions, but the old man, standing by the side of the chair and resting his hand on its arm, went on speaking quietly. 'His nephew found him – that's the boy there. He just looked in to see him, like he was always doing. He came to fetch us and then Sumitro's wife returned from school. Luckily we were just on the terrace when she came.'

'Now?' said Coventry.

'We're waiting for the police. We don't know who did it.'

Coventry was still stunned but his mind went racing on.

Could it possibly have been the communists themselves who had had Sumitro killed like this? From something that Leszek had said only yesterday, he knew Sumitro had been in disagreement with the leadership. But surely he wasn't so serious a threat to them that he had to be killed, especially at a time like this when they were riding high in the saddle? If it was a political killing at all, it seemed more likely that there was some connection with the attempt on Sukarno. There'd been that short story of Sumitro's mocking the Muslim *ulamas*. Had the Muslim Brotherhood decided to kill him as a sort of overspill of their excitement at the plan to kill Sukarno? Or – a peculiarly terrible thought – had they just turned to Sumitro as an easy victim after their failure last night?

In the room the only sound was that of Mrs Sumitro's sharp, half-stifled shrieks coming from deep inside her. The boy was motionless at her side, the old man still resting with his hand on the arm of Coventry's chair. The Party Secretary was standing stiffly by the window, staring at the ground. Coventry allowed himself to glance once more at Sumitro's diminutive head. Then he felt he had to get out of the room at once. His mouth opened and he sucked in air convulsively. He got up and hurried out of the door.

On the terrace the brilliance and warmth of the sunlight made him sob his breath in again. The people outside looked at him curiously. One man said, 'What's happening?' and he just managed to answer, 'Nothing.' He was walking slowly over to his car when a police jeep drove up, with people jumping back from the mud it spurted up. Two men in steel helmets with sten guns jumped out, and an officer in a peaked cap and a beautifully-pressed light khaki suit followed them with a springy but more leisured movement. The armed men ran up the steps and flung open the door of Sumitro's house. Several onlookers laughed. Coventry went up to the officer who was standing watching. 'Good afternoon, tuan,' he said. He tried not to let any tremor appear in his voice but it was strangely high-pitched. The officer, a smooth-cheeked boy, looked surprised and nodded faintly. Coventry persisted – he felt he had to. 'A man's been killed, you know – I think I may have seen the murderer as I came along, about fifteen minutes ago. You might like to have someone look into it quickly.'

'Who are you?'

'I'm a journalist.'

'Dutch?'

'English.'

The two policemen came back on to the balcony, and one ran down the steps again to where Coventry and the officer were standing. 'The body's inside and some witnesses, tuan,' he said. The officer didn't look at Coventry again. 'I'll come,' he said. 'Tell this man to wait for me. I've some questions to put to him.'

The subordinate glared at Coventry. 'Wait here,' he said, then followed the officer into Sumitro's house.

Coventry was in a rage now. But he couldn't help registering the irony of the situation. A moment ago he was deploring the fact he got special treatment as a white man, now what was he doing but resent the fact he didn't? He couldn't tell what anyone else in the kampong might have seen, yet here he was automatically assessing his own information as superior to anyone else's. It was the right kind of lesson for him. But he just stood there feeling stupid and exhausted after this. After a moment he went back to his car. He could hardly bear to stay but now he must, unless he completely defied the police officer's order, and he didn't have the courage to do that.

Sitting looking out of the car window he let his mind run over what he had to do. But that seemed a question of what he ought to do in quite another existence, nothing to do with his duties in this one. The sun was shining through the trees near the horizon now, and most of the people in the kampong had gone back to their houses; only a few boys lingered, talking excitedly, outside Sumitro's house. He could hear sounds from the badminton court. A fruit bat beat its way silently across the bit of sky he could see through the window. He had to write a piece on this, but he wouldn't hurry, he couldn't hurry – he'd tell Bill and the others, let Bill follow it up, just cable a sentence himself tonight. The death of friends wasn't news, the death of good men wasn't just journalists' copy. What he wanted to do was to see Leszek or Jane – one of that pair. It was strange – a couple of months ago he'd known neither of them. Earlier in the day he'd been feeling an obligation to get in touch with them after deserting them last night – but now, he simply wanted to see them.

The policeman who had come out of the house before to report to the officer appeared at the open car window. 'Come to the house,' he said. Coventry followed him. At the door he hesitated and asked, 'Is the body still on the floor?'

'No. It's been moved now.'

In the room there were only the policemen. The sarong that had lain across Sumitro's body was now on the floor covering the place where he had been. It was hiding bloodstains, Coventry supposed. The room was lit by a single light bulb overhead: it made the rattan furniture seem very bare and simple. He hadn't seen the others go out but he hadn't been watching the door: probably Sumitro's body had been taken into a bedroom, perhaps his wife or some of the others were still in there with it. The officer was sitting down and gestured to Coventry to take a chair facing him. He smiled at Coventry now and asked him for his name and address, then told him to tell them what he had seen. Coventry felt he scarcely had any interest in doing so now, but he tried to describe the man on the roadside as accurately as he could. 'Isn't it a bit late now?' he said when he had finished.

The young officer smiled again. 'We are collecting our evidence.'

Coventry didn't think it worth bothering about the matter any more. 'Could you tell me what has happened?' he said.

The officer's face was all smiles now. He visibly gathered his thoughts. Then he said, in slow English, 'Wait and see!'

Oh, what damned Dutch pedagogue ever brought that phrase to this land? thought Coventry.

CHAPTER SEVEN

Jane Summerson

JANE sneezed. Looking for Coventry, she had looked into the sun, streaming across miles of light green lowland. She was on one of the terraces of the Borobodur, the famous Buddhist monument she and Coventry and Leszek had driven out this morning to see. On this terrace, halfway up the great ornamented pyramid, the Buddhas sat, dimly visible, inside big bells of stone lattice-work. They were supposed to be slowly ascending out of man's sight: on the lower galleries they sat in the open air, while on the very top of the Borobodur the crowning bell, or *stupa*, was empty – the Buddha had vanished from mortal view. Jane had been peering at the black, courteously self-contained figure of the Buddha in one of the stupas on this terrace when she had glimpsed Coventry's lilac shirt through the lattice on the other side. She had straightened herself up to look round the side of the stupa, and the sun had caught her straight in the eyes.

When she had stopped sneezing, Coventry had gone again. She wanted to follow him, but she hesitated. Below her the elegant grey cages of the Buddhas rose all over the slope of the terrace. Beyond them a silent plain stretched out to the mountains – faintly outlined blue and green evaporations in the sky. Leszek had said on the way here that it had taken fifty thousand men twenty years to build and carve the Borobodur. All of them must have been buried beneath that pastel landscape, and their work still loomed there above them, hundreds of years later – a grandeur such as Jane had never seen before.

A few minutes ago she had been looking at one of the
carved stone reliefs on the gallery below – a king dancing
on tiptoe, legs bent, as he cut his hair before taking up
the ascetic life. It had made her wince, the grace with
which he was departing from the world where beauty
mattered. But suddenly, now, she couldn't look at any of
it any more. All she wanted was to follow Coventry. Still
she didn't move. She rested her hand on the cool *stupa*,
feeling faint. She couldn't stop thinking of Coventry for
more than a few minutes at a time today. She thought that
never in her life before had she wanted anything so much,
nor felt so powerless to obtain it.

Just then Coventry appeared again. 'Come and see
what I've found!' he said, his voice carrying across to her
without any effort. She felt a little pent-up breath leave
her. But she was struck by the difference in his manner
from the day she had first seen him, up on that other
yellow-lit terrace in the hills. He spoke softly this time, not
a showman but a man interested in something – yet in
a way, perhaps, less interested than when he was leading
Bertrand and her up to see the dinosaur. His attention
was sliding away again even as he spoke; he was more
preoccupied, not more interested. She remembered the
evening of Sumitro's death, a fortnight ago: how he had
come straight to see her from Sumitro's house, his voice
high-pitched and thin, surprising himself as much as it
had surprised her by its tones. She had propped him up
in an armchair against a pile of stiff Ministry of Works
cushions and he had talked, his voice slowly returning to
normal. Without a single word about his own emotions,
he had told her the story in great detail, from his drive
through the rain and the man's head appearing among
the banana leaves to the interview with the policeman
just before he left the kampong. One thought kept coming
uppermost in her mind while he talked – how glad she was

that Angela had been out. And when she had said he ought to have a holiday, he'd not hesitated before replying, 'Well, you come too, and I'll suggest it to Leszek, and then that'd all be quite proper.'

It was why the three of them were staying now in Jogjakarta, the old royal capital of Central Java, twenty miles from the Borobodur. But they had almost not got here. The last fortnight had been an anxious time for all the people she knew in Djakarta, with terrified Dutch leaving the country in large numbers and blood-hungry journalists swarming in. Coventry had been out and about continuously, drinking and cabling. Suddenly all the visiting journalists had decided it was a non-story, words without wounds, and in concerted movement, like a flock of birds, they had gone. 'Now I can get on with filing the news,' Coventry had said; nevertheless he had agreed to go to Jogja as they had planned.

She followed him back round the terrace now, and he stopped by another of the latticed grey bells. 'Look at that one,' he said, 'through that hole.'

Jane put her eye to the diamond-shaped opening, and could just make out, after a while, the smooth face of the Buddha staring calmly through her. She said, 'It's got a very worn face.'

'Yes!' Something like Coventry's old excitement was detectable in his voice, over her shoulder. 'The features are almost completely gone, but he's still got that marvellous calm expression! There's just a line of a lip, isn't there, and a line or two of the eyes? But it makes no difference to him, he's as bloody calm as he ever was!'

She peered. 'Yes, there's just the mouth and the eyes, they're just visible, they're closed almost, and the eyebrows – the eyebrows are still there, Cov, quite sharp somehow or other.'

'It's wonderful!'

She turned and looked at him and he laughed at himself now. 'I don't know,' he said, shaking his head, leaving the remark unfinished.

'Oh Cov!' The words came out of her without volition.

'Jane.' He said it quietly, and they stood smiling at each other.

Then they heard footsteps, and Leszek was there. He had got some country clothes at last: khaki shorts (something that Coventry, talking to her last night, had sworn never to wear) and a pink shirt. He looked smaller as well as more lithe in them. Even his face seemed more mobile.

'Now don't stand looking at each other,' he said, laughing. 'This isn't a holiday. There's work to do. We haven't finished looking at the reliefs yet, there's the bottom.'

Jane was irritated by the remark. It was like a bit of vulgar good humour not quite in Leszek's own voice, as though he didn't know what tone to adopt in this unusually cheerful mood of his.

'All right,' said Coventry. 'You lead the way.' He took Jane's hand, and, following Leszek, led her down some stone steps and under a narrow arch to one of the lower galleries. They walked round the gallery to a side out of the sun, which was getting very hot now. In the shade, Leszek began to point out how the background figures on the reliefs, musicians and soldiers, were all equally relaxed whether sitting or standing – there was no tension in any muscle he said, greater than that of an elbow resting on the arm of a chair. It was true, Jane thought – it gave all these scenes an extraordinary lightness and ease. But after a moment she said, 'I can't look at any more, Leszek, they're wonderful but there's a limit.'

'Yeah, we'll all go and sit down,' said Coventry.

Leszek laughed again. 'You're not really a traveller, Cov, you're just a tourist, I see it now.'

'You sod, I know more about this country than you do or ever will. You go on trying to catch up while Jane and I sit down.'

'All right.' Leszek seemed quite contented with this proposal – he was already looking at the reliefs again. Jane, in a strange state of calm now, was reminded of how it paid to be firm with the Hobleys' children. Once they knew for certain that you wouldn't do what they wanted, they got on quite happily with their own interests. She kept her hand in Coventry's till they turned away from Leszek, then let it slip out naturally as they changed positions.

'I've got something that mattered to me out of this place,' said Coventry. 'I can't get any more now.'

'No.' She nodded.

They went higher up the Borobodur again and sat on a block of stone on the shady side looking out over the palm groves and rice-fields. From here they could see two dusty tracks that approached each other on either side of a thin line of palms, and met to form a single road a hundred yards or so from the foot of the Borobodur. There was a betjak coming along each track: the two vehicles curved steadily towards each other as Jane and Coventry watched, and collided, both toppling outwards.

Jane shrieked. 'Goodness! They must have seen each other!' It had been an astounding spectacle.

'They were both as sure as we were that there couldn't possibly be a collision.'

That must have been it, Jane thought. All four of the men who had been thrown on the ground, the two drivers and the two passengers, were laughing as they got up. They started discussing the incident in shrill voices that came up to them clearly. Coventry smiled at her. 'Don't worry. When I first met Leszek he'd just been thrown out of a betjak.'

H 113

'Oh – where was that?'

'He was on his way to Sumitro's – that's where I met him, you know. The betjak man thought he'd seen a tiger and swerved.'

'Was it really a tiger?'

'It was a ghost.'

'Oh!' Jane felt as though she believed in that ghost. There was always something a shade sinister, or at any rate other-worldly, about Leszek. Especially this morning when he was so imperturbably cheerful. She looked at the sunlight shining on the miles of land below them and shivered slightly.

'Cold?'

'No, the ghost I suppose. Why's Leszek so cheerful today? Isn't he affected by – you know – Sumitro?'

Coventry's face became graver. 'Oh, he's serious.' He sighed. 'Don't be deceived. It's affected him more than it's affected me. The battle doesn't stop for him. This is just like stocking up with fresh ammunition here, you know.'

'You mean, we're frivolous people?'

'Yes. That's right. But he's got a little battle on with me as well, you know, a little mopping-up operation. Or perhaps quite a big one – it's more important to him than he realises perhaps. And perhaps I'm quite a big task, not that I want to be.'

'I didn't know about that.'

'I don't think I did really, not till just then!'

'Cov . . .'

'What?'

'Don't let him upset you – you know, don't let him change you in any way.'

'Hah!' She didn't know if it was a laugh or a sigh. 'Coventry Pearce is not so weak.'

'He's OK as he is.'

114

'Is he?' Coventry looked into her face for a long time. 'You are, anyway, Jane Summerson.'

Happiness suddenly seemed to be running through her veins, her whole body instantly affected by it. And it was as though Coventry responded at once to the fact.

'Let's go and have a marvellous lunch!' It was the man she'd first met, he spoke so eagerly. 'There's a little restaurant down there in the trees that has terrific Javanese cooking. I've been told about it. If only we had a bottle of hock, that's what we really want, it'd go perfectly with this landscape.'

'I'll steal one from Bertrand for you as soon as we get home!'

Leszek came up again as she spoke. He seemed to have forgotten his objections to their idleness. He sat on the stone floor at their feet and talked about what he had been looking at as though the Borobodur were a thousand miles away, not the very object they were all seated on. Neither she nor Cov spoiled this harmony by saying they must go and look at the reliefs again. As they went down, heading for the restaurant, she thought the three of them had not before been so contented together. For a moment, she thought that if friendship with Cov were always to be like this perhaps even friendship could be enough. Then her body instantly denied it.

The restaurant was just painted blue metal tables and chairs under the trees, and a wooden hut where the cooking was done. But from it they looked up at the great carved flank of the Borobodur, with the sun, high in the sky now, everywhere giving its grey stone a faint golden glow. Coventry had one of his moments of luck with the menu – one of those moments that, at any rate, he knew how to exploit so well.

'Look!' he said. 'Look at that!' He laid the handwritten piece of cardboard on the table and pointed to some words that she and Leszek leaned over and read: '*Bistek teosofi*'.

'A theosophical beefsteak!' said Coventry. 'For pilgrims to the Borobodur! You know what it means – a nut cutlet! Oh Leszek, I hand it to you, if the arts of commercial exploitation can penetrate to this coconut grove we need communism badly!'

When the waiter came, Coventry evidently spoke to him on the subject. Leszek was smiling. Coventry translated for her while the man stood patiently waiting for them to order. 'He's very serious about it. He says it's good to have it before going on the Borobodur, you get the full spiritual benefit from the Buddhas. It's like a delicious bit of fasting before Holy Communion!'

'Shall we have it?' said Jane.

'Oh no!' Coventry was scornful. 'Oh no, the waiter himself recommends the chicken, in spite of what he said. Anyway we've just come off the Borobodur. It's the kind of chicken we didn't finish that night, you know, the bomb-throwing. Let's have it, shall we? And some beer?'

He ordered, and the waiter beamed at them. '*Enak*,' he said, before going away – Jane knew that meant 'nice'. They all stared up at the Borobodur again, without speaking, for a moment. It soared serenely up into the blue sky, the great stone bell on its pinnacle shining, teasing the land around with the mystery of its dark emptiness.

'All the Javanese politicians employ soothsayers, or mystics,' said Leszek. 'The Russian ambassador is supposed to have been told by one of the Communist Party central committee that he could fix him up with the best mystic in Central Java provided he was paid through a Swiss bank.'

Coventry was looking excited and impatient. 'Well, I

recently heard a story about the Javanese on a still lower level. I was talking to a German woman who said that the Javanese made love like sparrows – they just hopped on, then they hopped off again.'

'But Jane, you know, they're not fools,' said Leszek. 'We may laugh about them being feeble and mystical and unrealistic sometimes, but they're also, many of them, very sharp and often – well, like Sumitro, often wonderful people.'

'Bertrand said something interesting the other day, Jane, something he said Angela had said to him. She said women appreciated an appearance of forcefulness in a man even more than real strength – anyway, the strong man who doesn't present himself as particularly strong doesn't go down so well as a fellow who they know is weak or lacking in character but who puts on a convincing show of strength to the world.'

Jane had an extraordinary sensation as Coventry spoke these words. It was like remembering a dream, yet far more uncanny. She herself had made that remark to Bertrand – using almost exactly those phrases – only a week or two ago. She remembered the occasion clearly: it was on the Club terrace, after she'd been watching Bertrand playing tennis. She hadn't told him so, but she was thinking of his style of playing. You found he was quite a good player if you watched carefully, but he always laughed and made such a show of it if he fluffed a shot, and giggled so much when he did well, that it was hard for people to take him seriously on the court. He'd been leaning closely over her as he bought her a drink, and something in his demeanour as he did that had irritated her and inspired this covert attack on him. But he'd sat opposite her staring intently while she'd been speaking – he couldn't have forgotten it was she who'd made the remark.

'He said Angela said that?'

'Yes. Why?'

'I said it to him!'

'Did you? How very odd! Perhaps he didn't . . . Oh God!' Coventry laughed loudly. 'Perhaps he's . . .' Then he stopped abruptly, blushing. 'Oh, I don't know, it's most odd.'

Truth after truth crashed into Jane's mind as he spoke. What Coventry had been about to say was that perhaps Bertrand had fallen in love with her. And Coventry was right, she knew it now. She knew it from everything that had happened in the last few days, from the time when he was leaning over her on the terrace. Bertrand had said that that was Angela's remark because to mention his conversation with Jane was to stir those feelings in himself – or was even, perhaps, in his own mind, to make some public admission of them. But that didn't matter. What mattered was that in contemplating Bertrand in love with her, Coventry had laughed. Coventry would never fall in love with her, she knew it now. There was no disrespect to her in his laughter, that was impossible – yet perhaps there was, perhaps there was some unconscious sexual disrespect that he had allowed to appear. The whole landscape shuddered as she thought that. She fought against the thought. Even if it wasn't true, even if it wasn't, one thing was plain: he wouldn't have been able to laugh like that if there'd been any feeling for her growing in him. Bertrand might be a ridiculous rival – though really why should Coventry think that? But any rival was something more than a joke to a man getting interested in a woman. There was something worse still. Coventry knew about her feelings. She was desperate at the thought. That was why he had stopped so abruptly, and blushed. Her feelings were not even very prominent in his mind, but after a moment he had thought about them and then he had stopped laughing. He knew about her love for him and yet he could take her hand without any love for her in him at all.

Tears pressed into her eyes but she managed to hold them back. She couldn't say, 'Excuse me' – there was absolutely nowhere to go. She managed to say, 'I'll have to challenge him, I can't have my best remarks stolen like that.'

Coventry put on a look of mock severity. 'Quite right,' he said.

But it was Leszek who eased the situation. He'd obviously sensed the change, though Jane didn't know if he'd understood it. He suddenly started speaking so intensely that she wondered if he hadn't simply responded in some obscure way to the emotion in her.

'My wife once said something similar to your remark, Jane, the one Bertrand repeated. But you know, you have to distinguish between a man being forceful and a man just being a bully – a woman might like force but there has to be some tenderness too, some quickness to see what will please and what will hurt. A sort of blundering forcefulness won't do – but then perhaps you'd say that wasn't really forcefulness.'

Jane and Coventry looked at him in what she thought was the same way: hesitating to ask Leszek to say more, but feeling he wanted to do so and showing that feeling in their attentiveness. It was like the time he had made his declaration on the way down from the bungalow. Jane found she had to fight back her own distress, in the face of his evident intensity, and she was grateful. He looked up at the Borobodur, then went on:

'I was proud of my wife and didn't care for anybody else, but I think I bullied her, I didn't usually make her feel that I was doing any more than just fit her into my life – fit her into my preconceptions. Perhaps I hopped about a bit like those Javanese sparrows, didn't linger enough over her.'

He sighed. It was clear he wasn't going to say any more. But Jane was very moved by what he had said. Some instinct had led him to make this revelation at just the right moment for her – so perhaps the right moment for him too. Love is hard, it seemed to say, and hard for everybody in a different way. But it was not only the message that was timely – it was also the way that, by opening out the perspective, he had brought the three of them together again, in a graver mood than earlier in the day, the only mood possible for the moment. She was still struggling with the pain, but she determined to go on struggling.

Their food came. It was as good as Cov had predicted, rice and chicken and the strange flavour of the pink breadfruit, just like what they'd been eating on the night of the assassination attempt. They fell back into light, rather impersonal talk, able to do so now. Jane couldn't add much to it. She was only wanting to go back to Jogjakarta to the hotel. The others must have understood this, since neither suggested that they should do anything else after eating.

In the car, she sat at the back while Leszek sat next to Coventry. She looked at the lilac shirt, sticking to Coventry's back when he leaned forward like a flower with a dark centre. If she'd been able to go on making some sort of conversation with him over lunch, it was partly because she couldn't condemn him. She liked him still—she loved him still, if that was what it was, and he had never proposed to her more than friendship, except perhaps for a moment this morning when he had taken her hand. She'd accepted that friendship and she had to go on showing acceptance of it, at least till she could leave Coventry and Leszek and get back to Djakarta. Behind their backs, though, she no longer resisted the tears in her eyes. She had big sunglasses on, so even if Coventry looked at her in the driving-mirror there would be nothing for him to see. The matter with Bertrand seemed trivial. She couldn't leave the Hobleys yet, with Christmas just coming, unless they themselves asked her to go; but she didn't doubt that by behaving perfectly correctly she could ensure that Bertrand would do the same. It wouldn't be a problem – but it added to the sense of waste, and to the pain.

She noticed out of the car window how extravagantly the horizon shimmered in the afternoon heat, trees and mountains moving all the time. If it had not been for that conversation they would probably have spent this hour lying on the grass in some cool spot, rather than driving under the sun. When they got to the hotel, they all went straight to their rooms to rest. Hers was a pleasant room, looking out on the courtyard at the front of the hotel, with its palm trees and flowering borders. But she closed the shutters and took her clothes off, and lay down naked on the bed.

She started to let her hand wander over her body – her breasts, then the inside of her thighs. But then she stopped abruptly. It was a long time since she had taken that bleak pleasure – the last time must have been in that unsettled month when she was deciding whether to come to Indonesia. You couldn't have sexual fantasies about someone you loved: it seemed too dangerous a denial of their reality, which you felt might not return again. And if you loved someone as she now loved Coventry, you didn't seem to be able to have more than the most meagre fantasies about anyone else. Her hand went back for a moment to her body, almost prepared to help create one of those. Then she got up angrily. She burst into tears as she walked to the bathroom. Tipping cold water over herself from the porcelain tank, still in tears, she decided she would go back to Djakarta on the train in the morning. She'd make herself sit through dinner with them tonight, but after that she'd find an excuse to go. She didn't think that Coventry would believe she was rushing back to see Bertrand.

CHAPTER EIGHT

Leszek Mylski

ON Christmas morning Leszek woke with a vivid
dream still in his head. There had been a baby in
a white frock sitting up and making the gurgles and cries
of a child who has not yet learned to speak. Suddenly its
mouth had opened and in a deep adult voice it had said:
'I promise.' Leszek knew in the dream that these were the
baby's first words.

He felt a deep sorrow for the baby weighing on him as
he lay on his bed, watching the still lines of yellow light
on the ceiling. The sun was pouring in through the ventila-
tion slots high on the wall. What a burdened baby! The
thought wouldn't leave him.

He got up and went to the kitchen at the back of the
house. This consisted of a gas-stove, a sink, a table and a
cupboard on a half-open verandah. The sun shone on to
a bare yard, where several chickens were strutting. By
some oversight, it had never been established whether
the chickens belonged to the Polish State or to the cook
and the washing girl: the eggs they laid, and the birds
themselves when cooked, were distributed by the cook
according to her own obscure principles of ownership.
Leszek could find no eggs anywhere, so he just made
himself some coffee. The servants had been given the day
off. One of the men in the house was on leave, and Leszek
and the other man had decided they'd not want much to
eat after last night's party.

Thinking about it over his coffee, which he drank sitting
on the verandah, Leszek was surprised at how much he'd

enjoyed that party. It had been given by some of the married couples at the embassy for the bachelors, and for the husbands whose wives were not out with them. The hosts had got hold of all the traditional Christmas Eve fare, from smoked eel to carp, and of course there had been floods of vodka. After they'd eaten, they'd begun to sing Christmas carols. For a while there'd been an unspoken agreement among them to forget that they were all representing a communist state. Idlinski himself had contributed a deep bass voice to one or two of the carols, and Tarski, the press agency man, had soon sung himself hoarse. The windows were open to the warm night, yet the dozen or so men and women seemed a beleaguered group as they sat round the table singing. Suddenly Leszek had found tears coming to his eyes – thinking of past Christmases, no doubt, but also responding to some revelation of courage in these colleagues of his whom for most of his time in Djakarta he had disliked or even despised.

Coventry was having his Christmas lunch today in very similar circumstances: some of the British embassy girls were entertaining all the British bachelors in Djakarta. Leszek tried to imagine the scene. What he could see most clearly was that that party of Englishmen and women would give no sign of having to harvest their resources, and live carefully with them day by day under every kind of strain. His compatriots seemed heroic by comparison. He was going round to see Coventry in the afternoon and was looking forward to it. Yet he had begun to feel that his friendship with Coventry was taking a new turn. Sooner or later, he was going to have to do battle with him. He knew when this feeling had had its beginnings: it was on the night when the bombs were thrown at Sukarno. That night, Coventry's capacity for pleasure – the quality Leszek had first been attracted by in him – had suddenly repelled

him. And after Sumitro had been killed the next day, and
Cov had brought the first news of it, Leszek had found
himself persistently associating Cov with some of the
responsibility for Sumitro's death. Realistically speaking,
it was ridiculous to connect Cov in any way with the half-
witted young Muslims who, it now seemed clear, had
been persuaded into throwing the bombs and killing
Sumitro. Yet Leszek couldn't help seeing one connection:
a kind of irresponsibility, some refusal to acknowledge the
proper virtue in certain lives or the proper gravity of
certain of men's actions.

One incident at the party had affected him in a different
way. At table, he'd been between Idlinski and Ella, Zosia's
old Warsaw friend. He'd talked more to Idlinski than to
her, but after the carols were over she'd put her hand on
his knee. When he looked at her she'd returned his look,
with watery blue eyes. He'd patted her hand affectionately
and with a half-smile she'd taken it away. He'd not wanted
to become involved with her, whether her action had been
a passing fancy related to the consumption of too much
vodka, or whether it had meant more. But the feel of her
hand on his leg had stirred him. He had not made love –
not tried to make love – with anyone since Zosia had left
him. But he had lain awake a long time in bed last night.
He had found himself thinking about another side of
Coventry's life. It was hard to imagine Cov living without
women. Leszek knew that some of the men in the Polish
embassy picked up girls off the streets, something he was
reluctant to believe of Coventry – yet now and then he
had noticed signs that this might be what Cov did. There
had been that night after the *wayang*. He'd noticed girls
lingering near the bar they'd gone to, then there had been
strange whisperings and disappearances into the darkness
by Cov and Achmad. Leszek's penis had been as hard as
iron as he lay in bed thinking, and all the area between

his legs was aching. Slowly the tension died away. The movements of the lizards on the walls kept startling him just as he was losing consciousness, and it was only when he began listening to them deliberately and imagining their movements that he had fallen asleep.

In the sunshine now, he remembered the Borobodur – the way the sun had seemed to permeate, unimpeded, the whole vast monument. On that trip to Central Java everything had been suspended for him: it was after Sumitro's death, after his first feelings of anger at Cov, but at the start it had all been ease and gaiety with Cov and Jane. Those hours on the Borobodur had given him a sense of the human capacity for creating beauty and serenity – in the figures of the Buddhas and in the reliefs, indeed, for being beautiful and serene – that he thought would never completely leave him. Yet even in the middle of that moment out of time there had been the curious clash between Cov and Jane that had resulted in them all going home the next day. He hadn't minded, himself: after seeing the Borobodur he had been happy enough to return. But it was another example, he couldn't help thinking, of Cov's irresponsibility. He seemed to have let Jane become very attached to him without being able to return her feelings – on top of that, he had let his indifference show at just the wrong moment. So, at least, Leszek interpreted the incident. He felt sorry for Jane, though he thought she'd been foolish and uncontrolled too. But it was the first part of the holiday that he kept remembering.

He went to the main room of the house, looking out on the front garden, and sat down by the window. On a table here he had some notes he had made on Sumitro. Idlinski had asked him to write a report on the political aspects of Sumitro's work and of his death, and it seemed a chance to pay a certain homage to Sumitro. At the same time he could repair the omission in his previous verbal reports – no harm could come to the man now. Christmas morning seemed as appropriate a time as any to do this service to Sumitro – though it would not be, Leszek intended, his last service, since he planned now to translate all Sumitro's novels and stories. He got up again and shaved in the kitchen, watching the hens, then settled down to work.

About half past twelve, he heard Janusz, the other man living in the house, come out of his room. He was glad of the sound. He pushed his papers and books back into the middle of the table, and leaned back in his chair. A few minutes later Janusz burst into the room. He'd only been in the house a week or two – he was the replacement of the man who'd left in November.

'Panie Leszku! Working Christmas Day?' He gave a high cheerful titter. He was too full of himself to tease more than perfunctorily. 'I like it here! Yes, I like it here. Feel the sun!'

He was a short man, very blond, with a small, pinched face, and had on a bright, brand-new sarong that needed a good many folds at the waist to prevent it going right up to his neck.

'Christmas present?' said Leszek, nodding at it.

'I bought it for myself! And they were right, I feel very comfortable in it. And you know what I'm doing in return! Ungrateful – ungrateful in the extreme! I'm trying to persuade Javanese women to wrap our scratchy textiles round their pretty bottoms. And ruin the batik industry at the same time!' He shook his head, his blue eyes glittering. 'But I'm glad to say I'm making some progress!'

'Do you want any breakfast?'

'Breakfast? Or lunch? Let's have something! Have you eaten?'

'I just had some coffee, a couple of hours ago.'

'Let's eat!'

Leszek's mother had sent him a tin of ham and a yeast-cake she'd baked for him. His offer to bring them out was enthusiastically accepted by Janusz, who went to his bedroom and returned with a bottle of vodka. Over the table he stared at Leszek with anxious eyes, and lowered his voice. 'I heard something about those little bottoms, you know. Authoritatively, Panie Leszku, authoritatively! Those black bottoms have little bright pink cunts in them. Hah!' He jerked back in his chair violently, once more quite relaxed, and gave his eager titter. 'Think of that, Panie Leszku! I've seen pink bottoms with dirty holes in them but the other way round, never!'

He didn't seem to need an answer. It was as well, since Leszek had none to give. Janusz started to eat his ham, staring at the plate, his thoughts far away. Then he looked up. 'You know that joke about capitalism is the exploitation of man by man, socialism is the complete opposite?'

'I've heard it, quite often.'

'I was travelling on the train to Cracow once and a man facing me was telling it to a friend of his. But this friend couldn't grasp it. So this chap took a piece of paper out and drew a circle on it and divided it in two with a line and wrote the word "man" in each half. Then he told the story again and when he said about capitalism he held the circle one way up and when he said about socialism he turned it the other way up. And still the man couldn't see. So he said, "You see, it's exactly the same both ways." So his friend said, "No, it's not, the word 'man' is upside down when you turn it upside down". Hah! Well, if the truth be told he had a point there. So I leaned across and said to the man who was telling the joke, "Why don't you write the word 'man' upside down in the bottom half of the circle?" So he said, "Oh, thank you," and did that. Oh dear!' Janusz munched away at his ham. Leszek said:

'Did it help?'

'Oh no! No use! His friend never saw!'

Leszek laughed. 'Well, you did your duty.'

'Yes, Panie Leszku, yes, I'm always talking, always joining in conversations. But I've got a friend who's worse, always talking about himself – his problems, you know, his housing, his wife, his job. I was amazed one day, he said to me, "I'm always talking about myself, let's talk about you for a change". Then he went on, "Tell me, what do *you* think I should do about my wife?" Hah!' Janusz shrieked with laughter.

Leszek was sorry when Janusz left – he was off to play bridge for the rest of the day. After he'd gone Leszek wandered about the house, then decided to go out. It was three hours before he was due to arrive at Coventry's. Down by the canal, in the afternoon heat, there was nobody about. On both sides of the canal, the high gates outside the gardens were shut. He walked along the concrete edge of the canal. It gave off a rank smell, and the still brown water looked very poisonous. But in the evening people would come to wash in it. He remembered the three little girls sitting on the bank shitting into it together, the night he had gone to Sumitro's and first met Coventry. It seemed a long time ago, and he'd not seen the sight again.

The canal curved slightly, and further on he found several betjaks under some trees, the drivers sprawled out in them. One man leaped out of his betjak as Leszek approached. He had nothing on except a pair of blue shorts and a dirty white cloth round his head. He landed on legs bent at the knees, his eyes shining, his finger in the air. 'Diponegoro Street,' he shouted – acclaiming Leszek as a passenger he remembered well. But it was all a brilliant act, a guess dressed up as a memory. Diponegoro was a busy enough street, and a common enough destination for the performance to have some chance of succeeding, of convincing the passer-by that in fact the betjak man remembered a previous occasion he had taken him there. But Leszek was sure he had never been to Diponegoro by betjak. As he shook his head, he smiled at the man, appreciating his performance, and the man gave a delighted grin.

'Tuan prefers to walk.'

'Yes.'

'No good, in the afternoon.'

The man turned and stretched himself out again in the seat of his betjak, and his companions laughed.

Leszek walked home again. As he sat down in the cool sitting-room he felt it pleasant to be there, but at the same moment he sighed. All his loneliness seemed to strike at him in that instant, through the fictitious familiarity of the betjak man's raised finger.

When he went out at five, he thought of walking down and seeing if the man was still there; but an empty betjak was passing as he went out of the door, and, lazily, he took that. There was more life in the streets now. Christmas Day was a holiday – Indonesians got both Muslim and Christian ones – and everywhere he saw servant women out wearing rich blouses and finely-laundered batik *kains*, with their hair done in gleaming black buns. They walked very upright, sometimes throwing their hands out with open fingers as they swung their arms. As he turned into Coventry's street he felt a moment's anxiety that Cov might not have come back from the lunch. But the car was standing outside the pavilion, and the pavilion door was open. He paid the betjak man, and walked up the garden and stepped inside.

Coventry was sitting in the front room with two other

men, Toby and a man Leszek didn't know. They must have all been at the Christmas lunch. Leszek found he was very tense. But Coventry got up at once.

'Leszek! Happy Christmas! Here, I've got a present for you: John Grayne. I've told you about him, he teaches – sorry, lectures – at the university.'

'Can I unwrap him?' said Leszek, letting his smile travel from Cov's face to Grayne's, and, as Grayne got up, taking his hand and bowing to him.

'No!' said Cov. 'He's one of those presents that look better with the wrapping paper on. Great disappointment without it.'

Grayne, a tall man, was wearing a dark blue suit of fine material. He beamed down at Leszek through his thick spectacles. 'But extraordinarily *enchanté et ravi*,' he said. Then he made a long, reproving face. 'My inefficient attempt to rise to Polish heights of courtesy and cosmopolitanism.' He slurred the last word and sat down again heavily. Christmas lunch was still obviously having a powerful effect on him – and there was a bottle of whisky and glasses on the table. Toby hadn't moved from his chair, but when Leszek looked at him, he gave Leszek a nod of his head that turned half-way down into a fall, his hair dropping forward. He left his head there and his hands slid further down between his knees.

'Oh, these soaks!' Coventry said. 'Here, have a glass, Leszek, and I'll have another one too. But not them, not yet.' He seemed soberer than either of the others.

Leszek sipped his whisky while Cov went off, carrying his glass, to the bedroom at the back. Grayne eyed him but said nothing; Toby seemed asleep. It was a dull little room – all bamboo furniture – except for a Balinese painting on the back wall, some slim, dark figures stabbing theatrically at turtles with their spears in the brown light of an *art nouveau* forest. Suddenly Grayne said, staring at Leszek:

'I – I'm sorry. I rather spent myself on that first wild outburst. That rather drained me dry, if you'll allow me the phrase. You're interested in the literature here, aren't you, Mr Mylski? No?'

'I'm studying that, yes.'

'Can't manage to get down to it myself, it's rather silly really.' He leaned back in his chair. 'You know, I spend the morning going into the finest detail about all sorts of English writers, after that I seem to feel the need for pleasure for the rest of the day, can't seem to get down to swotting up some other language and literature.'

'It's my job, you know. But no one's very interested, as a matter of fact. Sumitro – you know' – Grayne nodded – 'he was a communist, a real communist, but no one at my embassy has the least desire to hear about him.'

'Ooh, they wouldn't at ours, either!'

'Coventry was interested, in Sumitro anyway. He's the only one.'

'And his interest didn't end in pure pleasure, either.'

'No.' Leszek was silenced by this remark.

When Coventry came back he handed Leszek a small parcel in brown paper. 'You can unwrap that one,' he said.

Leszek did so: his present proved to be an old Dutch book on the Borobodur, with some fine sepia photographs. 'Oh, thanks,' he said, with intense feeling. He was silenced again. All he'd bought Cov was a bottle of Polish cherry brandy, and he'd left that at home. In the light of the book, he felt his present for Coventry was insulting.

Toby was stirring now. He shook his head and looked confusedly around him. He closed his eyes and shook his head again. Then, contemplating the foot of the door, he said slowly, 'I want to pedal a betjak. I want that for my Christmas present.'

'Oh Christ!' said Grayne. 'He's remembered that again!'

Coventry sighed. He looked rather low in spirits as he turned to Leszek. 'Toby heard someone say once before he came out to this bloody country that this chap had a marvellous time after a party pedalling betjaks. It seems to him just the right moment, every now and then, to experience that pleasure himself. I think he's always been dissuaded so far.'

'Why not, though?' Grayne suddenly said, jumping up. 'Presents are being given, why should we refuse Toby? A ride on a betjak saddle, an abstract pleasure, better than all your artefacts!'

'Oh Christ, you're off too, now, are you?' said Coventry. He looked no happier.

But Grayne laughed merrily. 'Come on, Cov, join in the sport. It's once in a lifetime.' He helped Toby out of his chair, and without waiting for Coventry led him stumbling into the garden.

Coventry looked at Leszek, his face drawn. 'I can't go and wrangle with them in the garden, it'd be too shameful. We must just go and see no mischief's done.'

Leszek got up but laughed. 'Grayne – he's a clever man, isn't he, a scholar?'

Coventry also gave a little laugh. 'A scholar, yes, a good critic too, I believe – you know how in England those Eng.Lit. guys always feel they've got to add that these days. Come on, Leszek, I know it appals you but we'll keep within bounds.'

In his turn, he did not wait for Leszek any more but hurried into the garden – the other two were at the gate by now, looking up and down the road. Leszek felt he had to join them.

A betjak soon came along the street, pedalled by a very young, smooth-faced boy. Grayne hailed it. As it drew up, they saw it had the name 'New York' in English on the mudguards. Toby peered at the betjak and suddenly noticed this fact. 'New York?' he said. 'No!' He waved his hands. 'I don't want this one, I want a real woggy one.'

'Liberal sentiments in abeyance,' said Grayne, waving the betjak away. But the betjak stayed, rocking, where it was, the boy pressing the pedals lightly with alternate feet. He knew something was happening, and wasn't going to give up the chance of a passenger so easily. 'Not enough air in his balloon,' he said, looking at Toby. It wasn't a bad description of Toby, standing there with his knees slightly bent and his shoulders drooping, and with Grayne's hand under one elbow. Leszek looked at Coventry, who laughed. Leszek couldn't help smiling too, after that. Grayne and Toby had not understood the boy's words.

'Come on,' said Coventry. 'You'll do just as well on this one, Toby, the boys'll quarrel if you take another one now.'

Toby was not up to protesting further, it seemed. He looked at Coventry without expression, and Cov said to the boy, 'We just want to borrow your betjak for a few minutes, just up and down the road, we won't damage it.'

The boy shook his head. 'Not allowed, tuan.'

'Oh, come on – we'll be very quick.' He turned to Grayne. 'In the garden, I think, eh, not on the road?'

'On the road,' said Toby plaintively.

'Oh, shut up, Toby, we're fixing it for you, now leave it to us. All right, John?'

'Wise, wise.'

'In the garden,' Coventry said to the boy. 'You can stand at the gate, it won't go out of your sight.'

'It'll cost a lot of money, tuan.'

'I knew you'd say that.' Coventry turned to Toby and said to him in English, 'It'll cost you a packet.'

Toby felt in the top pocket of his jacket and took out some small, dirty notes. 'Give him twenty.'

Coventry took two 10-rupiah notes from Toby's hand and held them out to the boy. But the boy leaned back on his saddle and shook his head very slightly. '*Ng-ga*.'

'Not enough?'

'*Ng-ga*.'

'How much?'

'A hundred.' He lifted his hands and lightly spread all ten of his dark fingers.

Coventry smiled at Leszek again. 'Good man, eh?' he said. 'Toby, it'll cost you a hundred. We don't want any bargaining this afternoon, we want to get a move on.' He took the rest of the money from Toby's hand, counted out 100 rupiahs, and gave it to the boy. He tucked the rest of the money back in Toby's pocket. The boy swung the betjak elegantly round, and sent it sailing, with one push of his foot on the pedal, into the garden. Then he got off and stood with one hand on the saddle. He only relinquished the betjak finally when Toby, having closed his eyes and shaken his head a few more times, was helped up on to the saddle by Grayne, with Coventry taking an arm and doing a little directing from the other side. Several Indonesian women and children, and another betjak driver, had now stopped at the gate to watch.

'Shall I let you go?' said Grayne. Toby gave him a sheepish smile, and Grayne and Coventry stepped back. Toby, who was leaning forward holding the back of the betjak's seat, pushed on the forward pedal, which was the left one. Nothing happened. He pushed again, turning his head and looking at Coventry. Suddenly he pushed at the pedal very violently with his foot. The betjak moved forward a few inches, and Toby lurched to the left and fell on to the ground. There were shrieks of laughter from the gate, and Coventry rushed to pick Toby up. The children at the gate were looking wide-eyed, but the

women were all smiling and one girl was bent double
with laughter. The betjak boy, who had stood watching
the scene without expression, stepped firmly forward and
leaped on to the saddle. '*Sudah!*' he said, 'Enough!' He
backed the betjak smoothly out into the road, turned it,
and soared away. Leszek couldn't tell whether he'd been
showing dignity and contempt, or whether he'd merely
been anxious about his money and eager to get away
before the white men changed their mind. Leszek had
thought for a moment of asking the boy to take him home –
but that would have declared his sympathies a little too
pointedly, considering that he was Cov's guest.

Coventry helped Toby to his feet; but Grayne didn't
move from where he was standing by Leszek's side. He
looked chastened by the event, his long face severe.

'Pathetic fulfilment of a long-held dream,' he said, then
turned and went back into the pavilion without waiting
for the others.

Toby was grinning even now – grinning seemed to be
his last barricade before total collapse, and he hung on to
it hard, Leszek thought. Brushing himself, he went un-
steadily back into the pavilion.

Leszek said to Coventry, 'Cov, I think I'll go. What are
you going to do now?'

Cov sighed again. 'They want to go to the Cosy Corner,
I must go with them. If only because they need my car.
You're right, you wouldn't enjoy it, though of course you
know you're welcome, Leszek.'

Leszek felt unspeakably priggish, suddenly. He'd been
complaining silently that Cov – however unwillingly – had
let him down; now he felt it was really he who'd let Cov
down. But he couldn't go back on his decision – it was
futile even to say he was sorry, too.

'You'd have enjoyed all that more without me here,' he
said.

'I don't think that's so. Only I'd have been less embarrassed.'

Leszek remembered his avowal to Coventry on their way down from the hills. 'I can still say what I feel to you – that's good, anyway.' He smiled, something he'd not expected to do in this garden again today.

'Right!' Cov was vehement. 'See you again soon, eh?'

They looked at each other and gripped hands for a moment. Then Leszek called the betjak man who had stopped to watch the show, and was still studying him and Cov. He told the man the name of his street. Sumitro could have what was left of Christmas 1957.

CHAPTER NINE

Coventry Pearce

ON New Year's Eve Coventry was giving a party. Almost everybody he knew in Djakarta was coming. He sat, after his lunch, thinking about them all, crowding into his house in the evening. They'd never get into his two little rooms – some of them would have to stay out in the garden. Luckily the drizzly days they'd had just after Christmas seemed to have passed, and this afternoon the sky was brilliant, the air still. He could hear the soft 'hoop hoop' of a bird from a banyan tree in a garden three or four hundred yards away.

He had this reputation in Djakarta, of being a man who brought people together. And it was true, he'd been talking about this party, throwing out invitations, for a couple of months past. But now the day was here he was not looking forward to it. Suddenly an idea presented itself to his mind, fully-formed: he wanted some space around him, with all these people coming, and he could have it if he went out and fetched a girl to the pavilion this afternoon. They'd swarm all over the pavilion but he'd still have the sensation of being alone in the middle of them with a stranger.

Once it had come to him, the idea was irresistible. And he knew just where he would go to look for the girl. There was a kampong over to the west of Djakarta, down below the high bank of a big canal. He'd been told by Macpherson that it was a thieves' kampong, but he'd been there once at night and no harm had come to him. It had been an uncanny experience, though – the only time in his life he'd been grateful for the moon's light. He'd walked along the canal bank at about nine o'clock in the evening. The water gleamed faintly on one side, away in the direction of the moon; down below the bank his eye had slowly made out the roofs of huts among the palm trees, whose tops rose a little higher than his head. There was no one on the bank where he first got on to it from the road, but as he went further along he came upon more and more people. There were girls in white or pink dresses which could be seen glimmering several yards away. But the men hanging about them were not visible till one was almost up against them. He passed several of these clusters, glad of even the short distance by which he was able to skirt them, with the help of the little light there was. The canal bank was eerily silent, except for an occasional high-pitched shout or burst of laughter, often from a group he had just passed. The girls made no attempt to accost him. Once a man stepped sharply into his path and he retreated a pace or two. But the man only muttered, '*Noni?*' – 'Little girl?' He shook his head and walked on, passing cautiously round the man. Suddenly he came upon three girls standing together. He felt he had to see their faces. He went closer and peered. They smelt strongly of coconut oil. Two of them were quite short, their cheeks fat, their eyes small, their hair rolled in small curls on the sides of their heads. Each had on a white dress – they might have been sisters, twins even. They looked up at Coventry, lifting their eyes in half-lowered heads. The other girl, who was wearing a red dress, was taller; her thick hair hung in heavy loops over her ears and was plaited at the back. She smiled straight at him: she had narrow eyes and a long, broad mouth. 'Tuan wants?' she said.

He didn't hesitate. 'All right,' he said. He put his hand out and touched one of her breasts through the dress. 'Don't!' she said, and laughed, slapping his hand down.

She beckoned him to the edge of the bank, and as he started to follow her down a muddy path, she put her hand out and seized his hard penis. 'The brake,' she said, giggling and giving her long plait a shake – and, indeed, when he slipped she pushed him back firmly, still holding him. In the hut she took him to he had stared in wonder at her long slim body, a very dark brown, with patches of almost black skin round her knees and elbows. It was marred only by a mottled vaccination scar, two or three inches long on one of her arms – the result of a bungled job by some Dutch doctor, he thought angrily. She felt him all over with her hands when he was undressed, continually saying, 'White!' and laughing. 'Haven't you seen a white man before?' he said. 'Hundreds!' she replied. When he came inside her on the bed, holding her hair, she laughed uncontrollably. Afterwards she led him back up the bank, taking his hand. He went back along the side of the canal more confidently than he had come, but still glad of the moonlight – he was conscious how easily he could be knocked out and robbed, and even tipped into the canal. But there was hardly any more movement in the groups of people he passed than there had been before – only one or two gestures of recognition and greeting as he went by, and murmured remarks like, 'He's going home now', 'The white man's had a *noni*', 'He's done it'.

Everything drew him back to that kampong this afternoon. The only other place he knew he could find a girl in the afternoon was the line of houses he'd been going to the afternoon Sumitro was murdered, and he'd no desire to go there. But on top of that he'd wanted for a long time to see the canal by daylight; and he couldn't help remembering the friendliness of the girl. He called out to Rochmet that she could have the afternoon off. She'd cooked the rice and got the glasses ready in the morning, and all she had to do later was to heat the rice and grill the sticks of *saté*.

At half past two in the afternoon he had the roads of Djakarta almost to himself. He'd often noticed how for twenty minutes or so after half past two the district round the pavilion fell absolutely silent. Everybody's siestas, the early and the late, were overlapping. Regularly at about ten to three he would hear the first purr, rising and falling again, of a car engine.

Driving with the windows of the car wide open, he was as cool as he would be anywhere at this time. The roadsides were baked pink, the roads themselves were dusty. The perfect moment for a *coup d'état*, he thought, if you could get anyone to take part. But though in the outer islands of Indonesia dissension seemed to be getting more and more open, in Djakarta the government and the army were working firmly together to keep the city quiet, and the whole of Java was peaceful, as far as he knew. The Dutch who had fled at the beginning of December had seen some of their businesses nationalised; apart from that, they had been driven out by shouts and slogans, nothing more, and since then the shouts had been resolutely silenced, the slogans scrubbed out.

When he got to the canal he realised that it was nearer to familiar territory than he had thought when he had approached it in the dark. On the opposite side of the canal from the kampong there was a railway line, and beyond it were more of the Dutch-built bungalows that most of his friends lived in. In this district, he realised, were to be found the military attaché at the British embassy, and a little nest of Italians he knew. But the canal divided them completely from the kampong. The Italians might make raiding parties across it for the same purpose as himself: otherwise, there was no chance of running into the inhabitants of the dainty gardens. It was a fine canal, broader and bluer than any of the others in Djakarta – he thought he remembered now that someone had called it the flood canal, taking away the waters from the Javanese hills when they threatened Djakarta.

The bank he had walked along that night was absolutely deserted, and was as hard as stone in the sun. Down in the kampong below him there was scarcely any sign of life. A man in a pair of shorts sitting in the shade of a hut looked up and grinned, showing his teeth. A radio in another hut was playing a wailing song, an intricate Eastern tissue of fine intervals buffeted by unmistakable tango rhythms. He came to what might have been the path down the bank that he had taken before, and went down it, slipping – it was still damp, the canal water seeping through, he supposed. And in the kampong, under the palms, the earth was muddy. He walked along a plank path in front of a line of silent bamboo houses with their doors shut. One door suddenly opened and an old woman stared out at him, her hair long down her back but quite grey, her crinkled face a curious patchy white as if its brown colouring was flaking away. Her expression was fierce, and anxious at the same time. '*Noni?*' she said.

He never liked to admit to anyone that he was looking for a girl, to seem to depend on them, but in this deserted kampong he allowed himself to do so. She didn't, as he had feared, invite him in – she gestured in the direction of a further line of bamboo houses, and shut the door sharply. He continued along the planks, and round at the back of another house he found three young men sitting in their sarongs. They looked at him without speaking, and he decided to ask them if they knew the girl he had been with before. He didn't so much mind taking the initiative himself.

'Do you know a girl with a red dress who lives here?'

Two of the men went on looking blankly at him. The third said, without expression, 'Yes.'

'Where is she?'

'Don't know.'

The eyes of one of the other men suddenly bulged. 'Dead,' he said.

Coventry felt himself stiffening.

'No,' said the other two men, shaking their heads energetically.

'Yes! She's dead! Her heart.'

'No!' The others were as vehement as he was.

Coventry relaxed again. There was no knowing who any of the men were talking about. There was no point in feeling distress just because *someone* had died, even if anyone had. But he found himself trembling slightly.

The men did not seem to be able to take the argument beyond these simple affirmations and denials. They fell silent again, then the man who had said he knew the girl, asked '*Noni?*'

Coventry nodded, and the man got up, beckoning Coventry to follow him. At the line of huts the old woman had indicated, he called out something in a language Coventry didn't understand – it must have been Sundanese, the language of West Java. They stood waiting. After a few minutes two girls came to the door of one of the huts. Coventry looked hard at them. He was anxious now to get out of the kampong as soon as he could. Both the girls were in rather sombre clothes – one had a brown blouse on and a deep blue and brown *kain*, the other a gingery-brown dress. The one in the *kain* looked soft-eyed and placid.

'Will you come with me?' he said. 'In a car?'

She nodded. 'How much?' said the man.

'A hundred,' said Coventry.

The girl stared at him, but the man shook his head determinedly. 'Two hundred.'

'All right,' said Coventry. 'Come on.'

Both girls smiled now and the one he had spoken to stepped out on to the plank. He gestured to her to go ahead of him but the man who had bargained with him turned aside when they got back to the other men, and sat down without saying any more. Once again Coventry tried to let the girl go ahead of him but she motioned him on with the back of her hands. She started talking now they were on their own.

'Tuan has a car?'

'Yes.'

'Tuan lives in Menteng?'

'Near there.'

'*Tuan senang noni-noni?*' – 'Tuan likes girls?'

Noni-noni, he thought – that has merrier connotations. 'I like you.'

As they passed the door of the house where he had seen the old woman, it opened again. In the darkness behind, he saw a man looking out at him. Coventry gasped, then started trembling from head to foot. It was the face of the man he had seen looking at him through the banana leaves on the road to Sumitro's house. Even in the feeble light that fell on the man's face from outside, he could see the square chin and the twist of hair on it, and the eyes wide and gleaming. The door shut as abruptly as it had opened.

'What's the matter?'

His mouth was trembling now and he couldn't answer. He couldn't take another step. The girl went on blandly and cheerfully: 'Tuan's frightened?'

Still he couldn't speak or move.

'Don't be frightened, tuan. It's all right. It'll be nice with me.'

144

He started running along the plank, which wobbled
from side to side – it just lay on the rough mud. But as
he neared the point where he had come down the bank,
he slowed down. It was all right, there was no one chasing
him except the girl, who was calling out, 'Wait for me!' – it
was all probably an optical illusion, created by his own
nervousness and ill-ease here. Yet the face of the man in
the shadows through the doorway still swam before his
eyes, and he trembled again. One or two other doors were
opening and people looking out. He pulled the girl with
him up the bank and strode swiftly along it, with her half-
running at his side. Suddenly he thought the car would
have been stolen, and he stood still again.

'What's the matter? Don't be afraid with me. Where's
your car?'

'By the bridge. Come on.'

The car was still where he had parked it. The girl got
in beside him. As soon as they were moving he ran his
hand across her thighs and touched her crotch. But it was
a mechanical act, and the girl's flow of talk went on as
uninterruptedly as if he had been wiping the windscreen.
'I went in a car with another Dutchman who lived in a
big house in Menteng. Cars are very expensive, you have
to have millions of rupiahs to buy a big one.'

'I'm not Dutch.'

'Are you Russian?' 'No, I'm English.' Something made
it hard for him to hold back that information.

'I thought Russians were black men but I saw them in
the parade and they were white just like Dutchmen. Nice!'
She tittered. 'But they're not rich, no one's rich there and
they have to work every afternoon when it's hot and all
night sometimes. They're called communists and I hate
them, but they say they'd make the poor people rich and
I don't know if it's true.'

When Coventry reached the pavilion he found he

couldn't remember the road he'd taken back. All was quiet around the pavilion. There was no sign of Rochmet. He unlocked and took the girl in, then drew the curtains over the glass door. He didn't want to allow the girl into his bedroom. He told her to take off her *kain*, which she did.

'I bought it last year for the New Year. It cost eighty rupiahs.'

Only when he took his trousers off did she stop talking for a moment and look at him.

'Stand facing the wall,' he said.

'Like a goat?'

'Like people.'

She showed no reaction to this liberal remark, just did as he requested and went on to say, 'This is a brick house, isn't it, not wood?' He made love to her standing up by the wall of the room. He didn't know why he'd gone on with the girl at all – some male pride, he supposed, that gave sexual desire an irreversible momentum. The girl was plump, her breasts pleasant to hold under the blouse she was still wearing. But afterwards his knees began trembling and he had to sit down. She smiled at him in a friendly way with her soft brown eyes, as she wrapped her *kain* round herself again.

'How shall I get home?'

'I'll give you something for a betjak.'

He let her slip between the curtains and out of the front door without pulling the curtains back. He held them aside to watch her trotting steadily down the garden path. Then he went back to his chair. An extraordinary feeling of depression was overwhelming him. But he didn't allow himself to sit down. He went on to the bathroom to throw cold water all over himself and wash himself down. Then he lay on his bed, glad it had not been touched. He told himself that there was nothing to fear, even if the face had been that of Sumitro's murderer. The man wouldn't have followed him there. Then in a panic he realised that they might get the girl to show them where he lived. But there would really be no point in the man following him and exposing himself again – presumably what he was trying to do now was just to hide. Would he, in any case, have known that Coventry had recognised him? Would he have recognised Coventry? Both seemed more and more improbable; on top of which, it was still quite uncertain that it actually was the man. He began to breathe a bit more easily again – he noticed the sensation. But he was still full of anguish. The episode with the girl had been lunatic and squalid. And he felt a coward as well. He hardly knew when he had lost so much self-esteem so quickly. There was only one person he could bear to be with now, and that was Toby. He thanked God for Toby, suddenly. He'd just catch him at the bank if he rang him straight-away – the bank staff had to go back for a late afternoon session. Toby could get himself dropped off at the pavilion by the bank car on his way home. He knew Toby would come. He remembered an afternoon drinking-club in Soho that he'd gone to from time to time a year or so back. Its charm, for those who sat on the wooden benches in the long, ill-lit room, was that the company around them expected nothing of them. It was a place for those who for the time being had stopped trying. Each talked or was silent, listened or did not listen, according to his whim, which was never questioned. Coventry had gone then as a cheerful tourist among depressed natives. But this afternoon it was the only atmosphere he could take, and Toby could provide it for him.

He got on to a Chinese employee at the bank who said that Toby was not available at the moment but that he would pass the message on. Coventry hoped it would be all right – it probably would be, those Chinese were all too damned efficient. He went back to his bed again and lay there, appalled at the thought of all the people coming for the party.

After a few minutes, there was a loud noise at the front door, someone tapping hard on the wooden frame. Coventry leaped off his bed. With the thin beige curtains drawn he could not see who it was without going right up to the door. He hesitated in the doorway between the bedroom and the front room. The tapping was repeated, louder. Still he didn't go. Then he heard a squeaky shout: 'Coventry!' It was Bertrand Hobley. Coventry's whole torso slumped as he breathed out again. He hurried to the door. 'Bertrand!' he called. 'Just a minute.'

When he drew the curtains he saw Bertrand standing there, his red walking-stick held in his hand like a club – obviously he'd been using it to knock on the door with. He was looking very cool and smart, in a light grey suit and open-necked white shirt. He grinned, his upper lip rising right up under his nostrils, and waved the stick at Coventry through the glass. Coventry opened.

'Coventry! I thought you weren't in. I didn't think you siesta-ed.'

'I did today.' Coventry could find no energy to put into the words.

'It arrived safely?' Bertrand stepped in.

'Oh yes, thanks.' Bertrand had arranged the drink for the party tonight, getting it from the embassy supply – the bottles were locked in a cupboard in Coventry's bedroom now. Was that all Bertrand had come to ask? It seemed not. 'Good,' he said. He looked round the room. 'How are you going to get everybody in? You'll have to have some in the garden, won't you?'

'I suppose so.'

'Good. Yes. You'll have to, that is, but that'll be nice.' He went back to the door and looked round the garden.

'How far does your garden stretch? Can you use the part behind the big house? I see there's no fence between your part and that.'

'It's all theirs really, but they're Chinese businessmen, they couldn't care less about the garden. I expect people will wander everywhere, as there's no fence, as you say.'

'Ah! Well, I'd better get back, just thought I'd see you got the drink all right.'

'Is Jane coming?'

'Oh! Yes – yes, I think she is. Yes, she distinctly said so at breakfast, I'm sure. Yes, I think you'll see her.'

'Tell her I'm really glad she's coming.'

'Oh yes! Jolly well will! Jolly well will! Bye-bye, then, Coventry, bye-bye. See you then tonight.' He grimaced friendlily at Coventry, then marched off down the garden.

Yet another reason for self-dislike: the thoughtless way in which he had treated Jane. He hadn't seen her since they had got back from Jogja. That silent drive back from the Borobodur had been a nightmare – Leszek lost in contemplation of the landscape or his past, Jane tight-lipped behind them, himself unable to start any talk going, since his realisation at lunch of how much she'd been expecting of him and how cheerfully he had swept her expectations aside. When she had said that evening that she was feeling unwell and wanted to go back to Djakarta, he'd felt he had to drive her back, he couldn't just put her on the train. But perhaps that was tactless, too – or more than tactless, an attempt, rather, to keep himself formally in the right even if it meant, in the end, that he was making things still more difficult for her. However, she'd agreed, and on the long drive back to Djakarta she had been very tough – talking mostly to Leszek, but putting extra energy into looking at things and taking in the interest of the journey. He was glad she was coming tonight, though puzzled: probably, as everybody she knew was coming, she didn't think it worth being left out if she was strong enough now to be able to face him again. It was another reason for wishing there was no party tonight. And his attempt to escape from his guests had failed abysmally. As for Bertrand, what had he been up to? He seemed to be spying out the territory. Perhaps he was hoping he would find the opportunity to make his own declaration to Jane this evening.

Coventry didn't, after all, feel like seeing Toby now. Bertrand's visit had changed his mood for him. Toby had missed his one chance to be of use: he was already becoming a burden again in Coventry's mind.

Toby arrived just after five. He opened the door as Coventry came into the front room carrying a tray of glasses. The glasses wobbled.

'Oh God!' said Coventry. 'You made me jump.'

Toby leaned against the door. He smiled broadly at Coventry but his blue eyes were clouded and hopeless.

'Oh God, you're drunk already! Where did you get it, Toby? Were you ill when I rang up?' Still he's come, Coventry thought, ill or not. 'Come on in then, old chap, come and sit down.'

Toby sat very stiffly in the armchair, Coventry looking down at him. The smile had gone from Toby's face. Suddenly he gave a slow sigh, then another. Hardly opening his lips he said, 'Old bloody Gregor.' The words just seemed to stir in the back of his throat. Gregor was the manager at the bank. 'No good. No good.' The 'n' was hardly audible – he might have been saying, 'Oh good,' if it hadn't been for the fact that everything indicated that he wasn't.

'What?'

Toby pointed to himself with a slight movement of his thumb. 'Me.'

'What's happened?'

Toby opened his lips and moved them from side to side with a little wriggle but no sound came out.

'You've got the sack?' Toby didn't answer. So that's it, at last, thought Coventry. He'd never really understood Toby's lethargy and melancholy, and the way he just let drink take his life over. There'd been some story of his being caught up with a middle-aged married woman in Hong Kong: behind her, Coventry supposed, loomed the figure of his mother. Coventry had even suggested once to Toby that if he found a nice Chinese boy that might do the trick – there was a man in the bank who'd set up a very jolly ménage in that way – but it didn't prove to be the word Toby was waiting for. That girl at the embassy, Jenny, had taken an interest in him for a little while, and he'd let her more or less look after him; but, understandably enough, she'd soon despaired of him. However, if he'd got the sack that was pretty serious. Those Eastern banks were indulgent to their staff and would always move a man somewhere else in the hope of reformation rather than sack him. Yet perhaps it would be best for Toby if he went home to England again.

He left him where he was and got on with bringing out the glasses and bottles. He wouldn't give Toby a drink till he asked for one. But Toby remained silent in the chair, dozing off for a minute or two from time to time. It's like that Soho club after all, thought Coventry, only the boot's got put on the other foot. It was Leszek he was looking forward to seeing now; yet he wouldn't be able to tell him about any of this. It was just that Leszek would make him feel there was still some order to cling on to in the world.

The first guest arrived soon after six. Rochmet was back and working, Toby was still dozing in the chair. Coventry had been standing at the door watching the snails on the lawn. They were three or four inches long, and made their way across the grass from one hedge to the other with more of a galloping motion than a sliding one, jerking their necks to and fro. Fruit bats were dotted about the pink sky, and as the pink turned to shadow some hawk of the dusk started swooping between the palm trees, making a sharp call. Into this array of wild life stepped John Grayne, out of a betjak.

'Join the snails,' said Coventry, as John came up to the door. 'Though you're too quick off the mark for them—you're the first here.'

John smiled at him. 'Always first in the line for pleasure, Cov.'

He looked more as if he were addressing Covent Garden, Cov thought, with his beautifully-cut dark suit and his dark-red bow tie. 'You're a tonic, anyway.'

'What, flagging, Cov? I thought you'd regard my boast as an insult.'

'Come on in, John, I can't banter any more with you, I'll give you a drink. Toby's there but he's more like the last of the day's visitors than the first of the night's guests. He's got the sack, I think.'

'Oh! Oh dear! What can we do?'

Coventry shrugged his shoulders. 'Let him be for the moment.' It was almost dark now, the night fell so quickly in Djakarta. He switched the light on and they could see Toby still in the chair. He half-opened his eyes, then his head slumped again. Outside there were car doors banging, voices, the grating ring of a betjak bell; suddenly there was a whole group of people coming into the garden.

'Mind the snails!' Coventry called from the doorstep. 'Shoo! shoo!' he cried. His style wasn't failing him, at any rate, he noted. As they came into sight he could see it was Achmad and Subekto, and Thomas and Christine, and a couple of other girls, one of them from the embassy, one working with UNRRA. These were a muscular couple who were always driving off to native villages in a jeep for the weekend, allegedly distributing urgent supplies of one kind or another. They were in heavy silks tonight. He hustled them all into the pavilion and told them to help themselves. There was whisky and gin and sherry, and lots of beer and water and soda-water and tonic, and a tin bath full of ice on the floor – it had contained a huge block that he had almost sprained his wrist breaking up with an axe just now. He grabbed both Achmad and Subekto by the arm. 'Go and talk to John now, don't be shy, you knew him before you knew me. He's not a bloody *guru* here, he's just a friendly fellow relaxing after work.' Achmad grinned through his teeth and gulped. 'We'll try!'

There were already more people arriving – another group of embassy girls, a tobacco crowd, Frank, some of Grayne's Indonesian colleagues. In no time they were spilling out into the garden. By darting about he managed to get away with just a word or two of greeting to them all. After a while he found himself fearing he might hear the sound of a snail-shell crunching under someone's shoe. He walked round the lawn gingerly, trying to see in the faint light if there were any still out, but either they were creatures of the sunset rather than the night, or else the vibrations of the earth under the heavy feet of Europeans had sent them packing – at any rate he couldn't see any left. People were being quick to relax and, apparently, enjoy themselves. He could hear singing coming from the pavilion while he looked for the snails. When he went back in he found the UNRRA girl and her friend standing by the wall, on the very spot he had stood united with the girl this afternoon, singing one of their party pieces arm in arm:

> Oh I'd like to be a fascinating bitch
> I'd never be poor and I'd always be rich

I'd live in a house with a little red light
I'd sleep all day and I'd work all night.

Carry on fantasising, he thought. There was a face
staring at him from his left: when he turned to look he
saw it was Leszek, and he started. Why was that? he
thought. He realised he'd had a glimpse of such a stern,
anxious look on Leszek's face, his small blue eyes hard and
concentrated before the face broke into a smile and they
softened.

'Hallo, Leszek!' He gripped the back of Leszek's half-
clenched hand. 'No drink?'

'I've just arrived.'

'Have something.'

'Well, a whisky, thank you, a long cold one – I'll get it.'

'No! I'll get it.'

After all, he couldn't talk to Leszek. In fact he was still
disturbed by the sight of him. But what a strange day,
when everyone he wanted to see proved to be unwelcome
when they came.

'There's another Pole here,' he said, 'a man called
Tarski, a journalist.'

Leszek looked startled, in his turn. 'You know him?'
he said.

'I met him in a bar.'

'He wanted me to introduce him to you once, Cov, I
somehow failed.'

'Dangerous, is he?'

'No – no, not that. I don't know.'

'Leszek!' Coventry scolded him, suddenly laughing. 'I
know you now – I don't know – you hug your friendships
hard to you. It's very nice, it's very unusual – oh, I can't
criticise you, can I?'

'You mean, not if you're the friend?' Leszek's eyes
sparkled.

'Oh, you roguish Pole, I meant nothing of the sort, except as I'm a friend of yours I can't criticise your general policy towards friends. Now go and talk to him or some- one, I'm hopeless tonight, we'll talk properly tomorrow or one day soon. Parties are for guests, not hosts.'

Well, he'd managed that all right, in the end. And as he went back to the door he saw he had something else to manage: Jane coming up the path with the Hobleys. Angela was in the middle, in green satin with a flower in her hair, Bertrand in his grey suit and a tie now on her right, Jane in one of her country dresses on her left. It was Angela who had timed their arrival, he was sure – so that they'd appeared after a good three-quarters of the people invited, but were not quite the last to come. He admired Angela for the way in which she always knew, and nearly always got, what she wanted – it was why he liked talking to her, even if she had got an etiquette book tucked between two lobes of her brain. 'A perfect night,' she said to him, beaming and glancing round the garden.

'Thank you,' he replied. He wondered if Bertrand would refer to the drink again, or to his afternoon visit. He thought not – he remembered Jane's account of breakfast in the hills, and Bertrand's ability to pretend he knew nothing of the preparations he had been so heavily involved in.

'Coventry,' he said now, 'my dear chap, how delightful of you to invite us!'

Jane could hardly be severe after that. And in fact she smiled very sweetly at him, though she only said softly, 'Yes, it's very nice of you, Cov.' If she was tense, she'd certainly mastered it for this moment. Their first meeting came back vividly to his mind, and as he took the hand she proffered him into both of his own for an instant, he wondered if he'd made a grave mistake that he could still redeem. But as he let go of her hands again he knew they were not hands he wanted to keep in his own, admire her immensely though he did. He was glad to see an Indonesian journalist hovering at the gate with his wife behind the Hobleys – it meant he could decently urge the latter to go in and help themselves.

When he went back into the pavilion again Rochmet was bringing the food in – it smelled good, he was glad to notice, but he didn't think that he could eat any himself. He drank a stiff whisky, leaning against the door. Afterwards he went to the gate and looked up and down the road. Nothing stirred in the darkness. He was not frightened any more; he was not feeling anything any more. He seemed as anaesthetised as Toby, who had not budged from his chair though people were leaning on the back of it and talking across his head.

He drank some more. Later, he went into his bedroom. There was no one in it except Willem, his Dutch friend, who was sprawled out on Coventry's bed, face down, his arms and legs stretched out like a cross, bounding up and down. He scrambled up when Coventry came in, and grinned through his newly-grown beard. 'I buy a new bed, Coventry,' he said. 'I make my researches, I try yours, I try everybody's, I want the right spring for love.'

'Buy it if you want it,' said Coventry.

'Ah-ah,' said Willem nasally, shaking his head. 'Very good, you get satisfaction all right, but I am perfectionist now.'

The girls were singing their song again. Coventry went out to listen once more. Now they were doing it for the benefit of a man called Len, a very fat man who spent most of his time on a bar stool in the British club, and whom Coventry had vowed to lure away from the club this evening just for the sake of the challenge. Not that he ever had anything to say to Len: Len himself rarely uttered a word, and when he did it rumbled up from deep in his stomach and was thought an event in the club. He was sitting in a chair, his head nodding in approval as the girls barked the last word of each line at him, shaking their heads in his face:

> Oh I'd like to be a fascinating *bitch*
> I'd never be poor and I'd always be *rich*
> I'd live in a house with a little red *light*
> I'd sleep all day and I'd work all *night*.

When they'd finished he clapped his hands slowly, beating the moist palms together, three or four times. His body started gently shaking, as though he were trying to suppress a belch; then he said, in a deep, extraordinarily slow voice, 'Girls will be girls.'

The girls shrieked with laughter; the UNRRA girl clapped the beaming Len on the shoulder and shouted, 'Hey, everybody, Len's made another Lenism. Listen, listen!' But this wasn't the club, and she didn't get much reaction. Christine, who was standing by, giggled and shook her blonde hair, and Thomas put his arm round her shoulder as though to approve of her response. Achmad and Subekto were also laughing, but Coventry knew it was just the whole strange scene that was fascinating them, and that they would go away and mimic it with rich embellishments. Above their heads he could see the reproachful face of John Grayne, whose ideas of pleasure were of a quite different order.

In the garden, now, he found Jane talking to Bill Macpherson. Bertrand was standing at Jane's side, taking a step forward and then a step back again from time to time. He looked worried. Coventry sat down on a chair someone had brought into the garden, just outside the square of light coming from the pavilion doors; he sipped his whisky and listened. James was apparently telling Jane about a cockfight he had seen.

'You wouldn't like it, speakerine, they kick up their heels and whoosh! that blade slits the unlucky one right up the belly.'

'Where did you see it?' Jane asked.

'In Bali. Want to come?'

'For the moment I don't want to go further than Cov's pavilion for another drink.'

They drifted off, after that, towards the pavilion, Bertrand still stepping awkwardly behind them.

People soon afterwards seemed to be leaving. Coventry couldn't remember how many whiskies he'd drunk. Hands were falling on his shoulder, kisses fluttering on his cheek. He sat where he was, knowing he was about to go to sleep. He was worrying about the snails. He had somehow to get to bed. If he got there, it seemed just possible that the world would be new and safe again in the morning.

CHAPTER TEN

Leszek Mylski

AT about half past ten in the morning, Leszek was sitting in his room in the embassy – a former bathroom, with a towel-rail against one wall that he used for resting small Indonesian paperback books on – when a message came for him to look in on the *chargé*. When he got to Idlinski's room he found Tarski sitting in a chair at the side of Idlinski's desk.

'Panie Mylski, good morning,' said Idlinski. 'Sit down.' Tarski was looking at Leszek and smiling, so he supposed that these couldn't be disciplinary proceedings somehow following Cov's party. But he'd been uneasy ever since he'd seen Tarski at Cov's. 'Would you be able to spend today doing a little job for us?' Idlinski asked. 'Or rather not exactly for us, rather to help us out in something we've been asked to do.'

'Of course,' said Leszek, 'provided the Party won't approve.'

'Someone in the Party won't,' said Tarski. 'Of that you can be sure.'

'Excellent! We're in accord, then,' said Idlinski. 'A German film team – GDR – is making a documentary about Djakarta and they can't find an interpreter. Would you do it? Pan Tarski here knows them, he'll take you along and tell you about it.' He exchanged smiles with Tarski. So there's something to discomfort me in this, thought Leszek.

'Of course,' he said. 'When do we go?'

'In a few minutes, if we could,' said Tarski. 'They

say the light's good for them between now and mid-day.'

Tarski had a Fiat parked outside the embassy with a ragged boy guarding it, sitting on the bonnet. Tarski punched him lightly with one hand and spun him a coin through the air with the other. 'Your friend Pearce seemed the worse for wear when I left the other night,' he said to Leszek as they got in.

'Oh, he was all right. He's been under a bit of a strain since Sumitro was killed.' Leszek remembered how Cov had fallen asleep in the garden, he'd drunk so much, and he and Grayne had got him into the pavilion when the last visitor had gone. They couldn't actually get him to bed, because he'd had to lock the pavilion from inside: they'd propped him up on a chair just inside the French windows, and seen him turn the key and stumble back into the darkness before they went. But all the evening, as Cov had moved about among his guests, he'd been as far away from them as Toby had been, sitting still in his chair with people passing round him. Leszek had not been able to exchange more than a few politely jocular words with Cov all the evening, and had only spoken briefly with him on the telephone since – they'd arranged to meet but had said no more. Toby, in his turn, had had to be taken home by Grayne in a betjak.

'I couldn't get much out of him,' said Tarski. 'I don't really understand. There were plenty of people there – they weren't just there for the food and drink and each other, were they?'

'He likes people, they like him, but he's changed lately, he's been depressed.'

'You didn't give him the chance of liking me, Panie Leszku. I got there under my own steam.'

'I'm sorry. Where did you meet him, in fact?'

'Oh, in a bar, the Cosy Corner. Drinking that filthy

Bols. Why does nobody else know about vodka except those Russian maniacs?'

'What's this film about?'

'Well, I can tell you it's not this bit of Djakarta they're filming today.' Tarski glanced out of the car window and Leszek did the same. The road they were driving down was lined with tall, silver-barked trees. Behind them stretched broad gardens, many with roses in bloom, and white or cream mansions showing between trees at the far end. Leszek had never seen anything quite to compare them with – they made him think of a picture of English houses round a golf course he had seen in a magazine Cov had, or pictures of Florida, perhaps. 'It's a propaganda film. We're going to see slums. Also some whores.'

That must have been what that look was about, Leszek thought. 'What's their line?'

'You know, anti-neo-colonialism, the new exploitation by the West and so on. Whores are good, they're well-established victim figures and they give everyone a thrill.'

'You'll be glad to hear I'm now an expert on Djakarta slang.'

Tarski laughed at that. 'Good for you then, Panie Leszku, we shan't miss any of the dirt.'

They were soon passing between smaller houses, then a bridge took them across a canal. 'The flood canal,' said Tarski. 'We're going down to the waterlogged huts the other side of it.' They turned on to a hard mud track that ran along the edge of the canal. Tarski drove a few yards, then stopped. 'If we hit a rut we could be shot into the water,' he said. 'I'm going back, I'll park under a tree, we won't come back to a furnace either. The Huns have done it but they've jeeps, they're suicidal anyway.'

Leszek preferred to walk. In fact it was an enchanting moment of the morning. It was hot already, and ahead of them along the path the air shimmered over the baked earth. But it was still fresh among the palms and banana trees growing in the village below, and faint leafy smells rose to them; while the sun, half-way up the sky behind them, shone steadily on the blue water of the canal, only occasionally gleaming and sparkling on some faint disturbance of the surface. The village was quiet, though a cockerel was crowing strong and clear: it soon became evident that most of the villagers who were about were gathered at the far end, where the German jeeps could now be seen standing on the bank.

When they reached the jeeps they ran down the bank. There were some sixty or seventy Indonesians, almost as many men as women, standing about quietly, the men wearing very little, the women mostly wearing their long batik *kains* and soft blouses, with combs in shining, well-plastered hair. In the middle of this crowd was a group of Germans, all in white shorts and white peaked caps, and three Indonesian men in shirts and slacks. The Germans greeted Tarski with loud cries. One shouted, 'How can you keep these ladies waiting?' and they all laughed. Leszek shook hands with everybody – there were five Germans. But he was less conscious of them than of the Indonesian men, who proved to be a reporter on a communist newspaper, a Ministry of Information officer and a technician from an Indonesian film company. Tarski took one of the Germans aside and spoke to him for a few minutes, then he came back to Leszek and explained the situation. The Indonesian journalist had been translating into English as they had gone round Djakarta the previous day, but it had not been satisfactory, since neither his English nor the Germans' was up to much. Leszek could translate directly into German for them, or else he could translate into Polish and Tarski would translate into German, which he spoke fluently. Leszek opted for the second choice: his German was moderately good, but he could go quicker and more accurately into Polish, and Tarski would be able to keep up the level of speed and accuracy with his German.

Apparently the team had already taken their shots of the village but wanted now to film a girl actually talking about how she had gone with a white man from the West. The Indonesian journalist had been speaking to the girls and had found one or two suitable candidates who were prepared to talk for a few rupiahs. The director wanted a sound-track of the girl talking, over which in the finished film a German voice – or a dubbed voice in the language of any other country that bought the film – would softly translate so as not to drown the Indonesian voice. This authenticity in detail was important to them – they wanted a film that couldn't be faulted by experts in some elementary way. The Indonesian journalist would put the questions, standing just out of the camera's range, with a boom microphone overhead; Leszek, standing slightly aside, would then translate for Tarski, and one of the Germans would write down what Tarski said. It was complicated, but they thought it should work – it was better than having it all translated afterwards, when half of it might be inaudible on the recording and none of it could be checked.

'We want a girl who talks as freely as she fucks,' the director said to Leszek, and his colleagues laughed again. 'Then the other way round,' said the one who had the notebook. 'But don't tell them that yet.'

'O.K.,' said the director. 'Let's begin.' 'Begin,' he said in English to the Indonesian journalist, who was called Marno – a slim man with heavy spectacles who frequently blinked and knotted his brow.

The crowd were immediately aware that something was happening: some of the men rose from where they had been squatting, women began to speak and giggle. 'Christ, are they all whores?' the director said to Leszek. 'They look more like vestal virgins.'

Leszek just shrugged his shoulders. He was finding the whole proceedings extremely distasteful. He couldn't withdraw now but he intended to say no more than was absolutely necessary. He didn't want to hear these girls' stories, let alone take part in recording them for others to hear – and in a film not even concerned with truth, only with a misleading authenticity. He went up to Marno, who was talking to one of the few girls who were wearing Western dress – in her case, a cheap white frock that was not so white as her thickly powdered cheeks. She seemed very young: her hair was fastened by green rubber bands into two small tufts, one on each side of her head, and she looked down as she spoke. Leszek was going to ask Marno if all the girls were prostitutes, but he was suddenly abashed to put the question in front of one of them. Marno said to him, 'Would you ask if this one will do – she has a good story, two Dutchmen took her into a room together.'

Without expression, Leszek reported this straight to the director – he'd go through Tarski when they began filming. The German spoke to his cameraman: 'What do we really want – a ragged girl or one of these goddesses? They don't look very exploited but they look good.' 'Try this one,' said the cameraman. 'She'll do if she's got a good tale to tell, she'll look interesting.'

They got the girl to squat on the ground outside a hut, with the unbroken sun coming down on her. The crowd were shuffling forward on all sides and the Ministry man shouted at them to keep back.

'Get her to look up, for God's sake,' the cameraman called out.

'She must look up,' Leszek said to Marno.

But nothing Marno could say, either promises or threats, would now make the girl lift her face or speak. Many of the crowd were smiling, and Leszek heard several people say, 'She's shy.' At last she spoke herself, still looking at the ground. 'I'm shy,' she said, her eyes wide and frightened. The crowd laughed, but not unsympathetically, Leszek thought: perhaps not especially sympathetically either, but at any rate appreciating the way in which a girl's natural feelings were making life difficult for these foreigners.

'Fuck it, it's hopeless,' said the director. 'We'll have to get away from this crowd if we're going to do anything. Get rid of that girl, we'll go up on the bank.'

It took half an hour to haul the equipment up from the kampong to the bank, and many of the villagers followed it. The Ministry official got some men to cut banana leaves and used them to mark off an area about twenty metres wide into which no one unauthorised was allowed. Two men were paid to patrol these borders. Leszek talked for a while to Marno, who explained anxiously in words borrowed from the Dutch that the long-term needs of the proletariat had sometimes to override the claims of its individual members. Leszek was thinking how much Sumitro would have hated it all – whatever activism he might have plumped for, Leszek was sure it would never have been anything like this. Then, as though a skin had suddenly fallen off him, Marno smiled and said, 'They're only whores.' An instant later, another skin had dropped, or appeared: a frown wrinkled his brow like a clenched fist and he murmured, with eyes like the girl's when she'd said she was shy, 'It's terrible.'

Leszek left him to his confusions. Soon afterwards Marno brought into the middle of the bounded-off space another girl, this one wearing a *kain* and a brown top, a plumper and slightly older girl than the last. She certainly appeared less shy, also. She squatted where she was asked in the middle of the dry mud path and smiled at Marno. Leszek thought it looked like bringing out a witch to be burned – he imagined the ashes being flung into the canal afterwards. The sun was high now and the air was quite still. Everyone was beginning to sweat heavily. A train went slowly along the line on the far side of the canal, and the smoke hung behind it in the air all along the bank like bunting. Behind it small houses stood in motionless gardens.

When everything was ready, the camera and the boom and the man with his notebook in position, Leszek and Tarski went out into the middle of the circle themselves. Marno seemed to have forgotten his doubts again. He began briskly and firmly, 'Tell us your name and how old you are.'

This girl didn't hesitate. 'Titi,' she said. 'Nineteen.' She held up the ten fingers of her stubby brown hands, then closed them again and tried to produce nine, but she had difficulty folding her right thumb in without folding her left thumb in at the same time, and laughed.

'What happened to you?'

'When?'

'You know, that time we were talking about.'

Leszek found he would have to concentrate hard. He had to translate each remark and listen to its successor simultaneously, since the director wanted as few breaks in the film as possible. 'I want as little ground for suspicion of the interview as I can get,' he had said.

'Oh, yes, the Englishman came in his car, it was the middle of the afternoon and he was very frightened.'

'Frightened?'

'Yes, we were going along down there,' she pointed below the bank, 'out of the kampong and he was very frightened, he stopped and couldn't speak. I told him not to be afraid with me and after that he wasn't so frightened.'

'Did he take you in his car?'

'Yes, it was only a small car.'

'What did you do in the car?'

'I don't know.'

'What do you mean, you don't know?'

'I don't remember.'

'Do you remember what happened afterwards?'

'Yes.'

'Where did he take you?'

'It was behind the Menteng cinema. I saw it as we were going and I got a betjak there to come home in.'

A fear that had been at the back of Leszek's mind ever since the girl spoke of an Englishman suddenly gripped his chest. That was where Cov lived, behind the Menteng cinema.

'He took you to his house?'

'Yes, it was a little house in a garden, he called it something, a pavilion.'

'And what did he do there?'

'He talked to me, I don't think he was frightened any more, then he made me take my *kain* off. There was no bed in the room, he made me stand against the wall with my back to him and he had *mek-mek* with me like a goat.'

The cameraman shaped his mouth like a whistle and blew silently through it. His blue eyes shone and they were wrinkled at the side with smiles. 'Timid and bestial too,' he murmured.

Leszek couldn't restrain himself. He said to the girl, in anguish, 'What street was it, do you know?'

The girl looked at him, surprised. 'I don't know, tuan. Oh, I remember, I went back down it in the betjak and I asked the driver.' And she named the street Coventry lived in.

There could be no doubt; it was Cov. No other Englishmen lived in little pavilions, he was sure; also he was sure there were no other pavilions in Cov's street. He turned to Tarski, and saw that he was looking at him, beginning to smile, with his mouth open wide. So Tarski had thought the same. The director was shouting to Leszek, 'What're you doing, what are you saying to her?' Leszek had not translated his own question and the girl's answer. 'Lay your hands off the girl, you're not here for that.'

Leszek ignored him. 'Did you like him, was he a nice man?' he said to the girl.

She beamed. 'He was nice! He gave me money for a betjak, he was very *halus*.' The word meant something like 'delicate' or 'refined' – it was used of the qualities found in Ardjuna and some of the other heroes of the *wayang* plays.

'Cut! Cut! Cut!' screamed the director. He came up to Leszek as though he were going to grab him by the shirt-front. 'What did you mean by that?'

'I had a question I wanted to ask her.'

'You aren't here for that, comrade.'

Having said this, the director seemed to lose interest in him. He said to the cameraman, 'I can't go on, that's enough anyway. We'll get something out of it. She wasn't much good, she enjoyed the fucking too much. Thank you, thank you,' he barked at the two Poles, then slithered down the bank to where the Indonesian technician was standing guard over some boxes.

Leszek looked again at Tarski, who was still standing there smiling. Suspicion, then rage took hold of Leszek. 'You knew about this!' he shouted at him.

Tarski's expression changed. He stared at Leszek coldly. After a moment he said, 'Panie Leszku, don't think you're the only person who knows how to behave decently.' Then he walked away by the side of the canal. The Indonesians who had climbed up to watch the girl being filmed were trailing out along the bank now or scrambling down it back into the kampong.

Leszek knew he had misjudged Tarski. 'I'm sorry,' he

called out after him. Tarski just lifted his left hand without turning round or stopping.

Leszek's mind was in a whirl. Now he felt humiliated and bitter. So that was how Cov lived! How, how could he do it? He hated Cov for it. There he had stood, unwittingly turning that man he cared for so much into an ugly, ridiculous image for cheap propaganda and entertainment. He recalled the picture he'd had in his mind as, translating the girl's words, he had described the Englishman as being frightened. It was that haunting view of the pale-faced, scurrying Kerensky in the Russian film *October*. That was the impression of Coventry that he'd had been trapped into giving to the world! It was worse than the almost unrealisable picture of him making love to the girl. But Leszek himself could now see the pavilion, and the girl standing in it by the wall, her bottom thrust out.

The sun was beating down on his head, and he felt he was about to vomit. He clambered down the bank to get under the trees again. The others were all down there – Tarski had rejoined them. The girl who had been interviewed was standing waiting with several other men and girls round her. The man who'd been writing the interview down in German came over to Leszek, with one of his colleagues behind him. He rubbed his mouth with the back of his forefinger, then said, 'Tell the girl we'll give her some more if she'll come with us now.'

Leszek looked into his eager face. 'I'm not a pimp,' he said.

The man's face dropped. Then he put his tongue out at Leszek. The man behind him looked at Leszek and spat. They spoke to each other, then went across to the girl. They hadn't approached Marno to be an intermediary, Leszek reflected: he wondered if it was through a last shred of delicacy or merely because they thought the girl would understand them better than Marno would in any case.

Marno was standing on his own, looking very disconsolate. 'Were all the girls standing there prostitutes?' Leszek said to him.

'No! No!' He spoke emphatically. 'Only about ten or twenty. But it's a very unusual kampong, that's why we came here – you know, it's not a typical kampong, it's a notorious one.' He was very concerned to make the point. 'Look,' he said sombrely.

The girl they had interviewed was walking briskly towards one of the huts, the two Germans following her. They had made themselves understood. One or two of the village people were watching them, but most of those still standing around did not seem to be taking any interest. A jeep was revving up loudly on the bank – it started all the cockerels in the village crowing. The only other person who seemed at all agitated by the morning's events was the simple Marno, still frowning at his side. But Leszek found one thought growing sharper and sharper in his mind: if what Coventry did could conceivably be right, then everything that he himself did was wrong.

CHAPTER ELEVEN

Coventry Pearce

AS Coventry awoke, it grew on him that he was in a
cheerful frame of mind. It was how many days since
his party? – four? – and this was the first morning since
then that he'd woken up like this. The very thought
stepped up his cheerfulness a notch higher. He turned on
his back. 'Rochmet!' he called.

Under the mosquito net he lay naked. He had an
erection that put no lustful thoughts into his head. His
penis jerked still tighter at the root, as he thought about
it, then began to subside. 'Stout man,' he said to it.

Rochmet knocked at the back door. 'Tuan!' Coventry's
penis trembled again, then finally flopped.

'Two eggs!' he shouted.

'Have you got the coffee in there?'

Oh, Christ. He'd bought some himself at a Chinese
shop he'd been passing the day before and still had it on
the table. 'Wait a minute!'

He opened the net and slipped across the room, unlocked
the door and dived back into bed. He tucked the curtains
in again behind him and turned with his back to the door.
'O.K.' He heard her come in and said, 'It's on the table.'
He wondered if she was taking in an eyeful of his behind
or not, and couldn't help smiling. He'd done this once or
twice before, though he knew he shouldn't. However, it
was not deliberate, he told himself, it was just a question
of laziness, encouraged by the fact that, far from offending
Rochmet, it probably amused her as much as it did him.
He looked over his shoulder as he heard the door close.

Rochmet was still peering through a small gap and as their eyes met, a strained exchange through the mosquito net, she grinned. He looked stern, and didn't allow himself to smile again till the door closed completely.

I'm getting slack, though, he thought, as he got up. The depression that had filled him on the day of the party started rising again in him. He went into the front room with his dressing-gown on and stood in the sunshine coming through the French windows. It was all right: his cheerful mood was going to prevail. And he'd go on being lazy. He'd have a large breakfast and leave his bath till afterwards. There wasn't much to do today. Revolt seemed to be brewing in all the outer islands of Indonesia, but there was nothing definite enough anywhere to justify his leaving Djakarta, where all remained peaceful. He'd file a story today that he'd got from one of the Indonesian papers about a man who'd been sent to prison in East Java for sitting on a copy of the Koran, claiming no harm would come to him. It'd probably get a couple of lines in his own paper, evoking in its liberal readers proportions of indignation and amusement close to the editorial ideal.

He opened the French windows, and stepped out. It was just detectably cooler outside. The gardens all round were empty, the grass in his own still dewy under the hedge. Birds were whistling and calling in every direction. When he went back inside he found that the cooler air had not flowed into the front room – it was so still. It was hard to believe that the days would go on like this in Djakarta for ever and ever.

When Rochmet brought in his breakfast she smiled shyly at him. 'Tuan,' she said, just before his hand reached his coffee cup.

'Yes?'

'I need some new sandals.' She looked down at her feet,

on which there was a pair of cheap leather sandals certainly more scratched and torn than any he'd noticed her wearing lately, when she'd worn anything on her feet at all. 'Could I have fifty rupiahs advance?'

That was what it was going to cost him, then, for not having dressed before opening the door this morning. She knew her moment and her price. He'd never get the money back. He'd already been obliged to acknowledge on previous occasions that she couldn't manage without her full salary every week, so those advances of hers just went mounting and mounting until one day, when some pretext for a noble gesture declared itself, they'd have to be written off. He took a fifty rupiah note from his wallet, which he always took from under his pillow and put in his dressing-gown pocket when he got up.

'Here you are, you'd better polish your other sandals up before you put them on again.'

She beamed. 'Thank you, tuan.' She ignored his last remark with perfect self-possession.

The boiled eggs were so fresh, the coffee so fragrant – he couldn't imagine a better start to the day. He remembered Sri, the girl he'd gone back with the night he first met Leszek: she was as sweet as an egg, he thought.

He went through his bedroom, and opened the back door to go out to the bathroom. The door didn't open easily and he gave it a firmer pull. Then his stomach turned right over: without looking, he knew what he'd done. He looked. In the crack between the door and its frame, just above his head, a wide-eyed lizard was slowly twisting its body backwards. Its tail was on the other side of the crack; its middle was crushed, and purplish blood was beginning to ooze from it. The slow, anguished curving back of its body went on until suddenly the lizard's eyes looked dead. Its front feet, like tiny white human hands in the air, stopped moving, their palms towards him.

'Rochmet!' he shouted.

She came out of the kitchen at once, barefooted now, he noticed. 'Look,' he said.

He was standing in the half-open door, and from her side she could only see the lizard's tail. But when she saw it she gave a sharp scream; her brow crinkled and her lower lip turned on one side in distaste.

'Will you . . .' He had started to say, 'Will you clean it up,' but looking at her face, still fixed in the same expression, he couldn't go on. He couldn't ask her. He'd have to do it himself. 'Will you get me a bucket of hot water and an old cloth,' he said, 'a big one.'

'Yes, tuan.' She shook her head in continuing dismay, and padded back to the kitchen. When she brought him the water and the cloth, he wrapped several layers of the cloth round his hand in order to take hold of the lizard's body. He was terrified it would have another dying spasm in his hand. But in fact something worse happened: the front half of its body came away separately – the lizard must have been cut practically in two by the door. He tried to catch the blood on the cloth. Then he went out into the side-garden and flung the contents of the cloth under the hedge. When he got back he found that the tail had fallen on to the ground outside the back door. He picked it up, also in the cloth, and threw it where he'd thrown the other piece.

But a strange elation was beginning to seize him now, as he mopped the remaining blood off the door. It was right that he had done this task, not left it to Rochmet. He felt he'd been forced back into a recognition of the way other people had to be treated. His life in Djakarta, he thought, had led him into all kinds of indulgence without him noticing what a transformation there'd been in him. Suddenly he'd been obliged to look at Rochmet as a human being with sensibilities and rights equal to his own. And this would tell from now onwards, he felt, in his relationships with other people.

He finished swabbing up the blood without any feelings of squeamishness – in fact, with a certain zest. He went back into the garden and threw the dirty water under the hedge. The lizard had died to save him – he was washed in the blood of the lizard! He thought his cheerfulness on waking up might have come from a dawning awareness, already, of this improved relationship with the world. But no, that was not so. His first act this morning had been an example of just the kind of slackness he was now planning to extirpate in himself. It had just been a natural, sensual good humour that he had started the day with: this was a better sort of pleasure he was now feeling. He was going to see Leszek for lunch, and he suddenly thought of the prospect with great satisfaction. Leszek had been trying to push him this way for quite a time: now he could report a triumph. Another thing he'd do: he'd start thinking seriously about the book he'd been wanting to write on Djakarta. In this frame of mind he could perhaps begin to see the city clearly for the first time.

On the other hand, he didn't feel like doing his cable this morning. It could wait till tomorrow – the story was a timeless one, and there probably wasn't another English speaker in the world who knew about it. Maybe just the British consul in Surabaja, who took an interest in these things: but there was no one down there he would leak the story to. Coventry thought he'd have a leisurely bath, ring up the Agency and make sure nothing important had happened, then go to see who was sitting in the restaurant at the Zoo before meeting Leszek.

It was half past eleven by the time he reached the Zoo. There was nothing else to do: the politicians of Djakarta were still exchanging public smiles. None of his friends were there, nor anybody else, but he took a table on the lawn and told a waiter he'd like an *alexandre*. The llama was still straining its neck to look over the bit of wire – Coventry couldn't think what to offer it, the food of llamas being a subject on which he probably knew less than any other matter. When the manager came hurrying along with his drink on what looked like a silver tray, Coventry urged him to sit down.

'Thank you, tuan, a moment with a respected guest.'

'You're looking well.'

The old, blotchy face went into an even more complicated pattern of smiles. 'Tuan, I went to my Chinese chemist this morning. His wife was in the shop and I asked if the medicine I buy for my stomach ailments was really any good. You know what she said to me, tuan: "It keeps you well, but I won't say it makes you better"!'

He got up and bowed, still smiling to himself, and walked away. Coventry felt he loved the man. Life seemed incontrovertibly good, this morning, as he took his first sip of the creamy, pungent *alexandre*. He browsed in the Indonesian morning papers, while exotic birds and animals, most of them probably captured not more than a few hundred miles away, sang a chorus. Remote problems offered themselves for his interest from the pages of the newspapers. The writer of a letter observed that if you had only one child, you had to arrange expensive ceremonies, including an expensive *wayang* performance, to protect it from evil influences. Was it cheaper, therefore, the editor was asked, to have one child or many? The editor invited readers' opinions. There was an announcement of the death of a five-month-old child, who obviously had not been protected sufficiently. The announcement ran half-way down the page, thanking everybody remotely concerned with the family – relatives, neighbours, kampong officials, numerous superiors at the government offices where the father worked, members of the police force, members of the army – for their sympathy and understanding. 'May God reward them.' The child's death had given its parents opportunities for ingratiation they could never have dreamed of while it was alive.

He thought about his lunch with Leszek. He was meeting him on the terrace of the Metropole Cinema. This was one of the most pleasant spots he knew in Djakarta. It was an open-fronted Chinese restaurant above a block of shops built on to the side of the cinema: you looked down on to a crossroads where good houses set among flowering bushes ran right up against a kampong on the other side of the railway line. A speciality of the Metropole was fried frogs' legs – like little crunchy bits of chicken that you dipped into a grey mixture of salt and pepper in a saucer. But after this morning's incident in the pavilion he thought he didn't feel like frogs' legs. He'd just drink a long, cold bottle of Heineken's, and perhaps have some fried rice afterwards.

He got on to the Metropole terrace a bit before one, the time at which he'd arranged to meet Leszek. Below, he could see the betjaks pulling up by the pavement – Leszek would come in one, he imagined, but there was no sign of him down there yet. The car park was filling up for the afternoon performance of *Love is a Many-Splendoured Thing*: on a hoarding in the car park, the giant heads of Jennifer Jones and William Holden leaned towards each other in a kiss, but a thick strip of black paper pasted down the middle between them hid the contact of their lips from the impressionable youth of Djakarta. On the far side of the road a particularly beautiful house – sturdy and richly tiled, but simple in line, with elegant shutters – stood in a decaying garden. It had belonged before the war to a Dutch sugar-beet millionaire, now it housed various families of university teachers, as Coventry knew from a visit he

had paid to a Javanese professor there with John. On the
lawn of the house he could see some ten or twelve swarthy
youths sitting: this was a well-known gang who sold black-
market tickets outside the cinema, mainly at the evening
performance. They were all Batak boys, from the north
of Sumatra – an enterprising race, head-hunters a century
ago and now mainly Lutheran Christians, which provided
scores of teachers and education officials in Djakarta and
also many members of the free-lance professions such as
these boys followed. The university teachers in the house
were all too busy, and probably too scared, to keep the
boys out of the garden, where they liked to sit and gamble
and watch the world go by when they were not working.
There was a large triangle of hard mud just outside the
garden, bare now but covered at night with little food
stalls, where Coventry had had many a dish of meat in
spicy gravy. The owner of the stall he usually went to
had explained why they removed themselves in the day-
time: 'Important people might pass by, tuan, and it
would look very untidy.' It was the story of the safety
pin at the back of the gold jacket, from another angle:
here the whole crossroads was a scene of rich chaos, but
the city authorities, and the stall-keeper himself, considered food-stalls members of that superior class of eye-
sore that also contained portions of posters showing meeting
lips.

He suddenly noticed Leszek getting out of a betjak. He
was small as it was, but foreshortened from above he
looked a very tiny figure. Coventry expected to see some
exchange of gesture between him and the betjak man but
Leszek appeared to pay him and move away without
saying anything. Coventry leaned over the balcony and
watched his narrow skull, with its closely cut blond hair,
pass directly below him. He felt a rush of affection for
Leszek: really he was the only man in Djakarta whom he

respected. He thought he must have grabbed Leszek when he first met him just in order to keep himself a bit steady: now he seemed to be steadier than at that time he could have anticipated being, and he thought he owed some gratitude to Leszek for that.

When Leszek appeared at the head of the stairs Coventry got up and went to greet him, smiling. 'Hallo! You all right? I didn't see you embracing the betjak boy.'

Leszek's blue eyes studied him closely. He smiled, yet his brow seemed tense. 'Hallo.'

'Come on, I've got a glass and a bottle of cold beer waiting for you.'

Leszek touched him softly on the arm: it was friendly, yet there also seemed to be something of sympathy, or perhaps penitence, in the gesture – anyway, as though Coventry somehow needed it. Coventry looked at Leszek carefully. 'All right, really?'

'Yes.' This time Leszek smiled more fully. 'I'm glad to see you.'

When they had sat down, Leszek said, 'Cov, you remind me this morning of how you were when I first met you. Very good at life.'

'Very odd – *very* odd. I'm feeling so different, I was going to tell you about it.'

'Well, you've gone up or down some spiral then – maybe you're on a different level but on one set of co-ordinates you're still in the same position. An attractive one.'

'Really!'

'I'm probably going to have to dislodge you from it but – I don't know, I like to see you like this. Anyway tell me how you've changed, if that was what you were going to tell me.'

'What are you threatening me with? – I'm not sure if I like this!'

'Nothing, nothing. Nothing that can't wait.'

Coventry felt unexpectedly alarmed. He remembered Macpherson's remark about Leszek being sinister, and it seemed a shade truer. Small and lean, with his pale eyes, and sitting leaning forward slightly in his bamboo chair, Leszek had something of that steeliness Sumitro had had for a moment the night they'd all been together and Coventry had challenged him. His own story about the lizard suddenly seemed rather absurd. He stumbled as he began, an unusual sensation for him.

'I had – well, a rather horrible experience this morning, yet I sort of benefited from it, I thought. I caught a lizard in the door as I was opening it, and I started to ask Rochmet to clear up the mess, and then I thought, no, I can't ask her to do that as though she's my slave and has no feelings or rights, so I did it myself. And I felt so much better in every way, I was going to say I was washed in the blood of the lizard, but now you make that sound ridiculous.'

Leszek looked at him unsmiling. 'It's a bit pathetic, really, isn't it?' he said.

Coventry's spirit slumped. There was a note of certitude in the voice with which Leszek had pronounced his verdict that he couldn't contest. He knew that to argue would sound petulant and small. 'I . . . maybe,' he said.

'I had a horrible experience yesterday, I think a good deal more horrible than yours. And it involved you, that's why I thought I'd tell you.'

'You wouldn't otherwise?'

'No, no, I'm sorry, I didn't mean anything like that – I didn't mean I don't confide in you or anything. I do. I just meant that's why I'm telling you especially.'

'What happened?'

'I had to be an interpreter for an East German film team who were making a propaganda film about Djakarta. I went with them to a kampong over by the flood canal to film some prostitutes – they wanted some true stories from prostitutes who'd been with white men, with Westerners. It was quite sickening, some of them went off with the girls themselves afterwards. But they got one up on the canal bank to film and as I translated her words it became plain to me she'd been with you. She described where you lived.'

Coventry's mind raced to take the scene in. It was that chatty girl he'd had in the pavilion on the afternoon of the party, it must have been. And she'd been up on that canal bank telling a crowd about it all! He'd been exposed – exposed, above all, to Leszek's severe judgment, and in a very stark way. Yet, as he thought wildly about the situation, he found a little of his self-possession returning. The scene had an unmistakably comic side to it, he couldn't help feeling. What an extraordinary way of being detected! What a drama for Leszek it must have been! When he looked at Leszek these thoughts faded. Leszek was trembling – his face had gone white.

'I'm sorry,' Coventry said. 'It must have been very unpleasant. And you were perhaps – well – rather disgusted.'

'It was awful! Awful!'

'I'm sorry, Leszek.'

'I had to stand there making these monsters laugh and clap their hands as I told a humiliating story about you. It was an unspeakable position to be in!' Leszek looked quite haggard.

'I'm sorry, I really am.'

Leszek was silent for a moment, looking down into his lap. Then his body relaxed a little, and he spoke more quietly. 'You can't blame yourself for that, it was just an accident really. That was only painful because you're a friend of mine, I can't blame you for pain caused in me simply because you've made me feel friendly towards you.'

'Still . . .'

'It did you no harm objectively . . .'

'No, let me say, if you were worried about me – I can't help feeling I've allowed myself to be very humiliated, especially, well – especially, Leszek, in your eyes. But the fact of being a sort of anonymous villain in a communist film – well, that I just find slightly comic, it's no more serious than appearing as a pinko-liberal or whatever it was in Macpherson's article.'

'Tarski was there – he identified you too.'

'Oh! Oh dear. But – well, people do know, Leszek, you didn't, but there are people, journalists, who do. I'm sorry, I really am.'

'Cov, it's not just a question of people knowing, it's not just a question of my being placed in a painful situation. It's the fact, it's the fact that I learned, whether people knew about it or not! This girl described how you took her home and made love to her. It was like a text-book story of humiliation – of her humiliation, I mean!'

'Oh. I don't . . .'

'I don't begin to understand it, even.'

It was Coventry's turn to be silent now. Then he said, 'Something I get out of it – or got out of it, I told you I'm changing. But something I got out of it, something I can't separate from all my pleasure in Djakarta. I love Djakarta – unlike anybody else I know. I feel some extraordinary excitement all the time here and I can't separate it from going with those girls sometimes. Can you understand that? I haven't really thought about it before, even, but can you understand it?'

Leszek again took a long time to answer. 'If I can – I don't know if I can, but if I can it means accepting a way of looking at things totally unlike any I've ever had before.'

'I can't say any more than that, I'm changing anyway.

You were scornful about that lizard business and I understand why, but it did mean something to me.'

'Oh, Coventry, what a way of putting it, though! It wasn't easy to take it seriously, not in the state of mind I was in when I came here. But I know you meant what you said.'

'I thought as a Marxist you didn't think all this individual morality important.'

Leszek looked quite ill again. 'Oh, that's a very unworthy remark, a slick remark. I'll only answer it in the same crude way, by saying that as a liberal I thought you did think it important.'

Coventry felt quite abashed. He'd been untrue to himself when he'd spoken then, and foolish in thinking that Leszek wouldn't immediately know it and demolish him. Oddly enough, he hadn't really supposed that Leszek wouldn't demolish him – perhaps in some way he'd been inviting Leszek to come down on him like a ton of bricks.

'There was something else, Cov. Something that puzzled me, but made it even worse for me when I was interpreting for those Germans. The girl said you were frightened.'

When Leszek said that, a fact became clearer to Coventry. They were not engaged in a moral argument. They were engaged in a personal battle, which Leszek was setting out wholeheartedly to win. And he had just delivered his hardest blow so far. Coventry looked round the terrace. Three Indonesian waiters, in their little brown hats, were watching him and Leszek, and smiling. One of them stepped forward as Coventry looked at them, but Coventry raised the palm of his hand to him to indicate that they wanted nothing. At the next table an Indonesian man was sitting with his small son on his lap, stroking the boy under the chin. The boy's large brown eyes surveyed the world calmly, as though his father's action was a genuine pleasure to him but one that he took as his natural right, with no need to acknowledge it. Leszek was still watching him, his narrow cheeks taut, his eyes anxious.

'Yes, I was frightened – in the kampong, that's where she said I was frightened, didn't she?'

'Yes.'

'You don't know why I was frightened?'

'No.'

'I'll tell you. I'd just seen a face through one of the doors, through the door of one of the huts.' He stopped. Leszek went on looking at him but said nothing. 'It was the face – I thought it was the face of the man I saw on the roadside that afternoon Sumitro was killed.'

Leszek's blue eyes grew large. 'Sumitro's murderer?'

'If the man I saw on the roadside was Sumitro's murderer. And if this was the same man. I was frightened, yes I was.'

Leszek shook his head slowly. 'It's not surprising you were frightened. What are you going to do about it? Or what have you done about it?'

'Done?'

'Yes. Don't you think you should do something? Don't you? It was – well, it was probably your friend's murderer.'

'I – I don't know.' Coventry found he was beginning to feel very frightened again, and helpless. 'What could I do?'

'Well, tell the police.'

'Oh! I don't know, it's all so uncertain – they wouldn't listen to me even on the day Sumitro was killed.'

'Should one mind embarrassment, even insult, in such a situation?'

'Well, if – well, of course, you're right.'

'Go and tell them, Coventry, go and tell them, it's something you can do, something.'

'I suppose I'd been trying to forget it.'

'Was that why you were like you were at the party?'

'What do you think?'

'Was it the day of the party?'

'Yes.'

'So in the afternoon you'd had that girl there?'

'Yes.' Coventry wondered whether to tell Leszek everything about his emotions that day – how he'd been feeling even before he set out on that dreadful visit to the kampong – but he had no energy now, he couldn't bring himself to say any more. He could scarcely bear to stay with Leszek any more, he was so shaken.

'Look,' he said. 'I'm going, Leszek, you're right, you're absolutely right, but I must go away and think what to do. I'm just confused now. Look, I'll leave 50 rupiahs there, I'll go, you pay.'

Leszek looked anxious now. But he seemed to understand Coventry's desire to go, and made no protest. 'I don't know, I'm sorry,' he said. 'I feel now perhaps I was wrong to say all that to you, I don't know what it's got to do with me.'

'No, you were right, that's our friendship, that's what it is. I'll phone you, all right?'

Coventry hurried down the bare concrete stairs. He was desperate now to get away. It was the hottest moment of the day, and he was sweating all over, but he strode fast across the car park to his car. He was glad to have the wind pouring through the window as he drove off. Home seemed to be the first place to go. He knew there was a decision he had to make, but he couldn't make it yet. His route home took him past a big police barracks; he stared at the lines of grey huts under tall graceful trees, but it was not yet the moment to turn in there.

The pavilion, properly condemned though it was, looked pretty in the sunshine. Walking up the path to it, he remembered again those ghost sparrows he'd seen in the chill morning in St John's Wood. He'd been thinking a moment before of his mother, and he reflected that she was a sort of ghost sparrow of a different kind. She was brisk and busy but she didn't want to know what went on in the world. He couldn't tell her about anything that really interested him. She'd have liked him to be a well-paid businessman, married and living near the Sussex village she'd moved to when his father died. She'd always resented slightly the fact that his father had left him a tiny income: not because she grudged him the money, but because she thought it had encouraged him not to settle down with a steady job in England.

He thought he'd write to her now, though. And a different memory came to him: how, when he was about 12 or 13, he always longed to find her at home when he got back from school in the afternoon. 'What's for tea, mother?' he'd shout as he came in the door: if he could see her hat and coat were not there, he'd hesitate in the hall, utterly miserable for a moment, the words unspoken.

Rochmet was out; the compound was silent. He didn't feel like lunch. He thought he might go round to the club in a little while and have some ham and eggs. He sat down in an armchair looking out through the French windows, and wrote the letter to his mother there. 'Dear Mother,' he wrote, 'Sorry not to have written for a couple of weeks but I've been very busy. Don't worry about stories of trouble in Djakarta that you might have read in the papers.' Unlikely, he thought. 'The English are very popular here and it's all terrifically exaggerated – except of course in my paper. I'm sitting at my French windows in lovely sunshine, looking out on the garden.' Could he even mention the bats, the snails, innocent things that he loved? Not even those, he felt, let alone whores, lizards, murderers, Polish friends. 'The hibiscus is still in flower, a lovely red, like sunlight shining through a glass of red wine. At night the flowers lose their crispness – they go soft and floppy and fold up.' He couldn't go on like this.

'One day you must come and see these things. Just a short note now as I've got to go out again on an interesting investigation – I'll tell you about that next time. Hope all is well with you, Mother dearest, Love, Cov.' He wrote the envelope but found he had no stamps; he sealed the letter and put it in his pocket.

After that he went on sitting in the armchair indecisively for quite a long time. He preferred not to think about what he ought to do. He listened to the afternoon sounds, all so familiar to him by now: that bird that went 'hoop hoop', still calling, far away; the chatter of three bulbuls that flew into his hibiscus bush, flirted their wings, and flew heavily on to the next garden; later, the soft whine of a rubber band between a betjak's wheels as it passed along the road, and the dry cough of the betjak man. A street seller, up early from his siesta, came along: Coventry could hear him for some while before he saw him. He was selling *tempeh* and *tahu*, two kinds of soya-bean cake – *tempeh* was like a biscuit, *tahu* consisted of soft mushy squares, and John Grayne used them as an analogy to teach his students the difference between pie pastry and pudding pastry. Coventry hated them both, but the *tempeh-tahu* sellers had a beautiful street cry. Twice they would call out '*peh-ta-hooo*', their voice dropping very low on the long last note; then in a way that startled you every time you heard it, they would cry the words in the opposite order, '*ta-hu-tem-peh*', their voice leaping an octave on the last two syllables so that they sang out in a high soprano. Coventry listened to this cry go all the way down the street. Then he got up, locked the door, and drove down to the club.

Traffic was on the move again, dust rising here and there on the roads. But there were only a few cars at the club gate when he got there, and when he went in he found the big hall of the club empty. The waiters in their white suits glided inquiringly by him, but said nothing. He went to the little room called the library where one could eat ham and eggs at any time of the day, and called out to one of the waiters to fetch him that. *Mata sapi* – bull's eye – a fried egg was called: his pair came to him on the plate shining from their bath in deep oil. Afterwards he walked out on to the terrace. The cricket field did not seem to have been mown today: it too shone in the strong sunlight. Four people were already playing tennis on the grass courts at the side of the cricket field. He suddenly realised that the broad back of the girl on the near side of the net belonged to Jane. He stared at it: yet more reproach seemed to stare back at him from it. He felt the fried eggs and ham turn over in his stomach. The white square of Jane's back was like a signal. Before she could turn, he must go – must drive to the kampong, and look for the man himself.

As he drove back through the gardens of the houses round the club, he asked himself at last why he was going to do this, when he was so frightened. The answer was a simple one: there was a pride in him that would not let him rest now until he'd made a real effort to find out the truth for himself, risking the consequences. His decency, and his courage, both had to be proved again. Perhaps some impulse to punish himself was present there also. He rejected that, with his intellect, as a proper reason for going, and insisted to himself that the other motive was the important one; but he had to admit that some urge to seek retribution for his own misdeeds might be forcing him on too.

He realised that he had not thought about Leszek since he had left him. Leszek, in the end, had nothing to do with this – no more than the lizard had. He was glad of that. He was on the road now that led to the bridge. When he got there he stopped for a moment and looked out of the window. The canal had only a dull grey shine on it, from the position of the sun in the sky now. To the right of it, though, the railway line glittered; down on the left the dark tops of the palms roofed the kampong for a quarter of a mile. He drove off the bridge and turned the car on to the track along the side of the canal. He wouldn't leave it and walk this time: he'd drive it right along to the point where he would have to go down the bank.

It was a bumpy ride along the bank, but a clear one – there was no one up there at this time in the afternoon. He could see car tracks in the dust in some places, probably left by the film team. He stopped where there was a great deal of disturbance of the dust on the bank: it must have been here that he had been publicly arraigned. He sat for a while looking down on the kampong, though it was very hot in the stationary car. He saw a woman in a long *kain* and a pink bra walk slowly across from one hut to another, her back and shoulders shining greasily; after that there was no other movement. What was he going to do? He didn't really need to do much. He would go and knock on the door of the hut where he had seen the face, and look in again on the pretext that he thought he would find a girl there. He wouldn't see anything. But he could walk round the kampong after that and then go back and tell the police what he'd seen and done. He wouldn't look too much of a fool if he did it that way and played it down, rather than simply went to report to them four days after he'd seen an obscure face in a doorway. The face he'd seen on the afternoon of Sumitro's death came back to him, though – the dandyish twist of hair on the chin, with the eyes of a desperate man above it.

He got out of the car and slammed the door loudly, then scrambled down the bank. The earth was drier in the kampong now, but the planks were where they had been before. He knew which hut he wanted: he fixed his eyes determinedly on its dirty yellow bamboo door, in the shade of some trees twenty yards away. A boy and a woman, the boy in shorts, the woman, like the other, in *kain* and bra, appeared from behind a hut just by him. The woman smiled broadly, showing some gold teeth.

'He's looking for rice,' she said to the boy, loud enough for Coventry also to hear. He knew what she meant; with the price of rice going up rapidly of late, there had been laws hastily passed against hoarding.

He smiled back at the woman. 'No,' he said, and she laughed. What a lot I know about Djakarta, he thought – far more than any other white man he'd met in the crazy city.

He walked rather slowly towards the hut he wanted. When he got to the door he tapped on it lightly. His knuckles didn't make much sound on the bamboo, but the door shook. Then it opened abruptly, and he saw the old woman's flaking face, her eyes wide and fearful, her mouth open.

'Girl,' he said.

She shook her head fiercely.

'Yes,' he said. He stepped forward, and she tried to push her frail body up against his, but he pushed her back gently by the shoulder and took another step forward to look into the hut. It was dark, only a little light coming in through the door. Then the old woman quickly moved back – he got the impression she'd been pulled and looked, alarmed, over her shoulder. The door was slammed and he was in the hut in the dark.

He then experienced a sudden bewilderment that was never explained.

CHAPTER TWELVE

Leszek Mylski

LESZEK was in his office, in the middle of the morning, trying as usual to work on a translation. But ever since Coventry had left him on the Metropole terrace the previous day he'd been full of unusual excitement and tension. He didn't know what outcome he could possibly be expecting from his conversation with Cov; he had started to tell himself that he had exaggerated its effect on Cov, that the whole incident with the girl would quickly dwindle in importance, both for Cov and himself. Yet he was waiting all the time for a phone call, or even to see Cov bursting excitedly in at the door. Just now, as he had sat listening to the insistent ringing of the betjak bells on the road outside, he had been reliving an incident with Zosia before they were married. He knew why it had come to mind: it was another occasion when he had given some advice that was not entirely welcome, and he'd hung about waiting to learn what the consequences would be.

Zosia was a student, doing Polish philology, when they had begun to take an interest in each other. One day that first summer she had said to him, sitting on the desk in his office in the university, 'I'm going out to have coffee with Kowalczyk, Monika and Natasha.'

This Kowalczyk lectured at the Faculty in the history of the Polish language. Leszek knew him slightly: a vain but insecure man, always talking about his friendships with actors. Leszek smiled at Zosia, who was in a light white dress cut at the front in a semicircle to show the faint rise at the top of her breasts. She looked keenly back at him, smiling too, but visibly holding on to thoughts she was not quite ready to express.

'Good. When?'

'You don't mind?'

'Not at all. I believe in good relations between staff and students.' He raised his hand, pretending to stop himself. 'Need I say?'

She leaned over the desk, stretching out her torso till it was almost horizontal, and kissed him with half-open mouth on the lips. Then she slowly sat up again, and the look she had had before recomposed itself in her face. It was asking him to ask a question.

'Why this sudden contribution to good relations on his part? Or on yours?'

'On ours actually.' She looked a shade more uneasy.

'You're inviting him?'

'Yes, they want to take him, they say he doesn't even know but unconsciously he gives good marks to students who've made some attractive impression on him, or anyway some pleasant impression, I don't mean sexual – you know, darling.' She stopped, her eyes pleading with him now.

'I don't think I should go if I were you.'

'Oh!'

'I shouldn't, really.'

'But you know, I can't tell them I'm not coming, it'd look so priggish, and what does it matter, can't we be nice to our teachers? You know I've worked hard, I deserve a decent mark.'

'Then you'll get one.'

She shrugged her shoulders, making a face. 'You know how it is, and if they get a five it won't be fair, and I only get a four or three, because they haven't worked at all, they haven't done a stroke this year, they're both as good as married.'

'Your mark'll be worth having, then. That's if what you say, or what they say about him's true.'

'It's probably not true, so there's no harm in going at all really.'

'Nor any point.'

'Oh!' She hit her clasped hands on her knee and grimaced. 'Don't be ironical. I know you're right, really, I don't care about the damn mark, it just seems unfair, that's all, and also it seems priggish if I don't go.'

'Don't go.'

She'd been looking down at the desk, but now she raised her eyes to him again. She was still gritting her teeth, but she gave a grunt and began very slowly to smile at him. Then she leaned over flat across the desk like she had before, and kissed him lightly on the nose. 'All right, I know you're right, sweet one. I don't want to displease you anyway. It doesn't really matter. You'll have to take me out somewhere much nicer at exactly the time they're taking him out, so I've got an excuse and to reward me.'

He stared at her. 'Anywhere in the world, Zosia,' he said. 'I love you.'

She jumped off his desk, blew him a kiss and was gone. And he remembered now how he had sat there thinking that if he had loved her for that first kiss across the desk, he had had no expression to convey how much he loved her for the second one. Yet that had been a mistake: and a forerunner of all the mistakes of his that were to follow. It was the first kiss he should have loved her for most – and now, far too late, he did.

Yet in the days immediately following that scene in his room everything had gone well. They'd been to see *Swan*

Lake the evening the girls were meeting Kowalczyk, and had dinner after at the Bristol Hotel. And in the oral exam they'd all had with Kowalczyk the week following, Natasha and Monika had each got their five, but Zosia had got hers too. Examiners told candidates their marks immediately at the end of the oral, and Leszek had been waiting for Zosia in the street outside the Faculty. She had rushed down the sunlit steps, flung her arms round him and burst into tears, kissing him all over his face. She was full of new trust in him, and at the beginning of those summer holidays they had gone to bed together for the first time. But he still remembered, sitting in the embassy this morning, how he had stood on the pavement fearing she would get a lower mark than the two other girls, and picturing her walking down the steps to him slowly and sadly, not wanting to return his look.

The phone rang on his desk: the odd rising and falling sound, beginning like a squeak and ending abruptly like a belch, of all the Djakarta phones. It was Tarski.

'I've got some bad news for you,' Tarski said.

'What?' Leszek felt the muscles in both his arms go rigid.

'Your friend Pearce was killed last night.'

'Oh! Oh!'

'He was stabbed in that kampong we visited. I don't know what he was doing there. I don't know any more than that.'

Leszek felt himself fainting. He pressed the edge of the desk hard with the hand that was not holding the phone.

'If I hear any more shall I come and tell you? I probably shall.'

Leszek couldn't raise his voice above a murmur. 'Yes. Yes. Thank you.'

'I'm terribly sorry, Panie Leszku.'

'Thank you.'

His body seemed to be falling apart under the impact of Tarski's words, yet his mind was empty. He could not formulate any picture of what Tarski had told him. He noticed that the betjak bells seemed to be ringing very loud and fierce.

He stayed sitting at his desk, scarcely moving. Tears once or twice came into his eyes, but each time his head began to throb and the tears stopped. Slowly he began to wonder how Cov had died, and he found himself trembling. He thought of the terror of death, of Cov fighting with a man who had a knife in his hand he was going to use, and the knife going in. He almost vomited, and his thoughts refused to return to the picture.

After a while he knew it was true that Cov was dead. He saw again Cov's sweaty back as he hurried down the steps of the Metropole terrace and a new horror seized him. He had sent Cov to his death – he was an angel of death! He would probably never know what had been in Cov's mind, but he knew in that moment that Cov had gone back to the kampong because of him. Probably he had been looking for the man himself. Probably it was that man who had killed him. Cov wouldn't have gone back to find a girl, in the state of mind he was in when he left the Metropole. He might have done, by a sort of reaction, if he hadn't done something similar on the day of the party. But he wouldn't have repeated that act. Or if he had, it was still Leszek's words that had driven him to it.

At last Leszek found himself sobbing, his forehead resting on his arms on his desk. But there was no comfort in the tears: his anguish seemed to grow as he cried. His own life seemed to have been utterly empty: Cov had put the sap in the Indonesian trees, the blood in the arms of the betjak men, the animation into the dark in the Djakarta streets. Now Cov had gone, the city was like those piles of dead wings the flying ants left under his lamp every night. And Cov, who had enjoyed Djakarta more than any other white man – he remembered him saying it – would not enjoy it again.

The telephone rang again. He looked at his watch. It was over an hour since Tarski had telephoned. Idlinski was on the line.

'Panie Leszku, I've just heard the sad news of your English friend's death. I gather Tarski informed you.'

'Yes.'

'Would you mind coming across to talk to me about it? Leave it a little longer if you want to.'

'I'll come now.'

'Thank you.'

Idlinski got up from his desk when Leszek went into his office, and came forward to lead him in by the elbow. His black eyebrows shot up and down with his attempts to express genuine emotion through a face painfully trained to convey neutrality and false feeling. 'Come and sit down, dear Leszek. I'm grateful to you for coming.' He sat Leszek in the chair Tarski had been in the morning they had gone out with the film team; then he sat down himself and looked at Leszek closely, his eyebrows rising and falling once or twice more, his smile turning into a grimace and back again.

'I'll tell you my position in this sad matter before I ask you anything,' he said, after a moment. 'Your friendship with – with Pearce is no concern of mine. An interest has been taken in it, you'll understand, but with no unfortunate consequences to you or to us, and – well – we needn't trouble ourselves with that now. But, my dear Leszek, we just like to know what's happening, and Pearce's death would seem to have some political character, it seems plausible to connect it with the death of his friend, and

your friend, Sumitro. Is there any connection you know of?
If I may ask you, my dear Leszek.'

Leszek told Idlinski what he knew about the man Cov
had seen on the afternoon of Sumitro's death, and the man
he had seen in the kampong. He also told him he had
urged Coventry to go to the police.

'Do you think he went to the kampong instead?'

'Yes.'

Idlinski looked at him hard – Leszek had never seen an
expression on his face so near to surprise. There was a long
silence. Leszek looked away. Torments of guilt were taking
hold of him, and he tried to press his tears back. Idlinski
started speaking again very quietly.

'I see. Believe me, Panie Leszku, if I say I have nothing
but sympathy on the personal side. But you mentioned the
police. Would you mind if we looked after any communica-
tion with the police ourselves? I feel you might want to
help in the tracing of – er – the man responsible. And
probably your information could be helpful. But I'd rather
you trusted us to see it reaches the police through our
own connections. You'll understand we have no interest
in protecting the Muslim Brotherhood. But I would rather
there were no risk of any public interest in your connection
with Pearce.'

'All right.'

'I should go home now. Come in again when you feel
like it.'

'Thank you. You've been very kind.'

Idlinski's mouth and eyebrows worked more energetically than ever, and as he shut the door Leszek thought how
relieved Idlinski must be to see the back of him. He went
out and found a betjak. They had their hoods up now – the
sun was blazing. He thought of Cov's body already losing
its shape. He didn't know where it was; a desire to see it
once more fought in him with repugnance at the thought.

At the house he found the two servant girls in the front garden, trying to knock down a papaya fruit from a tree with a broom. They were both just too short to reach: the small one was rolling on the grass laughing at the other's efforts. The tree was like an open umbrella, with a frail crown of leaves and the single dark green fruit hanging just under it on the trunk where the top ring of the umbrella would be. The head of the broom was oscillating a few inches below the fruit, and both girls cried out to Leszek to get it for them.

He knocked it down with a single blow and went on into the house. There it was cool, and he lay back in an armchair. One of the girls brought him almost immediately a glass of iced syrup – a mysterious sweet drink that tasted of mangoes and pineapples but whose composition he had never known for certain. Suddenly he was glad of the luxury. He sank back deeper into the armchair and his body shook with sobs again.

He sat there for a long time. He wanted to do something, but Idlinski had forbidden the one thing he might have done. The sense of his own emptiness was mounting in him again. Some thought or remark of his about being 'entirely without content' kept coming back into his head; he couldn't remember what it was about. He noticed, with a start, that he was again beginning to wait for the door to fly open and for Coventry to step in, hailing him as he had always done with a half-mocking laugh. He saw then that what he had been expecting after their conversation on the Metropole terrace was not a change in Coventry but a change in himself. He had not seen it at the time – but that outburst against Coventry was something he had expected, in the end, to come boomeranging back in some form against himself. Coventry had not seen that either; and it had sent him to his death.

There was a loud knock at the front door. He trembled:

a desperate hope came into his mind. The door of the living-room opened, and one of the girls came in with Bill Macpherson towering over her shoulder.

'Mr Mylski!' Macpherson's eyes were staring, as though he were either frightened or putting on a show of deep feeling. 'I guess you've heard.'

'Yes. Sit down.'

'I just heard. I rang you at the embassy and they said you'd gone home so I guessed you'd heard. Who told you?'

'Tarski . . .'

'That gink. Did he know how it happened?'

'I don't think he knew very much.'

Macpherson gave him a piercing look. 'Do you?'

'I know – well, I know a few things that might be connected with – with it. Yes.'

'I hear he was killed in a kampong where you'd been with some film men. What did that have to do with it?'

'Nothing, really.'

'Oh, Jesus!' Macpherson jumped up from his chair. It seemed he couldn't keep up his keen almost considerate manner any longer. 'Jesus, there must be some connection. I can't believe there's not!' But he sat down again, leaning as far forward in his chair as he could, his eyes fixed on Leszek now. 'Leszek, we want to find the guy who did it, don't we? Those creep-arse police'll get nowhere, they're dandies, they don't want to get their denims dirty in the mud. You help me! You help me and that way we'll find out what happened. You know something, I can see you know something. Eh?'

Leszek studied the eager figure bending towards him. He didn't trust his reporting – as for Macpherson's emotions and his motives, he supposed they were beyond sorting out now. But he had been prevented from talking to the police, and he felt an impulse to take into his confidence this man who had at any rate known Coventry and was interested in his death.

'If I tell you anything, will you keep my name out of it? You know where I work, you understand. If you agree, I'll tell you what I know, for Coventry's sake. Or for mine.'

Macpherson had his fists clenched in front of him. He gave a sharp nod, without taking his eyes off Leszek. 'Shoot!' he said.

'How did you know about the film team?'

'Some guy at the Ministry of Bumpf couldn't contain himself. The bitch we've got assigned to us wasn't helpful but this guy had been down there with these Germans and he thought he was on to something, he was excited.'

Leszek remembered the little man who had organised the boundary-line of banana leaves. 'He didn't tell you where it was?'

'No, they didn't want to tell us, they didn't want us going. You know, don't you?'

'I'm sure you know the place, it's that kampong on the side of the flood canal.'

'Jesus! There! My Christ!' Macpherson looked really worried for a moment. 'If we go there let's go before dark. I knew something like that would happen there some fucking day.'

'Your idea is that we should go down there?'

'Well, yes, Leszek, that was the idea.'

'Oh.'

'Will you come? You can talk the lingo, you know the way.'

'Perhaps I will.'

'Work on that "perhaps", Leszek. Now shoot. Was it a girl he was after?'

'No.'

'No?' Macpherson shrieked the word.

'No.'

'All right, all right, you tell it, I'll shut up. Shoot.'

Leszek told Macpherson about the face Coventry had seen on the afternoon Sumitro was killed – which he found Macpherson already knew about – and about Coventry's belief that he had seen the man again in the canal kampong. Macpherson knew nothing about this – Leszek felt it was likely that Cov had spoken to no one about it except himself. He added that he thought Cov was looking for the man when he was killed. He didn't say anything about the filming of the girl or his own attack on Coventry at the Metropole.

Macpherson listened intently but quietly. When Leszek stopped he said, 'Where does the film team come in?'

'I told you, it doesn't really. It's just that I told Cov about my own visit to the kampong yesterday and that led him to tell me about the face he saw there on New Year's Eve. After telling me that he must have gone back to the kampong.'

'Did he say he was going back?'

'No.'

'Did you say anything to him?'

'I told him he should go to the police.'

'The damned police! He went to the kampong instead. It makes sense. He wanted another look round. And what was he doing in the kampong the first time? – wait, you don't have to tell me, I know. A fucking bint that time.'

'I think so.'

'Shocked you, eh?'

'No.'

'Well you'll see some more this afternoon. Look, we'd better go about half past four – I've got to file now, after that it'll be too hot, everyone sleeping their mutts off.

But I don't want to be there after dark. All right? I'll come here half past four?'

Leszek hesitated, but he knew what his answer would be. 'All right.'

Throughout the afternoon he was impatient for Macpherson to return. He couldn't eat any lunch, though the girls urged it on him; he worked for a while on translations – he had books to translate, and dictionaries, everywhere. He had accepted by now that Coventry was dead. As the afternoon passed, to go to the kampong where Coventry had died seemed more and more plainly to be the one thing for him to do: he was grateful to Macpherson for proposing it, and wondered whatever he would have done if Macpherson hadn't come. He took good care to be in his bedroom when Janusz arrived home for lunch – he didn't want to meet him now. He went out of the house quietly just before half past four, and sat on the wall of the next-door house, where rose-bushes hid him from the windows of his own.

The sun poured down on the roofs and gardens; the street was still. From another street, out of sight, he could hear the call of a man selling soya-cakes: '*Peh-tahu! Peh-tahu!*' – then the voice suddenly rising an octave and singing out with unexpected melody: '*Ta-hu-tem-peh!*' An empty betjak freewheeled by, the boy giving it an occasional push on the pedal with one foot; he gazed inquiringly at Leszek as he passed, but said nothing.

When he heard the sound of a car engine he was sure it was Macpherson. A moment later the jeep swung, squealing, round the end of the road and revved up loudly before stopping in front of him. Macpherson was grinning. 'Hup!' he said. 'Got your kris in your sock? – we're going to find that guy.'

It seemed so improbable an idea as he said it that Leszek wondered after all why they were going. What could they find out? He wasn't really going with that purpose, and Macpherson couldn't honestly be hoping for any more than a bit of background detail for his story.

Macpherson drove very fast, but he concentrated on his driving, with his chin almost touching the wheel. He only spoke to swear at objects in his path. They soon reached the canal bridge. Leszek looked at the long, dull shine on the water, disappearing far away among palm trees. He thought it must have been the last decent sight Coventry had had of the world. He'd have looked as he crossed the bridge, Leszek was sure, and it must have appeared much the same as now – it was just about this time yesterday, he supposed, that Cov had reached here. He didn't know why he supposed that: probably he'd assumed that Cov's mind had worked as Macpherson's had done.

The jeep swung on to the canal bank. 'Where did Cov leave his car?' Leszek said suddenly. The question had come abruptly into his head.

'Oh, he must have taken it along the bank, it was just by the kampong, I heard from a Dutch guy, Willem, just now. But he didn't know which kampong!' Macpherson gave a high-pitched laugh through his teeth. 'Yeah, the poor mutt must have driven it along the fucking bank to have it near him. Let's hope ours is more fucking use to us.'

'Did they take it away? – the police, I mean.'

'Yeah, something like that, I think so. How far do you think we should go?'

Leszek's instinct was to go up to where he had been with the Germans – it was where they had found the girls, so probably it was there also that Cov had found his girl, or girls if there'd been other occasions before New Year's Eve. 'I'll tell you,' he said.

'You'd better.'

Leszek recognised at once the place where he had interpreted for the Germans. There were still a few lifeless-looking banana leaves on the edge of the bank, and marks in the dust – in any case, he could remember some of the huts and trees they had stood amongst down in the kampong.

'What shall we do?' asked Macpherson, looking down on the kampong from the now motionless jeep.

'I don't know. What do you want to do?'

'Find out where he was killed, I suppose.'

'We'll go and ask.'

It was not a difficult undertaking. As soon as they had got down to the bottom of the bank they saw an old man sitting with his back against the wall of a house. His face was wrinkled so thoroughly that even his eyelids were full of creases and puffed up round his eyes, and he only had two or three teeth in his bottom jaw. But he wore a strip of batik wound jauntily round his head, and grinned with open mouth at the two men. Leszek asked him if he knew where the white man had been killed the day before.

'Yes, tuan! Yes!' He struggled to his feet, beckoning and smiling as if he were leading them to some pleasure. He took them along some planks that were lying on the moist ground and about fifty yards along he stopped outside another small bamboo house. There was a big iron padlock on the door.

'Here! In this house! That's where he was found!' The old man was nodding and chuckling, looking for their approval. Leszek wondered if he wanted any money, but he couldn't bring himself to pay the man anything. Macpherson, obviously very used to such situations, threw a 10-rupiah note at him. The old man dropped it, and fumbled in the mud to pick it up. Some children, and a couple of younger men, were standing watching them now. So it was in that little house that Coventry had died. Leszek felt himself growing faint again, and put his hand out involuntarily to lean against the door of the house;

but as soon as he touched the door, he recoiled, tense but fully conscious again.

'Christ,' said Macpherson. He was shaking his head fiercely. 'I've had nightmares about dying in a place like that. The poor fucker. Can we go in?'

'Why's it locked?' Leszek said to the old man, who was still standing smiling at them.

The children shouted out together. 'There's no one there.' 'The police locked it up this morning.'

'Who found the white man?'

'A man.' 'The door was open and a neighbour went in.' 'He's with the police now.'

'Did he kill the white man?'

There was a chorus of 'No' from the children, and one of the men said gravely, 'No, tuan.'

'Who killed him?'

The children were silent this time, and the men looked back at Leszek with blank faces. The old man had stopped smiling.

'Is he still in the village?'

The silence continued. Then the young man who'd spoken said, 'If it was the people who lived in the house, they've gone.'

'Where?'

'No one knows.'

Macpherson was looking anxiously from face to face. 'What's it all about, for Christ's sake? Come on, cut me into this conversation.' Leszek told him what the little group had said. 'So that's that,' said Macpherson. 'They won't talk.'

'The police have been here, I expect they were cautious even then. Now they'll be even more cautious. Anyway I don't suppose these know anything. Anyone who knows anything will be keeping out of the way.'

'What do we do?'

'Just go back.'

But they stood there uncertainly, Macpherson silent for longer than Leszek had known him before. Down here, among the trees and houses, the light above their heads was fainter. A fruit bat made its heavy way across the sky between the trees. Just then, a girl came out of one of the huts. She had a white dress on, hanging slightly loose so as to suggest at once the nakedness of her body underneath. She smiled at Leszek and Macpherson with her thick lips, darker than the rest of her face.

'Christ!' said Macpherson. 'That's what we do! Jesus, that's what we do, we screw ourselves silly.' The girl, watching Macpherson now, gestured with a shake of her head towards the hut she had come from. Still looking at the girl, Macpherson said, 'It's a sign, Mylski, old boy, read it aright. I'll see you in half an hour! Use it well!' He gave a long whistle, a mixture of relief and amazement. 'Come on, *noni*, give me the whole *buku-buku*.' He moved forward, put his palm on the small of her back, pushed her round towards the hut and went in with her, stooping to get through the low door.

All the villagers standing round were laughing. 'A proper cockerel!' one of the boys said. Leszek didn't know what to do or feel. He found a mysterious respect growing in him for Macpherson. Then another girl came round from the back of the hut into which Macpherson had gone. It seemed as though someone had told her Leszek was there since she looked hard at him straightaway. Leszek took in the red dress, the pale brown skin of her face and shoulders and legs, the soft eyes holding his. The men were laughing again. He was finding it hard to breathe, he was so attracted to the girl. 'Tuan wants?' she said, smiling, with a slight jerk forward of her shoulder so that one of her breasts trembled slightly under her dress. His penis was like an iron hook between his thighs. Suddenly he

knew that he would go with her. In the same moment he
saw with equal clarity that he would not have done so
had Coventry been alive. He stepped forward decisively
now. The girl beamed, holding out her hand, and the men
burst into delighted laughter again.

He followed her to a hut behind the one Macpherson
was in, the girl glancing flirtatiously at him over her
shoulder as they went. Leszek felt himself no more than a
shell, some inner wind driving him lightly along. In the
hut everything happened very swiftly. The girl had nothing under her dress, and lay down naked at once on the
small bed. She lifted her legs and opened them wide once
or twice, still smiling at Leszek: he noticed the thin pink
line Janusz had spoken of. He had had a strong desire to
clasp his hands together from either side between her
legs and lift her up when he had got into the hut, but she
had moved too quickly for him to have had time to do
that. He undressed completely and lay by her side, a hand
across her breasts, which were cold. 'A hundred?' she
said, and he nodded. She drew him into her with her
hand and he ejaculated almost immediately. She tweaked
his nose. 'Good,' she said.

He washed in a bucket, dressed again and sat on the
bedside. He had no desire to get up. Coventry was dead;
nothing seemed to exist any more outside this bamboo
hut. It was enough to do, just to sit there with his hands
on his knees. The girl appeared to sense something of his
state and started combing her hair unhurriedly, looking
in a small round mirror hanging on one of the wall-poles.
His head was full of the sweet coconut oil she had rubbed
into her hair. He was sitting waiting for something to
happen, with an absence of anticipation and an absence
of will utterly unlike anything he had known before.
He couldn't imagine what the next event in his life
would be.

What happened was that the door opened with a crash and three policemen in steel helmets rushed in, one holding a sten gun. 'Hands!' this one shouted. Leszek got up slowly, lifting his hands. Behind the policemen were several other men in civilian clothes. The girl had stretched her hands as high as they would go, and her dress was lifted to her thighs. One of the other policemen ran his hands over Leszek and the girl with equal impersonality, then they were told to go outside.

Macpherson was there, doing up the buttons of his shirt, with two more policemen by him. A lot of villagers were standing about now. There was a murmur of recognition from some of them when Leszek came out. Macpherson was looking very indignant, but when he saw Leszek his expression turned to one of astonishment: 'Jesus, you went in too! The big time! Thank Christ you did, boy! Tell 'em who we are, Leszek, they think we murdered Cov or something.'

The policeman with the sten gun said to Leszek, 'Papers.' He had lowered his gun now. Leszek found his diplomatic pass. 'I'm at the Polish embassy,' he said. The men in shirts and trousers who were with the police all showed interest at this, and one sniggered. When he had examined Leszek's pass, the policeman said, 'You'll have to come to headquarters with us to confirm your identity.'

'My friend here?' said Leszek.

'He must come too.'

'Tell him we were friends of Pearce, for God's sake,' said Macpherson.

It seemed an absurd observation to make but Leszek found he had no interest in resisting the suggestion, any more than he had resented the policeman's instructions.

'We're friends of the man who was killed here yesterday,' he said.

Almost everyone standing watching laughed at this.

'Burning the corpse,' a voice said, and the laughter rose again.

'What about my jeep?' said Macpherson.

Leszek translated for him. The policemen conferred for a moment, and it was agreed that Macpherson could drive to the police headquarters himself with two policemen accompanying him. 'Jesus, these nuts! See you there, then, Leszek boy.' He scrutinised the girl Leszek had been with – she was standing, uneasy and subdued, on her own, evidently uncertain whether the police had lost interest in her or not. Macpherson gave Leszek a big wink. 'Nice bint!' he said. 'One of them's screwing my little bitch already.' Then he scrambled up the bank with the policemen hastening after him.

The other policemen told Leszek to come with them. He saw a police truck waiting on the far side of the kampong – it must have come in by some other road. The girl was being left behind. Leszek looked at her, wondering whether to smile, but she was obviously too frightened to make a movement or gesture of any kind till the police had gone. He glanced round the kampong – the low huts, the dark palms above them, the little crowd of its poor inhabitants looking steadily at him in the dwindling light. It had acquired an extraordinary importance in his life in the last three days, but he knew he would never see it again.

CHAPTER THIRTEEN

Jane Summerson

JANE sat in the garden, still trying to finish *Room at the Top*. Leszek was due any minute, and she kept listening for the latch on the gate to clink at the front of the house. But the afternoon was silent, except for birds calling and, just audible sometimes, the sound of a dry leaf brushing the foliage as it drifted down through the thick banyan above her head. The family were all at the club. They'd had the tact to suppose that both she and Leszek would rather meet in an empty house. She didn't know what she was going to say to Leszek, but she had felt she had to talk to him if he would come and, slightly to her surprise, he had answered her letter to say that he would.

She had first heard the news of Coventry's death in the club, and, before she could escape, it had been garnished by three or four people with stories of his immorality. It was all new to her, but standing there, stunned already, she had been forced to believe in the truth of at any rate some of what they had said. For an hour or two afterwards, it seemed, she had felt more outrage at his life than grief at his death. Although he hadn't loved her, and she had had to stop seeing him, she had gone on thinking of him as an unusually outgoing and sincere man, who would have been a wonderful friend if her own feelings had not run away with her. Suddenly, learning how he had gone about with prostitutes and actually died in a brothel, even that surviving tenderness of hers towards him seemed to have been fraudulently inspired. Physically, the memory of him had become revolting to her. Yet the

210

next day, playing with the children while Bertrand and Angela were out at the Dutch cemetery where he was being buried, she had suddenly cried uncontrollably, imagining the day they first met. And in the evening, Bertrand had heard from the Foreign Ministry quite a different story of his death – a suggestion that he had been in the kampong in search of Sumitro's murderer, and had been killed by the same man. Most of the British in Djakarta had quickly accepted this account of his death as the true one, for Cov had been popular. Bill Macpherson, and short reports in one or two British papers based on his agency messages, had supplied confirmation. Coventry had become a new British hero, dying in the brave and private pursuit of justice. But Jane had just remained confused.

Then there had come the story that Leszek was leaving Djakarta – and a new subject of gossip had occupied the diplomatic community. Jane had found herself going through a series of emotions about Leszek almost identical to what she had just gone through about Cov. Leszek had been arrested in a brothel in compromising circumstances, along with Macpherson. There had been remarkable press coverage of the incident in Djakarta. Bertrand had come home one evening with copies of two newspapers, and translated a news item from each of them for her and Angela. One was a Muslim paper, which had said: 'LOVE OF THE PEOPLE! A communist diplomat from Poland was caught naked by the police earlier this week in the house of a "night flower" in the notorious kampong by the Djakarta flood canal. Many of the inhabitants of the kampong witnessed his shame. Love of the people, in the Warsaw style? Note – Warsaw is the capital of Poland, the biggest "little brother" to big brother Moscow.' There was no mention of Macpherson. The Communist Party newspaper wrote: 'A Canadian journalist working for the

American Press, Maceprson, has been seized by the
police in the embrace of a young girl corrupted by money
in a house of vice in Djakarta. We insist on the expulsion
of such men from our beloved Indonesia.' There was no
mention of Leszek.

Jane had felt nausea when she had heard all this, yet
it had not lasted. When the fact came out that the kampong
Leszek had been found in was the one in which Cov had
been killed, she started wondering once more what had
really happened. She thought again of that day at the
Borobodur, when Leszek had let her see something of his
own failed marriage as an oblique comfort to her, and it
suddenly made it as hard to judge him as it had been,
in the end, to judge Cov.

A couple of days ago, now, Bertrand had told her that
Leszek's departure had been fixed for a week hence. She
had known at once that she had to act. She couldn't let
that period of happiness with Cov and Leszek end in such
doubt about them both.

She looked up from her book, in which she had been
trying to make out the meaning of some simple sentence.
There were voices at the front of the house. Then *coki*
appeared at the back door with Leszek behind her. He
must have closed the gate quietly. The moment she saw
him her uneasiness about the meeting faded. His face was
pale and small, and his eyes fastened on her anxiously, as
though he was afraid she might not be friendly to him.
She heard with surprise the ring of pleasure in her voice
as she greeted him – 'Leszek!' At that he smiled quickly
and with evident relief, and hurried forward to seize her
hand and press his lips to it. 'Jane, hello!'

They looked at each other in silence after that, and Jane
gestured to him to sit down with her at the garden table.
They still went on looking at each other in silence. A round
yellow leaf fell with a faint tap on the metal table top.

Jane spoke first. 'You know, that little group of people when we first met in the hills. . . . Do you remember Thomas and Christine, the man Cov called a dinosaur?'

'Of course.'

'They've broken up, and do you know why? He found out she had a Greek or Roumanian or something grand-mother, and he just stopped seeing her. He was a fantastic racialist, it just killed everything for him that she wasn't pure English. It was terrible for her, she still doesn't know what happened.'

She remembered how Christine had sobbed in the home of one of the embassy girls for hours and hours, till her face was a mass of dark lines. None of her friends had had much comfort to give her, and they had been in a worse dilemma since the talk had reached them of the reason for Thomas's action. Should they tell Christine of what they had heard or not? The general opinion was that they should tell her but encourage her to believe that this was just a fanciful explanation of some incompatibility that Thomas couldn't admit to. However, nothing had yet been done to enlighten her. Jane winced to think of Christine's unhappiness, past and doubtless to come – but speaking of Christine she had managed to express uncannily well what she and Leszek couldn't immediately say about themselves and Coventry. It was funny – she'd not done it deliberately. 'Toby's going home too.'

Leszek's blue eyes pierced her. 'How did he take . . .'

'Cov's death?' She could help him now.

He nodded with a tiny movement of his head.

'He was already pretty far gone, you know, drinking. Since then he's been almost, you know, beyond human reach.'

'Oh.' Leszek's sigh had no note of surprise in it – as though it were just the latest in a long series of sighs.

But Jane could speak plainly at last. 'Tell me, Leszek,

tell me what really happened to Coventry. I must know.'

Leszek sighed in the same way again, and gave her a long, uneasy look. Then he started speaking softly but rapidly. 'Of course I haven't seen any English people, I don't know what you all know or what you've been thinking.'

He stopped. But this time Jane couldn't help him – she couldn't bring herself to answer that question, if question it was. He studied her and seemed to be summing up for himself what she would want to know.

'It was true about him going to the brothels – if you want to know about him you must know that. But perhaps you knew? – I only found out very late.'

Jane shook her head.

'But when he was killed he was looking for Sumitro's murderer – it's true what they've been saying, I'm sure of it. I had lunch with him that day and I sent him there – I killed him myself, you might say, by sending him! I didn't know of course. But maybe I wanted to put him in danger.'

'How?' Jane could scarcely understand what he was saying.

'I learned – I learned in a strange way that he picked up those girls. I was very dismayed and – and shocked. Then he told me that he'd seen Sumitro's murderer again, in a sort of brothel village, and I told him he should do something about it – tell the police or something, of course, that's what I said, but I think he went back there himself and I wonder, I keep wondering, if I didn't want him to. I wanted to harm him in some way, I believe.'

Already Jane had heard enough. It was a good enough picture of Coventry to be left with – she didn't want to think about him any more, she didn't want to remember him any more. That would do, that would do for good. All at once it was a desperate need with her to stop Leszek talking on. At the same time she knew that it was probably hopeless to try to stop him now. He hadn't come just to answer her questions, she saw it: he had come because she was the only person he himself could talk to about Coventry. She didn't care, she felt no sympathy for him. It must be a fantasy, this, of his having killed Coventry in some way, but even if there was any truth in it she didn't want to know.

She got up. 'Excuse me just a moment. I'll call *coki* to bring us tea.'

He stared up at her. In the tension in his face, she could see politeness warring with his need to go on talking. She waited to see which would win.

'Jane – would you mind if we spoke a little more first?'

She sat down again. There was nothing she could say but 'Of course.'

'Jane – after he was dead a very strange thing happened to me. I went down to look for the murderer myself – I went with Macpherson. I didn't know why I was going – he wanted to go, he wanted me to show him where it was and tell him what I could find out, but that wasn't why I went. I had a much greater desire to go than that. When we got there, there was nothing to see of course, just the house locked up by the police. Then two girls came out and Macpherson went with one. And I couldn't stop myself going with the other. I was dragged to her, as if I was being sucked in by a vacuum. And I realised it was as if I was taking Coventry's place. It was horrible, of course, the whole thing, just horrible, but it was as though, at that moment, as though I'd killed Cov, moralised him to death – just that, moralised him to death – just so as to take his place and do the things he was doing. I don't know. You heard what happened, the police broke in, they were really looking out for some clue to Cov's murder, they weren't interested in – you know – the girls. And there were some journalists with them and they wrote the thing up in the papers and the embassy decided I was a liability. But I don't mind about going home, what I can't bear is the thought of all I've done!'

Jane suddenly felt insight flooding into her mind. She was appalled at what she was thinking yet it was like a revelation. She hated both Coventry and Leszek.

'I've just seen it!' she said – she could hear herself, she was almost shouting. 'You and Cov, you don't know anything about women, you have no feeling for women – you don't understand what it is to please a woman, to make her respond to you, perhaps you've never known it. You didn't know it in your marriage, I can see that. You seemed so different, you and Cov, but you were both the same. I'm not saying you're homosexual or anything like that, but you're cut off, you seem so lively and strong and yet you're terrified and right outside everything that's natural and really strong.' She felt exhausted and hopeless, and started to cry. 'And you're the only people I ever liked being with here! The only ones!'

She buried her head in her hands, weeping. She felt Leszek lean over and touch her forearm with surprising tenderness. It made her sob all the more violently and she shook his hand away. He said nothing. When she looked up at him again, rubbing her tears away, he was contemplating her, his face very drawn.

'I'm sorry,' she mumbled. 'It's nothing to do with me. It's just been a strain, that's all – obviously it's been far worse for you.'

He answered in the same way as when he had begun to talk, speaking quietly but rapidly. 'I think I'll go, Jane. I understand what you say, you touch on some truth. I know. But we can't say any more to each other now, we've seen each other more clearly, we've learned a bit from each other – that's the important thing, isn't it?'

He got up, and she nodded. 'I'll ring you before I leave Djakarta,' he said.

She nodded again. 'Thank you,' she said, very softly.

'Thank you, Jane.' He lifted her hand from the table and kissed the back of it, then walked briskly away round the side of the house. She heard the front gate clink this time as it closed.

After a while she got up and walked slowly round the garden. She stopped to pull some brown petals out of some roses, and showers of petals fell to the earth. She was going to look at men in a quite different way from now onwards. She wasn't going to sit and admire them up on their hilltops, and wish she was allowed up there with them. She wanted attention, attention to her as a woman, and those who weren't prepared to give it to her weren't going to interest her any more, however attractive they might seem. Let them show that they understood and cared about women. She'd once thought that all men did, virtually – now she thought that perhaps very few did. Anyway, it was those, however many or few, that she was interested in now.

Coki came to the door and called out, 'No tea?' Jane had mastered such domestic expressions by now. 'No, thanks,' she called back. *Coki* laughed, her hand on her side. 'Tuan's gone?' 'Yes.' *Coki* moved her hand from her side to the edge of the door. 'He didn't stay long.' She bent double with laughter, holding on to the door. *Coki* had moved her hand anticipating her laughter, Jane thought. She relaxed for a moment, noticing that. But after a minute or two she was feeling as tense and depressed as she had been before.

She was still cleaning the roses, more carefully now, when she heard a footstep on the grass behind her. She turned, startled. It was Bertrand. He was in his tennis shoes and white shirt; his glasses were off, sticking precariously from his shirt pocket. Without them his head was rather a noble construction, the back round and massive, the profile deep-cut. But he was blinking, and pulling at the hair that grew in the hollow in his neck.

'My dear!' he said breathlessly. 'My dear! I thought there might be an hour now when you might be alone, when I'd be able to talk to you, after Leszek had gone.'

'He went early. Otherwise he'd still be here.'

He ignored the remark. 'My dear!' he said, and stretched a hand forward towards hers.

She jumped back violently. His upper lip shot up, revealing his teeth. 'Jane!' he cried, anguish in his voice. But she wasn't going to allow him to say a single word, not a single other word.

'Go away, Bertrand,' she said to him fiercely. 'Just stop hanging around me, just stop it.'

'Oh but . . .'

'I know, I've been conscious of you hanging around me, breathing on me, leaning over me. I don't like it, I don't want it.'

'Jane!'

'Just go away now, look, I won't show a trace of this, come back to supper tonight and you'll find me absolutely normal. I'm going, I'm leaving, but I'll announce . . .'

'Don't go!'

'I'm going, Bertrand, I was going anyway. It's nothing to do with you, but as far as you're concerned it's better too.'

'But . . .'

'Not another word!' She just stopped herself shrieking – *coki* mustn't hear. 'Not another word! If you do I'll make such a frightful fuss!'

She thought that would arrest him; but she was sorry it did, in a way. He went on standing there, looking at her with wide-open eyes, his mouth open too, but saying nothing.

'Go on now.'

He gulped, then said in a very small voice, 'Can't I say anything?'

'No. Look, I shall remember that you reached your hand out to me, I shall count it as a compliment, but there's nothing more, Bertrand, there's nothing more that can possibly be. Just go, please.'

He turned and walked away slowly round the side of the house. Just before he passed out of sight she saw him put his glasses on. She breathed out heavily. Perhaps in some way he was relieved too.

She had just been about to deal with a very dead rose. She snipped it off, and most of its curling petals fell at once. She threw what was left in her hand on to the grass. She knew she would regret, later, the rough way in which she had spoken to Bertrand, but for the moment she was exulting in it. She decided she would go in and do something else that she would not previously have imagined herself doing. Angela had put away in her desk a long letter she'd been writing, doubtless to her mother. She'd go and look at it and find out once and for all whether Angela's performances were put on for her mother's distant eyes.

Angela's writing desk was a beautiful piece of furniture, in walnut, that she kept in the drawing-room. It stood out rather too splendidly among the government furniture, but even Angela couldn't manage to furnish a whole house in a short posting to the tropics. She kept the desk unlocked – she'd said to Jane on her first day, 'I don't lock anything except the safe, I'm not going round the house perpetually warring against the servants, or thinking that's what I'm doing.' It was a bit of the performance that Jane admired, and it made her feel guilty after all when she took the letter

out. She looked to see if *coki* wasn't at the door; but she
was alone in the cool room, with its little latticed windows
against which red hibiscus pressed.

She unfolded the large thick sheets of blue writing-
paper. At a glance she could see that Angela told her
mother nothing. The dutiful, mundane phrases sprawled
across page after page: 'the garden's looking nice, almost
English, though some of the roses are turning brown';
'the children are keeping well, though Rupert's had a
slight cold, what you might call a summer cold if it wasn't
always summer here!'; 'we've had quite a lot of friends in
this week, and have been about a bit more ourselves too'.
As Jane read on, she felt a terrible misery overcoming
her. So Angela did it for no one – no one except herself.
Jane felt the time she had spent in the house, watching
Angela go about her life, was like time spent at the peep-
hole in a cell-door, the prisoner in it unaware that anyone
was there. She suddenly remembered dinner the evening
they had learned of Cov's death, and the single remark
Angela had made when Bertrand and herself had at last
brought themselves to speak of the subject: 'He'll be badly
missed.'

CHAPTER FOURTEEN

Leszek Mylski

T HE embassy car slowed down to pass through a flock
of betjaks. In the back, Leszek stared out at them, the
drivers shouting and grinning as they swerved away from
the car. One driver lifted his leg and waved a scarred foot
at Leszek through the car window – his passenger, an
Indonesian woman, with a square, dark jaw that must
have meant she had Dutch blood in her, was sitting up
stiff and alarmed. Leszek was glad Idlinski had let him
go to the airport on his own. He tried to see the small
pictures painted on the backs of the betjak seats – a
landscape of palms in pinks and blues on one, a semi-
circular tiger with large eyes leaping through an egg-blue
sky on another. There was so much he hadn't thought
about, or even looked at, in Djakarta.

Now there was nothing ahead in the sunshine on the
broad concrete road. He leaned back again. He was still
remembering Idlinski's smile, in which worldliness and
kindliness had blended inseparably, when Leszek had been
leaving the embassy this morning. 'Panie Leszku,' Idlinski
had said, 'we all thought you were going to be a political
problem, not a sexual problem. Fortunately the latter is
not taken so seriously in our country.'

With the other members of the embassy it had not been
so easy. To Leszek's surprise, Tarski had proved to be
the most decent of them. He had gone to Idlinski, so Leszek
had gathered, and told him what a strain Coventry's
death had put on him. Leszek was far from understanding
himself, so he doubted if Tarski and Idlinski had under-

stood him: however, Idlinski had played the incident
down, and though instructions had come from Warsaw
that Leszek was to go back to Poland, the fact that
Sumitro, his chief contact, had died figured among the
official reasons for his recall. Many of the other people in
the embassy had been embarrassed, not knowing what
tone to adopt with him, so he had worked at home these
last few weeks. There the atmosphere had been unfriendly
but somehow more acceptable. Janusz was simply in a very
bad temper with him – he had laid extensive plans for
sexual pleasure in Djakarta, and now felt he couldn't
risk going ahead with them.

But leaving the embassy was unimportant to Leszek.
He'd been lucky – he even had his university job waiting
for him still. The losses went far deeper than that. He
looked out of the car window again: two buffaloes were
walking slowly across a dry field, their heads down. He
studied their appearance – but it was an effort of the will.
After all, was it worth trying to collect these last few
impressions of Indonesia? He'd thrown so much away
already.

Those first days in Djakarta, six months ago, he'd been
for a short while a different man from what he'd been at
any other time in his life. He could still remember the
sweetness of those days. That, he had soon lost: and afterwards there had been such confusion. Jealousy, fear, the
urge to act rightly – he didn't know what parts they'd all
played in what he'd been doing since then. There'd been
ill-chance, of course: Sumitro's death could not have been
foreseen, and all that followed from it. But he knew that
he had had a share in spoiling everything. In so far as he
was the loser, there were times when he could almost
accept the fact: it meant no more than that he was his
old self again. What was still as bitter as ever was the
thought of Cov's death. He supposed he felt less guilty than

he had done immediately afterwards – he had to allow
Cov the dignity of having chosen his risks for himself. But
he still believed that Cov had had an exceptional capacity
for pleasure in the world and in people, and it seemed to
be a quite pure grief that Leszek now experienced at the
thought of that capacity being extinguished – grief for
Cov in so far as it made sense, grief for the world itself.
And less pure, no doubt, but sharpest of all at times, and
not reprehensible, was his misery at what he had lost
himself when Cov had died. It was a grotesque moral
situation: he still couldn't give up the belief that a more
responsible life than Cov's had been was a better one – yet
when he thought that his holding of that belief had contributed in the least degree to Cov's dying, he was filled
with agonising remorse. As for the other motives he seemed
to have detected in himself, that day on the Metropole
terrace and the day after in the kampong – well, time
alone, he now thought, would tell him the truth about
those.

That startling conversation with Jane was also constantly
in his mind. He didn't know how far her condemnation
really applied to Coventry. She was right, Cov's bold-
seeming dealings with whores must in fact have reflected
some timidity towards women – yet he thought that, when
the time came, Coventry would have known how to
manage with a woman he was in love with. It was for
himself that Jane's words had rung true. He'd conducted
his friendship with Cov in much the same blundering,
bullying way that he'd tried to control his marriage with
Zosia. But with Zosia the failure had gone further. He'd
never been tender enough to her – it was true, he could
see it now – and perhaps if he had been, she would have
accepted all the rest of him. Or – the thought of what he
had lost was so painful! – his preachings would have been
transformed into some gentler influence of a kind she would

in turn have exercised on him. He sat with his fists clenched for a moment. Those were things he was already realising before Jane had said what she did – things, indeed, that he had in part learned from his relationship with Cov. But Jane had made them very clear. So perhaps he was not quite the same man he had been before – perhaps he was going back to Poland with a few lessons taken in.

Yet he resisted that thought too. There was something so ugly in learning from mistakes of which other people were the victims. When he thought of his life in Poland – starting again, though he could scarcely believe it, to-morrow night – every twinge of hope seemed a vulgarity, after what he had seen and done.

In Poland now it was very cold: in Warsaw the brown snow would be heaped at the edge of the pavements, and people would be hurrying along, most of them also of bulky, brown appearance. His fellow-countrymen dressed well most of the time, but the wintry streets defeated them. Coats that were thick enough to be warm, and also elegant, were too expensive for all but a very few people. But Zosia would be sleek, in the dark fur she had had as a wedding present from her family. He knew she would still be wearing it.

He had got out of the car now, and the Indonesian driver had given his bags to the porter to carry off to the airport reception. The sun was as fierce and brilliant as he'd ever known it in Djakarta. 'I'll leave you, tuan,' said the driver. He was an alert boy with friendly ways, who was supposed to be a communist, but never showed it except in making rather cheerful jokes against the rich and the Americans. 'Betjaks for Warsaw this way,' he said, pointing in the direction the porter had gone.

Leszek laughed. 'Thanks,' he said. 'I'd prefer one back to Djakarta.'

'This city?' said the driver. He held his nose between two fingers and blew a lump of snot on to the ground.

Leszek gave him a hundred rupiahs – it was the last bit of Indonesian money, apart from a few coins, that he had. The driver smiled and saluted him, and waved again from the car as he drove off. Leszek stood where he was. Aeroplanes of the world glittered out on the airfield; over to his left, in front of the airport buildings, the terrace restaurant was crowded. Three girls were walking away from it, one of them in a dress in three bands of colour, green above, then red, then yellow. Nowhere except in sunshine like this could she have looked so right in such a dress. The girl next to her was in a white blouse and a yellow skirt; the third girl was in Javanese dress, looking very slim, the roundness of her breasts under her muslin blouse like swellings on a tree. They passed Leszek, talking and laughing softly, without looking at him.

He walked in the direction of the terrace. He could see that many of the Indonesian men sitting at the tables were in their *pitjis*, their little squat brown fezes. He remembered an evening sitting with Coventry and Subekto and Achmad at a big open-air café outside a cinema near Cov's house – the Menteng cinema. It was just after six: the daylight was fading fast, the tall trees opposite them loomed like heavy clouds, a dusk hawk was swooping between the trees with sharp, regular squeaks. Leszek had suddenly had the impression that most of the men sitting at the tables had had the tops of their heads cut off. Then he realised what it was: the dark *pitjis* they were wearing had blended with the night, and only their faces under the *pitjis* gleamed in what light there was left. He and Cov and the boys had sat on and on there that evening, drinking one bottle of the cold Heineken's after another. It was the evening Cov had described to them the silhouette map of Indonesia in solid gold on the wall of Sukarno's palace, and had added, 'Malaya's also on the map with gold outlines, like a pair of hands reaching out for it.' The boys had laughed, then Subekto had said, 'Cov, you say more about politics in one sentence than enters our heads in a year.' Achmad's merry laugh spluttered out again through his teeth, Subekto leaned back in his rattan chair and laughed low and long in his belly.

Leszek suddenly wished that someone had come to say goodbye. He stood still again; he couldn't move. He let the heat pour into his head and shoulders and back. Just then, he heard some shouting. He looked round. A jeep was bumping across the grass on the other side of the road, and two airport officials in khaki were running towards it from different directions. It wasn't clear how the vehicle had got there, but it was obviously in a place where it was not allowed to be. The jeep was heading straight towards Leszek. Suddenly he realised that the driver, smiling crazily at him through the windscreen, was Macpherson. The jeep swung on to the road and stopped, about fifteen yards from Leszek. Macpherson raised his arm high in the air and waved it, still looking at Leszek.

'Goodbye, Russky,' he shouted. 'See you in the Kremlin!'

The men were on the road now, just behind the jeep. It roared and leaped forward again, and the men stopped running, their hands dropping to their sides. Tears that he could never have imagined were in Leszek's eyes. He watched the jeep rapidly dwindle in size till it reached the junction of the airport road and the main road. It merged with the low palm trees on the horizon. Invisibly, Macpherson was speeding back to Djakarta.